MURDER ONE
In
Midvale Corners

BY

ALEXANDRA
HAWTHORNE

Murder One in Midvale Corners
©2018 Meech Road, Ltd.

Cover by Designs by Dana

Published in USA by Meech Road, Ltd.

Dedication

Dedicated to all the small towns across America
and the four people who read the first version of Murder One:
This one is shorter and better.

Chapter 1

Penny Johnson, newly licensed attorney, briefcase on her shoulder and JD's leash in her hand, heard a phone ringing as she unlocked the door to her two-room suite of offices above Maxi's Delicatessen. She reached in her pocket for her cell phone, realized it wasn't ringing and dashed across the reception area to her desk and picked up her desk phone.

Before she could say her usual "Penny Johnson, attorney at law," she heard, "Penny is that you? It's Horace Appleworth. I think I'm in a bit of trouble. The police are at my house to arrest me for the murder of Dick Boswick. I don't know what to do."

"Why, what, how---don't answer." Penny quickly got herself into her lawyer mode. "Let me talk to the officer."

"Sheriff Nicholson here," said Bill Nicholson, acting like he hadn't known her all her life and coached her when she played on Midvale Corner's softball team.

"We're arresting Horace and taking him to the jail for booking. You can meet us there in an hour or so." He hung up.

Penny placed the phone on its cradle. She stood, her mind turning over the short conversation. She dumped her briefcase on her desk, crossed the outer room to retrieve the keys dangling from the lock. JD, her big German shepherd, padded along behind her dragging his leash. She stopped, unsnapped it and picked up the local paper that had been shoved through the mail slot. She saw the headline: Dick Boswick, City Manager, Found Dead in His Office.

After getting her keys, she stopped to read the story, which informed her that Sally Boswick, Dick's wife, discovered him sprawled across his desk, shot twice in the head.

"Did you hear about Dick Boswick?" asked Althea Riversmith bustling through the still open door.

Althea, retired school secretary and now Penny's legal assistant, accountant and maker of the best coffee on Main Street if not in the county was holding a copy of the extra edition of the Midvale Courier, Midvale Corner's local paper.

Penny nodded. "I heard. Horace Appleworth has been arrested for his murder and is on his way to jail. He wants me to represent him. I am to meet him at the jail in an hour."

Althea stared at Penny, then said in her efficient way, "Good grief. Horace couldn't kill anyone. I'll start his file. You'll need an appearance for the court and the prosecutor's office. I'll get on it right away."

She hung up her royal blue raincoat, placed her tapestry bag in the bottom drawer of her desk, sat down and booted up her computer. Her blue rain hat was still perched on her grey curls.

"Right," Penny said returning to her desk. "I've never represented an alleged murderer. She picked up the phone to call Gordon Swanson, family friend and one of the best criminal lawyers in town.

"I heard Appleworth was arrested," said Gordon, after Penny got through his secretary

"You can do this," he went on, addressing her concerns about representing such a high-profile case. "Take it one step at a time. Don't let Horace talk to the police, if you can stop him. Get him bonded out if you can. You know what to argue for a bond—long standing member of the community, evidence all circumstantial, will appear for all hearings, you know the drill."

Penny hung up. She knew she was a decent—maybe even a good lawyer. She had successfully represented folks who got in bar fights. She had even managed to get a couple of not guilty verdicts—but this was murder and Horace was a longtime friend of the family--what if she messed this up?

Realizing that despite her personal trepidations, Horace needed a lawyer in his corner now and she was the lawyer he wanted, she opened her briefcase gathering up the items she thought she would need. She put in a clean yellow legal pad to take notes, a couple of blue, not black, ink pens and her lucky Petoskey stone. She snapped her briefcase shut, walked through the reception area and to Althea's desk. Althea handed her the documents she needed for court. Penny put them in her briefcase, gave JD a pat on the head and said, "I'm off. Thank you."

While Horace was traveling in the back of a police car, Penny was driving her Pepto-Bismol pink ancient Ford Escort to meet him. She drove a few short blocks, and she was quickly at the jail. Like many public buildings, the jail was brick faced with an awning over the door. Inside, Penny deposited everything on the conveyer belt, and made it through the metal detector without causing it to ring. Relieved, she picked up her briefcase and moved on.

"Hi, Penny," said a voice. "You here to see Horace?"

The voice belonged to Jerry, high school friend and now the officer guarding the desk at the Sheriff's office.

Penny nodded.

"I'll let them know you're here. Wait there."

Penny sat on the hard bench in the waiting area. It was visiting time. Mothers were trying to corral children who, bored and no longer able to sit, were running around in circles. Lawyers sat off to the side, on their phones, staring at their computers or talking to each other.

"Hey, Penny," said Frank, chair of the local bar association criminal law section. "You going to represent Horace? There will be a lot of press on that one, you know. They will be dogging you. I heard they'll all be at the arraignment."

"Oh," said Penny, thinking of another reason to try to convince Horace to hire a more experienced attorney. She had no idea how to handle the press who had never been interested in her bar fight clients. She was musing on a clever way to say 'no comment' when she heard her name being called.

"Penny," said Jerry. "You can see Horace now."

Penny followed Jerry through a series of doors. Sticking to jail procedure, one door is closed and locked before another is opened. Finally, she was ushered into a large room. Facing her were three large holding cells, one for women, and two for the men. The last night had been busy in the community. Some men paced, others banged on the bars only to be told to shut up by the police guarding them, and still others, trying to sleep it off, curled up on a bench. The women were fewer, some in bright colored tube tops and skirts so short that their bottoms were barely covered while others sat looking like they were trying to disappear.

Opposite the cells was a long counter enclosed with protective glass, behind which were three officers, busy with paper work, oblivious to the organized chaos around them. Along a sidewall were five small, enclosed spaces equipped with a table and two chairs, where attorneys could meet with their clients. The offices, if that is what they could be called, had large glass walls so that the officers could see but not hear what was going on between the lawyer and the client.

"Here, Penny," says Jerry. "You can use this one. I'll get you another chair. Horace will be along shortly."

Penny sat on one side of the table. She got out her yellow legal pad and a pen. Breathing in, smelling the odor of fear and disinfectant that permeated the space, she waited.

"Here he is," said Jerry, pushing Horace ahead of him into the chair across from Penny with his back to the glass wall. "Do you want to keep the cuffs on him?"

"No," said Penny looking at Horace in his orange jump suit with the words "County Jail" printed in black streaming across Horace's chest.

Horace sat down tentatively in proffered grey metal chair, attempting to smile at Penny.

"Orange is not my best color," he said. "And look at how this bags—I need a belt. And the style leaves a lot to be desired."

Penny understood. Horace, a compact man who worked out regularly and who, even when on the messiest of job sites, dressed immaculately—was reduced to looking like a common criminal. Which, in the eyes of the law, he was.

"Horace, forget about the jumpsuit. We need to talk about what will happen next."

"They took my picture, and not from my best side, and my fingerprints," said Horace. "What more do they need, and when do I get out of here?"

"Horace, listen," said Penny using the tone of voice she used with JD when he was not behaving.

"You will be going to the court this afternoon for your arraignment. I…"

"Do I have to talk? When do I go? I didn't kill him you know."

"Yes, you will have to talk but, you won't be actually in the courtroom. I'll be there. You will be here on a video monitor. You will be able to see me and the judge and the prosecutor, but you will actually be here."

"Judge Hancock will call your case—he will say 'The People versus Appleworth,' then he will ask if you are Mr. Horace Appleworth. You say yes, I am Horace Appleworth. Then I'll tell the court that I am your attorney. The judge will read the charge and will ask you how you plead. You will say 'Not guilty, your honor."

"Can't I tell him I didn't do it and that this is all a big mistake?" Horace leaned forward, his hands palms up.

"No, he doesn't want to hear anything except that you are Horace Appleworth and that you are not guilty. We will deal with the rest later. Then we will talk about a bond to get you out of jail until the trial."

Penny jumped as one of the male prisoners started yelling and banging on the bars. When he stopped, she went on. "The prosecutor wants no bail, he will argue that this is a murder charge and you are a menace to the community. I'll argue that you have a business to run, live in the community, and are not a flight risk. I am hopeful that we can get a reasonable bond set so you can get out of here. How do I reach your partner, Ryan? It would be good if he were in the courtroom."

"Ryan is probably at the hospital; he's in charge of the trauma center during the day. How much will they want for a bond? Where do I find a bail bondsman?"

"The bail bondsman will come to the jail, but in case they don't, I'll give Ryan the information he will need to get you bonded out."

"What if the judge won't let me have a bond?" asked Horace. "What if I have to stay here? In this horrible place? Do you have any idea how hard this is for someone like me? I've been called names I haven't heard since high school."

"I know, Horace, but we can appeal if your bond is denied. Now are you clear—I'll be in the courtroom and you will be on the TV here. You will say your name and answer 'not guilty' when asked. We will argue bail. If the judge grants it, we will get you out of here as soon as possible. I haven't seen any paperwork on this and don't know anything except that they are charging you with murder in the first degree."

"I didn't kill Dick Boswick. He wasn't a nice person, but I didn't kill him."

"We will talk about all of this later, when you are out of here," said Penny. "Now sit still, I'll get a jailer to take you back to your cell."

"I don't have a cell—I have a spot in one of those cages over there," said Horace pointing to the holding cells across the room.

Penny stood and called to the closest jailer to take custody of Horace. She patted Horace on the shoulder.

"It will be alright," she said. Horace rolled his brown eyes at her as he was led away.

Penny gathered up her things, walked across the room and knocked on the door at the end of the hall to be let out. Jerry opened the door, took her visitor's badge and nodded.

Penny walked down the hall to the outside door. She rang the bell to be let out. Jerry rang her out.

Once in the fresh air, Penny breathed in to get rid of the jail odors. She climbed into her car and headed back to the office, that awful image of Horace and the enormity of what she faced in defending him lingering in her mind.

Althea looked up when the door opened and Penny walked in. "I made some fresh coffee. Did you eat lunch? It's almost two o'clock— do you want me to go get a sandwich from Max's? Oh, and, this came from the prosecutor's office. It was hand-delivered. I signed for it."

She handed Penny a large envelope.

"Thanks," said Penny. "Coffee would be good. No sandwich. I have to be in court shortly for Horace's arraignment. Could you call the hospital and try to locate Ryan? I would like him to be in court."

"He has already called three times," said Althea, holding the pink message slips out to Penny.

"Ask him to meet me at the district court—the one here in town. I'll be there in an hour."

Althea, in her usual efficient way, nodded and picked up the phone.

Penny went into her office, put her briefcase on the client's chair and gave JD, who had been waiting patiently for some attention a treat from the treat jar on her desk. After several pats, he went to his bed. She sat, stretched then opened the envelope and started reading the preliminary police report on Horace's case.

"At approximately 9 pm on Thursday, August 20th, a 911 call was received from Sally Boswick, wife of deceased, Richard (Dick) C. Boswick, saying that her husband had been shot. She was at his office in the city office building. An ambulance was sent. Detective Dunlap also responded. The victim was sprawled across his desk. It appeared he had been shot twice in the back of the head."

Penny scanned all she could since it was imperative that she be on time for court. She knew the arraignments started at four and she suspected Horace's case would be first up. The report said that Andy Clinton, the custodian, heard Horace and Dick arguing. He heard a popping sound when he was leaving around nine. He didn't see Horace leave.

Penny also learned that Horace's fingerprints were on the desk along with some smudged unidentifiable prints. Horace was the only person they saw entering the building on the security tape.

The Report noted that Horace was a life member of the National Rifle Association and had won a number of pistol shooting matches. The police knew this because they had competed against him and lost.

Penny wondered if that fact had anything to do with the speed with which Horace was arrested. The clock in the courthouse building chimed three times indicating three o'clock.

Althea stood in the doorway. "Ryan is on his way to court and will meet you there. He is most anxious to get Horace out of jail. He is concerned about Horace's well-being. 'You know how they treat homosexuals in the jail and it is so dirty there, he said.' I assured him you would do your best to get Horace out as soon as possible."

"I hope Judge Hancock is in a good mood," said Penny looking in her briefcase and going through her mental checklist—court rules, yellow legal pad, two blue ink pens, police report, and her lucky Petoskey stone in its special pocket.

After saying good-by to Althea and JD, Penny dashed down the stairs on her way to save her client from another day in the "dirty jail." And, to start her defense of Horace. While there was always some doubt with any client, her intuition told her that Horace didn't kill Dick and it also told her that if she lost, her legal career in Midvale Corners would suffer a serious setback.

Chapter 2

Alex Jeffries, attorney at law, eased his 6'4" frame out of the black Mercedes, thinking that it needed a wash, which meant a trip into the big city since there wasn't a decent car wash in Midvale Corners. He stopped and looked across the parking lot at the squat building that housed the local district court, he recognized three reporters milling around the front of the building. Two of them were from the local TV channels and one from the newspaper. All three had photographers with them and were pacing around looking for someone important or not so important to interview. The big white television vans were parked at the curb in front of the building.

He watched as they talked to Sally Boswick, Dick Boswick's wife. What is she doing here, he wondered? Her husband had been killed—shouldn't she be home with her daughter or making arrangements for the funeral? The reporters finished with Sally so they started looking for someone else.

Alex reached in and got his old briefcase out of the car. His client was to be arraigned on a drunk driving charge at the 4 o'clock call. It was his client's second drunk driving and it was going to be hard going to keep him out of jail this time. The judge would not be happy that he had failed the fancy rehab program the county had paid for. It looked like his client would lose his license and be walking for a long time.

As he stood up he noticed a pink car pulling into the parking space two slots down from him. There was only one person he knew who drove a bright pink car—Penny Johnson. Alex and Penny graduated from Midvale High the same year. She beat him out of the valedictorian's spot by a slim margin, not that he ever thought about that.

His mother, Mabel, who was living with him, had said something about Penny just that morning at breakfast—Alex couldn't remember exactly what it was.

Penny got out of the car, grabbed her briefcase and pushed the door shut with her hip. Then he remembered Penny was representing Horace Appleworth.

The reporters fixed their predatory gaze on Penny.

He watched Penny walk toward the courthouse. Her long legs made quick work of the distance but it was easy for him to catch up. As he got closer he could hear them shouting.

"Ms. Johnson, over here, can we get an interview?"

"Penny, is your client guilty?" asked the reporter with the camera man.

"Ms. Johnson, this way."

Penny looked at the three reporters with their photographers and bright lights and microphones being jabbed in her direction. She kept walking, trying to get past them with a simple 'no comment.'

Suddenly she felt a hand at her elbow pushing her along. Alex was there, smiling.

"Let's see if two of us can get through this trial by reporter safely," he said.

"No comment," said Penny to the closest reporter. "I want to try my case in the trial court not in the court of public opinion."

Penny and Alex pushed through the crowd, opened the door to the courthouse moving quickly into the security area.

"You can let go of my arm now," Penny said unloading her briefcase onto the conveyor belt. "But I do appreciate your help."

"Reporters can be persistent," said Alex coming along behind her.

Alex saw an assistant prosecutor standing with an armload of files in one corner of the reception area. He knew she was there for the misdemeanor arraignments. He went off to stand in line with the other lawyers trying to get a good deal for their clients.

"Is Penny Johnson here for the murder?" asked the lawyer in front of him in the line. "Has she ever handled a murder case?"

"I don't know," said Alex, his hazel eyes narrowing, looking at the shorter man. "She's smart, she'll figure it out."

Why am I defending her, he asked himself? He had been attracted to Penny when they were in school as kids, but that was a long time ago.

Glancing out the front window of the courthouse, Penny saw Mike Pritchard, the prosecutor, talking to the reporters. He looked like he was enjoying the attention. She was sure that he saw this as a big opportunity, since he was up for re-election in the fall.

She went into the court to see the clerk and the list of arraignments for the afternoon. Horace was first on the list.

"The judge wants this one up first," said the clerk, taking a copy of Penny's appearance for the file. "This is a big case, you know. We don't have murders here—it's just not done in Midvale Corners."

She took a seat at the defendant's table to the right of the judge's bench. She wouldn't have a live client; he would still be at the jail. Mike Pritchard came striding into the room. Penny got up to go have a word. Maybe she could get him to agree on a low bond.

"Your client is guilty," Mike said. "He should plead guilty and save us all some time. And don't even think about getting a bond. Horace is menace to the community."

"Why don't we let the judge decide that issue," said Penny walking away. She saw Ryan Nelson, Horace's partner, motioning to her.

"Oh, my god, Penny, have you seen Horace? Is he all right? How can anyone believe that he killed Dick Boswick? How do I get him out of that dirty jail?"

Penny put her hand on Ryan's arm. "Ryan, Horace is okay, be calm. We will argue bond before the judge. I'm afraid he'll set a high bond. Dick was the City Manager, killed in city offices and the judge will not want to let a killer loose."

"But, Horace is not a killer," said Ryan, using the tone of voice he used with an anxious patient in the trauma center. "I have found a bail bondsman—a guy in the hallway had a card. I can raise some money and Horace and I have some investments, the house and Horace's business. We can't leave him in that horrible place."

"Let me see that card," Penny said. 'We are Your Friend Bonding?' I don't think so, Ryan. There is a reputable place right here in town. I have their card here in my briefcase."

"There's Horace," said Ryan, pointing to the large monitor on the wall of the courtroom. "He looks awful."

Judge Mortimer Hancock came through the door behind the bench. "All rise."

"You may be seated."

"Mr. Prosecutor, what do we have here?" Judge Hancock asked.

Mike Pritchard rose slowly to his feet; aware all eyes were on him. "We have a heinous crime here, your honor. This is the matter of the People vs Appleworth. Last night Dick Boswick, our City Manager, was brutally murdered in his office while attending to the city's business. After long hours during the day, he was back at night to do what needed to be done. Between eight and nine p.m., Horace Appleworth came up behind him and..."

"Enough, Mr. Prosecutor. This isn't a trial and you don't need to make an opening statement. This is an arraignment. I have the charge."

He looked at Penny. She jumped to her feet.

"Penny Johnson, representing Horace Appleworth," she said.

Judge Hancock, aware of the reporters in the room, turned to the video screen. "Are you Horace Appleworth? Can you see the courtroom and the people in it?"

"Yes," said Horace. "I can see and I am Horace Appleworth and I didn't."

"Not now, Mr. Appleworth. Do we need to read the charge, Ms. Johnson?"

"No, your honor, we waive the reading of the charge and enter a not guilty plea. We ask that the matter be set for a pre-trial as soon as possible. And we would like to discuss bond."

Mike jumped to his feet, also aware of the press covering the hearing and the coming election. "I object to any bond being set, this is an awful crime, one not seen in our little village for a long time. This man should not be allowed to run rampant in our streets."

"Your honor," said Penny, cutting off Mike's barrage of words, "my client has lived in the community his entire life. He has a home here and a business to run. He assures the court he will appear for every hearing and abide by any terms and conditions set by the court. And he's never been in trouble before—except maybe some speeding ticket years ago--and..."

"Your honor," said Mike, interrupting Penny, "this is a murder – not some little misdemeanor—the court has a duty to keep him locked up to protect the community. Appleworth should sit in jail until he is convicted by a jury of his peers."

"I know my duty, Mr. Pritchard. This is a serious charge", said Judge Hancock. "I agree with the prosecutor on that point. However,

Mr. Appleworth is known in the community. Will your client agree to wear a tether and abide by rules set by this court, Ms. Johnson?"

"Yes, your honor."

"Bail is set at $500,000, cash or surety. Mr. Appleworth will wear a tether and will be in his home every night from 7 pm to –what time do you go to work in the morning, Mr. Appleworth"

"Depends, but usually about 6:30."

"6:30 it is then. You understand that you need to be in your house from 7 pm to 6:30 am. And, if you have any weapons in your home, you need to turn them over to the Sheriff until this matter is resolved."

"Counselors, will there be a probable cause hearing in this matter?"

"Don't see the need, your honor, but if Ms. Johnson thinks she…'

"Ms. Johnson does, your honor," said Penny. "We believe we can resolve this matter when all the facts become clear."

"We'll set it for Wed., Sept 9 at 1:30. That's two weeks away. Is that it, counselors? Okay, next case is People v Ladybird Smythe."

Penny put the date in her calendar. While most in her profession used an electronic gadget or smart phone to keep track of dates, she felt better to have it written in her calendar. She could look at the whole week and see what was up. She gathered up her file, yellow legal pad, pens, and notices given to her by the court clerk and stuffed them back in her briefcase. She walked toward small wooden gate in the bar dividing the people from the lawyers and the judge. Ryan came up to her once she was on the people side.

"Penny," said Ryan, "Where do I find this bail person? I need to get Horace bailed out and get back to the hospital. We are short staffed."

Penny saw Ryan's concern but she also sensed he would stand by Horace through all this. Rummaging in her briefcase she found a card for the local bail bond agency. She handed it to Ryan.

Ryan smiled his thanks rushing up the aisle and out of the courtroom his cell phone at the ready.

Penny followed. She came out the courtroom door to find Detective Dan Dunlap standing in the middle of the hall, still looking like the football player he was in high school. He held up a stack of papers.

"Penny, I have a copy of the autopsy and some photos for you," he said. "We'll probably have more in a couple of days. They are still processing the crime scene."

Penny knew Dan from the days when her father began his legal career and Dan, a beat cop then, came to the house to bring reports to him.

Penny placed the files carefully in her briefcase, which was starting to bulge, a new experience for it. "Bar fights don't have as many reports," she said.

"Nope, and there will be more. We're just getting started," said Dan.

Mike Pritchard came over. "Can we talk about a plea?" he asked Penny.

"I think it is a little early for that," she answered. "I am sure you are investigating other possible defendants."

"No," said Mike. "I am sure we have our man."

Dan's face was blank. She decided to let that go.

"Well, no plea? Then I'll see you in couple weeks," said Mike walking away. Dan followed him out of the court and into the spotlight of the press. Penny dreaded the thought of running that gauntlet again. She looked to see Alex moving toward her in that easy way of his.

"How did the arraignment go?" he asked.

"Okay, at least I got bond for Horace but he has to wear a tether."

"My guy didn't fare so well; he won't get out jail until I can get him in another rehab program."

Penny nodded, noticing that Alex had hazel eyes—why hadn't she noticed that before? In High School, he'd seemed so awkward, but now he was… But, no time for that now, she had a murder charge to deal with.

"I have to get back to my office," she said. "and I still have to get through that bunch of reporters."

"I know a back door and the bailiff who can let us out if you want to sneak out of here. Follow me."

"Thanks, that will be a relief. Those reporters are vicious. I know they're simply doing their job but still…."

Penny followed Alex down a hall. At the end was a door with an intercom. Alex pushed a button and a metallic sounding voice said, "Yea,"

"Hi, Ford, it's Alex Jeffries. Penny Johnson and I want to get out the back door."

"Oh, hi, Alex, how about those Lions—you think they'll have a good season this time? I don't know about them—I don't want to give up but..."

The crackling sound told them to push the door and make their way into the back hallway.

Ford smiled at them from behind his desk by the door. It seemed his job was to guard the door and talk sports. Penny and Alex thanked him and went out the back door of the courthouse.

They walked along silently until it was time to split up in the parking lot. "I'm over there," said Penny.

"I know," said Alex. "I saw you come in—isn't that the car Maureen drove when we were in high school?'

"Yes, and I know the color is horrible, but at least I can always find it and my clients can find me—they recognize the car."

They both stopped.

"Well, see you," said Alex. "Good luck with your case. If you need help, let me know. I haven't done a murder in a while but I do remember some things."

"Sure, see you," said Penny. "Thanks for the offer." Penny climbed into her car, throwing her briefcase on the passenger seat. Despite its age, the car started right up. She drove away.

Alex watched as she left. Driving out of the parking lot, he turned left to go to his office. He didn't think he would tell his mother, Mabel, that he had run into Penny. She was after him to settle down and thought Penny would be a good match for him.

He could hear her say, "And Penny's mother, Kitty, thinks you two would make a good pair. After all, Penny's husband died well over three years ago. We both agree that it is time for her to move on. And you can't be flitting from girl to girl all your life. It is time for you to think about settling down."

No, he didn't think he would tell Mabel he had seen Penny. But he might think about seeing some more of her. After all, they were both members of the legal profession so it could be best to offer to help her with this trial.

Chapter 3

Althea watched as Penny left for court. "She'll do just fine," she said to JD. "And didn't she look nice in her grey linen pants and beige jacket. The white silk blouse is a nice touch. And she had all her notes. Oh my, this is a big case for her. She'll need our help."

J.D. looked up at Althea and then at the door. "Okay, let's go for a walk around the courthouse square."

J.D., short for Juris Doctor or Just a Dog, depending on Penny's mood, stood still while Althea attached his leash to his collar. She led him out of the office, closed the door behind her and headed for the stairs.

Out on the sidewalk, they turned to the right to get to the corner.

"Althea?" said a voice, "Is that you?"

"It is indeed," said Althea turning toward the sound. She saw her friend, Rose. "What are you doing out of the library?"

Rose, a short, plump woman wearing her usual dress slacks and blouse –the better to climb around looking for books or so she said-- gave J.D. a pat on the head, her reading glasses swinging from her neck.

"It's the end of August," Rose said, "it's hot and most folks are on vacation so I'm taking a stroll. Ricky is there to check out books."

"I'm so glad to run into you—can you walk along with us for a bit? I think we have a puzzle to work out."

"Oh, another one?" Rose said. "How fun."

"Well, this is what I know so far. Penny has a new client—Horace Appleworth—you remember he owns the renovation business. He and his partner live in that big old Victorian on Elm Street. Anyway, you know that Dick Boswick was murdered last night. Horace has been charged with the murder."

"Horace Appleworth." Rose stood stock-still. "He couldn't hurt a fly—why I remember how he brought one of his tall ladders over to help me get Cinder out of the tree. Why that cat climbs so high up, I'll never know. But Horace—no way he killed Dick. Why would he? What do you want us to do?"

"I think the Midvale Corners Literary and Investigatory Society needs to meet. Can you get us together tonight at the bookstore," Althea said, "around 7 pm?

"Of course, I'll call Mary. Can you call Arney?" Rose said.

JD stood up and started walking away.

"Yes," said Althea, feeling a pull on JD's leash. "Oh, dear, JD needs to walk. See you tonight."

Althea and J D made a trip around the 100-year-old courthouse, situated in the center of town with its bell tower 300 feet in the sky. Horace's company, Appleworth Construction, had refurbished the outside of the building several years ago. Even the eagle at the top of the tower had been re-gilded. It gleamed as the sun danced over its outspread wings.

"Excuse me," said a small voice. "What happened to the dog's ear? And what's his name? Where does he live? Is he friendly?"

"You're full of questions, aren't you," said Althea looking down at a little girl dressed in pink shorts and t-shirt with pink tennis shoes. J. D. was standing patiently, all his business accomplished.

"Oh, Mrs. Riversmith, you know me. I'm Mildred, Rose's niece."

"My goodness," said Althea, taking a closer look. "Of course, you are. My how you've grown."

Mildred, not interested in vagaries of adults, turned back to the dog. "Can I pet him? Does his ear hurt?"

"Yes, you can pet him and thanks for asking. No, his ear doesn't hurt anymore. It did hurt when the bomb went off and blew part of it away. He was a bomb-sniffing dog, but he had to leave the police force when he didn't sniff that particular bomb. His name is Just a Dog or J.D. for short."

"Oh," said the girl, her blue eyes wide. "Poor J. D. I bet that did hurt."

They walked along, the girl with her hand on J.D.s head, Althea thinking she should get back in case Penny needed her and she had to find Arney, and J.D. thinking whatever dogs think on a hot summer day.

"Mildred, there you are. Be careful, that dog could bite you," said a young woman hurrying toward them. She stopped when she saw Althea.

"Mrs. Riversmith, it's good to see you again. We just moved back to Midvale Corners and I haven't had a chance to see all of Rose's friends."

"Rose said you and Randy were back in town," said Althea. "She is so thrilled to have her only niece near."

"No, he won't bite, Mother," Mildred said, answering her mother. "He is a retired police dog. He helps people. Like that nice policeman who was talking to Dad this morning."

"Well, come along, we need to get home. I do hope Mildred hasn't been bothering you," she said turning to Althea.

"No trouble at all. JD likes the attention," said Althea, thinking Mildred was the perfect name for Roses' busy niece. She looked like a Mildred. Wondering why a policeman was talking to Randy, Althea hurried back to the office, where she saw Penny deep in thought at her desk.

Picking up phone she called Arney.

"Arney, Althea here. Can you meet tonight at the bookstore around 7? The Midvale Corners Literary and Investigatory Society need to meet."

"Certainly," said Arney in his perfunctory manner. "Does this have anything to do with Horace Appleworth and Penny representing the NRA so as far as Mike is concerned, Horace had means and opportunity and that's that—no need to look elsewhere. But, why would Horace kill Dick? Mike doesn't seem to have an answer to that question," he said hanging up.

Althea got up and walked into Penny's office. Penny looked up.

"I don't know, Althea," she said. "This is a big case. I'm not sure I can take this on. I've never defended an alleged murderer and I believe Horace—what if we go to trial and I lose and he goes to jail for a crime he didn't commit? I'd have to leave Midvale Corners. My practice would be destroyed."

"No, it won't be. You will do just fine," said Althea. "What about Kyle? He's a great private investigator. And your friend, Gordon

Swanson, will help. He's tried murder cases. I'll help in any way I can. I know you can do this."

"Well, the good news is that I managed to get bail set for Horace. Ryan was on his way to get the money. The judge made him wear a tether but at least he will be out of jail."

Penny stood up to her full five foot ten-inch height stretching her arms over her head.

"I'll call Kyle. He was in the CIA. I'm sure he will be able to help. And JD likes Percy."

"Why he likes that big old grey tomcat, I don't know," laughed Althea, "but they do get along. Do you need anything else? I think I'll head on home. You better go to, there is nothing more you can do today."

"I think I'll stay here for a bit. The office is quiet and I can read the reports again and do some research. We have a probable cause hearing in a couple weeks. I need to be ready for that."

Penny watched Althea leave then began taking all the paper from her briefcase. She stacked them up in piles, turned around and booted up her computer. It was time to get all this organized. JD sighed, sensing his mistress would be busy for a while.

"I won't be long," said Penny, smiling at the big dog.

When Althea came into the bookstore, the clock tower chimed 7. She saw Mary Taggert, Midvale Corners City Clerk, and Rose sitting at their favorite table in the center of the café section of the bookstore, discussing whether to have decaf or regular coffee. Arney stood leaning on his cane, waiting patiently for their decision so he could go order the coffees.

"And you Althea—having your usual decaf latte?" asked Arney when Althea came up to the table.

"No, I'll have regular," she said. The others agreed that regular was needed. Arney left to place the order.

Althea sat, put her large tapestry purse on the floor and turned to her two friends. Mary and Althea had known each other since they were girls. They played together, were in each other's weddings, and helped at the funerals of their husbands. The physical contrast between the two women was striking—Althea, barely over five feet, with snow white hair that stuck out at odd angles—Mary, taller, thinner with hair still dark and cut in the same bob she had worn in college.

Arney returned with a tray of coffees and some little cookies that shop owner and baker Belinda sent over for the group. After each had a sip of coffee and a bite of cookie or two, they turned to Althea expectantly.

"Do we have another puzzle to solve?" asked Mary. "We did so well on the last one."

"I don't know that Detective Dan was too pleased with us. I'm not sure he appreciated our efforts," said Rose, "but I noticed he used our suggestions to find the person who took that World War I helmet out of the display case in the courthouse."

"And, remember, a gas mask was missing, too," said Arney, shifting to adjust the crease in his seersucker slacks. "I am glad it was all returned. But, let's get down to business. Althea, what's going on?"

"This is a far more serious problem—this time Penny's client is charged with murder. And she is not sure she can represent him. She's not sure she is up to it and I want to help. This is what I know so far and it's not much. Horace Appleworth has been charged with First Degree murder of Dick Boswick. According to the paper, Dick was shot in the back of the head in his office last night around 8:30. Horace was heard arguing with Dick by Andy Clinton, the cleaning man and he was the only person other than Dick and Andy seen on the security tape."

"The first question is 'what do we know about Dick.'"

"I've heard rumors that Dick was having an affair with some girl in town," said Rose. She paused as a group of teen-agers walked by on their way to a table in the back where they could talk without the prying ears of adults. She continued "I also heard that he spent a lot of money and I don't know that he made that much as City Manager."

"He wasn't really liked by the people who reported to him," said Mary. "I didn't have that much to do with him, but I heard people complaining about his abruptness. And I did wonder about the people he recommended to do work around the city. Those contracts were worth a lot of money. The bids for the contract to renovate the interior of the Courthouse are in. The commissioners were going to announce the winner today. But then there was a big flap this morning—the assistant manager was sequestered with the commissioners. They finally decided to wait until after Dick's funeral to award it. I heard some talk of re-opening the bidding."

"Who was bidding this time? Was Horace one of them? And what about this affair rumor? Did Sally Boswick know? Jealousy can be a strong motivator for murder." Althea said, leaning back in her chair, listening to the swoosh sounds of the espresso machine. The bookstore was busy.

Arney spoke up, "I can research the past contracts—those are public records. It might be harder to find out the current bids—they are kept sealed I think—but I know the city accountant—we're in Kiwanis together. I'll see what I can find out."

"I'll keep my ears and eyes open for developments in the city offices," said Mary. She looked pensive, as if trying to remember something she'd heard. She had known Horace for many years and there was something in his past, but she couldn't quite dig it out.

"I'll see what I can find out around town," said Rose. "Everyone passes through the library during the week."

Penny and I haven't had time to go over them. How about we meet in a few days to compare notes. Our book club meets then so we can stay after," said Althea.

They all pulled out their paper calendars—except for Arney, who pulled out his I-Phone, found the calendar section, entered the date, punched some buttons and put it back in his pocket. By this time, the ladies had put everything away and were ready to go. The little group bustled out of the bookstore; nodding to people they knew, ready to take on the new task.

Chapter 4

Penny sat at her desk on Friday listening to the frequent ringing of her phone. She knew it was the press. She let it go to voice mail. Should she convince Horace to hire a more experienced attorney? Like Gordon, who had represented many clients charged with murder. And he knew how to deal with the press. Maybe if Horace hired Gordon, she could sit second chair and learn how to handle a murder trial.

She stood and stretched, deciding it was time to go home. JD, ready for his dinner, was heading for the door.

The phone started ringing again. Penny didn't answer.

"Penny, Horace here. I am out of jail. Thank you so much."

"Horace," said Penny grabbing the phone. "Sorry, I'm avoiding the press—they keep calling and calling. I am so glad you're out."

"Well, I am out but I have this ugly thing on my ankle. But that is much better than prison. What happens next?"

"Can you come in tomorrow so we can talk. How about around eleven? Will that work?"

"Okay, I'll see you at eleven,"

Penny hung up the phone with a sigh. She picked up J.D.s leash, clipped it onto his collar, grabbed her purse and headed for the door. "Let's go home, buddy. It's time to call it a night."

Promptly at eleven on Saturday morning, Horace came walking into Penny's office. Penny got up from her desk, shook Horace's hand and directed him to a chair by the round table that was in the corner of the room across from her desk. After Horace was settled, she sat down across from him, yellow legal pad and pen at the ready.

"Horace, are you sure you want me to represent you? You know that I have never represented anyone charged with such a serious crime. I've only been out of law school a short time and I'm just not sure I'm the one to be with you in the courtroom."

"Penny, let me ask you one question. Do you think I murdered Dick?"

Thinking that it really didn't matter what she thought, she said, "No, I don't.

Horace went on, "Good, and because of that, I am sure you will do the best you can for me."

"Thank you, I appreciate your confidence, but a murder trial is complicated with many things to consider. And, in this case, we have public figure in Dick Boswick, City Manager, known by practically everyone in Midvale Corners; we have a prosecutor, Mike Pritchard, who is up for election and wants to put this matter to bed as soon as he can and we have a police force that is convinced they have found their man and won't dig too hard to find the real killer. And then there is the media—they will be around at every turn."

"Penny I realize all that. I'm still confident that you can do this. What happens next."

Penny explained.

"Our next hearing is the preliminary exam. I hope that will be the end of it. If Mike can't present enough evidence to convince the judge that Dick was murdered and you did it, the judge won't continue the case."

"I don't understand," said Horace, looking confused.

"Okay, I'll explain. You are charged with murder in the first degree, which is a felony. Felonies are tried in the circuit court. The court you were in—well, you weren't actually in it, but you could see it—is the district court. That court has one part in the trial of felonies. The district court judge has the power to decide if there is probable cause to believe that the felony—here, murder—was committed and that you, Horace, committed it. To prove probable cause, the prosecutor only has to show that 'maybe' the crime was committed and that 'maybe' you did it. He doesn't have to show much. But if he doesn't meet his burden, the case can be dismissed by the judge, which is what I would like to see happen."

"How do we do that?" asked Horace.

"We cross examine their witnesses and we can put on our own witnesses. For example, did someone see you at the time of the murder?"

"You mean do I have an alibi?" asked Horace, leaning forward, hands clenched in front of him resting on the table, "I'm afraid not. I did go to Dick's office. I heard that Victor Miller had been awarded the contract and I knew his wasn't the lowest bid. But when I left, Dick was alive. I was so upset; I didn't go to the concert and walked the other way to cool off before I went home. Ryan was at the hospital so when I got home, there was no one there to give me an alibi."

"Do you remember seeing anyone while you were walking around?" asked Penny, making notes on her yellow legal pad.

"No," said Horace, eyes staring at the table, shaking his head slowly.

"Tell me more about Dick and the contracts,"

"You know that whenever there is work that needs to be done for the city, a Request for Proposal or RFP is posted in the local paper and on the bulletin board at the city offices. If a company wants to bid on the job, they get the specs from Dick and bid on the job. Dick gets the bids. The theory is that the lowest bid wins."

"But it didn't always work that way. Dick would present the commissioners with the bidder who promised him a kick back. I was getting tired of doing business with that crook and I told him so."

Penny sat up straight in her chair and stared at Horace. "What? What kick-back? How long has that been going on? And why didn't anyone report it? Who else knew?"

"I don't know how long; I think since he became the City Manager. It seems like it's always been that way. It wasn't fair, but if we wanted the work, we had to pay up."

Penny looked out the window, hearing the street noises below and seeing the people of Midvale doing their Saturday morning chores. After a moment, she turned back to Horace.

"Does Mike know this? It's a strong motive for murder, but you aren't the only one with a motive. We need to do some investigating. Can you write out the names of other contractors that might have been involved with the kickbacks? One of them could be the real murderer. I want Kyle Lafferty on it."

"I guess so but I don't want to get them in trouble," said Horace. They're my competitors but also my friends."

"Horace you are charged with murder. I want their names. They have nothing to fear if they didn't kill Dick Boswick."

"Okay," Horace took the yellow legal pad and pencil Penny handed him and began writing.

While Horace wrote names and looked up address, Penny picked up the reports she had received from Dan Dunlap, went to the copier and started making copies. While the copies were spitting out of the feeder on the copier, she searched for her cell phone under the papers on her desk. Smiling to herself, she thought of Althea who would be horrified if she saw the files all over the table and floor.

Horace came over, handing her the list of names.

"Thanks, Horace. I'll get Kyle Lafferty started on this right away. It will be an additional cost, but I think we need him. Kyle is a retired CIA operative and an excellent investigator

"How much more do you need?" asked Horace.

Penny told him three thousand get started. After Horace wrote out the check, Penny walked him to the door.

"Try not to worry too much," she said. "I'll be in touch soon with what we have found."

Horace left and Penny returned to her desk. Picking up her phone she punched in Kyle's phone number and waited for an answer.

When Kyle answered, Penny said, "Kyle, I need a P.I. Horace Appleworth, who has been charged with Dick Boswick's murder, is my client and I need help. Are you in your office?"

"No, I'm fishing. I'll be back tomorrow. Why don't you leave copies of what you have under my door and I'll see you Monday morning? Around ten? I'll bring the bagels."

"And I'll make the coffee—well, Althea will—she is much better at it. See you then."

Penny took the copies, stapled them in the right order, put them in envelope and slid them under Kyle's office door down the hall.

Going back to the office, she put the files away, grabbed her criminal law book for some light reading that afternoon, called J.D. and they left the office, heading for home. The decision was made. She would represent Horace. Now she had to do everything she could to defend him.

Monday morning Althea arrived at the office, opened the blinds, put her red straw hat on the hall tree in the corner and went into the small kitchenette in the corner of the office. It had been converted from a closet with the installation of a dorm-size white Kenmore refrigerator, a two-burner electric stove, and a small stainless-steel sink. After starting the coffee, she went back into her reception room/office.

She checked the phone for messages. There were 11, many from the press and a few from clients. She booted up her computer. She heard a scratching at the door. Looking down and smiled at Percy, Kyle's cat, sitting patiently waiting to be let into the office. "Come in," she said. In he marched, tail straight up, heading for the windowsill in Penny's office, one of his favorite sitting spots. He jumped up, looked down at the street waking up on a lovely August morning, settled himself down, paws tucked, ready to wait for J. D's arrival.

Kyle poked his head in the door. "Hi, Althea, tell Penny that I have the reports she left and I'll see her at ten. Is Percy a bother?"

"He's waiting for J.D and no bother at all," Althea said. She watched Kyle walk swiftly down the hall to his office, his compact frame the result of thrice-weekly workouts at the police gym. Althea closed the door then went to check that there was plenty of coffee, which Kyle lived on when he was working on a case.

The door opened with a swoosh. Penny and J.D. came in, armed with files and a new bone.

J.D. went up to Percy, giving a quick sniff, making sure it was his friend and then went to his bed. Percy followed, and began a careful washing.

Penny smiled hello to Althea, put down the files and bone, and went for her first cup of coffee.

"Kyle said he has the reports and will be here at ten," said Althea.

"Good, Horace is out on bond, but we need to start his case right away."

"By the way," Althea said, "you have to be in court this afternoon. Jimmy Harper was arrested again. He was found wandering around the courthouse square naked as a jaybird and covered with post-its and toilet paper. Here is the report."

"But he was just released from the jail last week. He must be off his meds again. Why was he covered with toilet paper and post-its?

Oh, I see, it says here that he was protecting himself from the electronic probes the police inserted in his body while he was in jail. His sister is not going to be happy. She has a family to raise and is at her wit's end. I think she needs to think seriously about an adult foster home for him. Would you call the Department of Social Services?"

"Of course," said Althea, picking up the phone.

Penny put down the report, noted the court time on her calendar, and went back to her musings about Horace and his problem.

She opened her book on criminal law from law school, which didn't seem so far away today. Penny completed law school after her husband, David, was killed in the automobile accident. She opened her office in Midvale Corners, her hometown, almost two years ago after graduation from law school. She liked the small-town practice—she felt she was helping the folks in Midvale Corners.

She read the definition of first-degree murder in her criminal law:

A person who commits a premeditated killing of another is guilty of first degree murder and shall be punished by imprisonment for life. Malice aforethought is as essential an element of the offense of murder as the act, which causes the death and the presumption of innocence applies to both ingredients of the offense. The prosecutor must prove both elements of the crime beyond a reasonable doubt.

"You are deep in thought," said Kyle, standing in her doorway holding a box from the Maxi's Deli. The smell of warm bagels wafted toward Penny.

Penny jumped and then smiled. She got up, walked around her desk, peeked in the box and took out her favorite, a cinnamon raisin. Coffee poured in their favorite mugs, they moved over to the conference table in the corner of Penny's office.

"Althea," said Penny, "please join us, we need your help."

Althea sat down. Both women turned and looked at Kyle.

He straightened. "I read all the reports you have so far. The coroner's report is preliminary—but it says that 'he was shot twice in the back of the head from a short distance. There were powder burns on the left side of his neck meaning the gun was held right against his neck. One bullet went through his neck and was discovered in the wall. The other rattled around his brain. He died instantly. He was shot with .22 caliber pistol. The police have not found the gun yet."

"After Horace was arrested, the police confiscated all his guns. He hunts and he's a champion pistol shooter. He had one .22 caliber pistol, which they sent off to the state police lab to test. They also took all his ammunition."

"Horace isn't happy about that," interrupted Penny. "Those are valuable weapons and he's worried the police will keep them."

"Well, they can't keep them if the charge is dropped or he's found Not Guilty at trial," said Kyle.

"That's all we know right now about the gun. We know that Horace was there—he admitted as much to the police. I know," Kyle said holding up his hand to silence Penny, "you told him not to talk, but he did. They always do. I can't tell from the report whether he was Mirandized before he talked to them. I'll check that out."

"We also need to look at motive," said Penny. "Murder in the first requires malice aforethought, which means that the prosecutor must prove beyond a reasonable doubt that the act of killing was intentional."

"Then we need to look at the victim. Why was Dick killed?"

"Kyle, trace Dick's days before the killing," said Penny. "Look more closely at who Dick Boswick really was and what he was up to. Horace said that Dick awarded contracts to the bidders that paid kickbacks. He gave me a list of the contractors."

Kyle and Althea stared at Penny. For a moment all was still.

Then they both spoke at once. "What? Do the police know? Isn't that a motive for murder?

"I don't know if the police know. And, yes, it could be a motive for murder," said Penny.

"I'll get on it right away," said Kyle, putting a copy of the list in his file.

"I'll research the law. I want to see the affidavit for the search warrant for Horace's house. I am quite sure Ryan would not give permission for them to search. Did they search before or after Horace was arrested," asked Penny? "And, does it make a difference."

Althea returned to her desk. This was news the Society needed. They were working hard to help Penny. She was sure her friends would come up with some answers.

"Keep me posted on progress," said Penny. "I better get ready for my hearing this afternoon. I need to go to the jail to talk to Jimmy. I hope he is wearing some clothes. I don't want to see him covered in post-its and toilet paper."

"Goodness, I hope not. That would not be a pretty sight. I'll see what I can discover from DHS," said Althea, hurrying off to her desk.

Kyle collected his files and headed out the door. "Percy, are you coming?" he said to the cat, that stood up, stretched and slowly ambled toward the door. J.D. looked up and watched his friend head on out the door. He put his head down and with a sigh went back to sleep.

Chapter 5

Mike Pritchard, prosecutor, looked out the window of his corner office on the second floor of the courthouse. He saw the citizens that he had sworn to protect going about their business. It was Monday morning. They moved quickly, occasionally stopping to exchange pleasantries and catch up with the news.

Mike suspected the big news was Dick Boswick's murder. Midvale Corners rarely had a murder—the most recent one a family feud that resulted in a death and was over ten years ago. At the time Mike was still on the police force during the day and attending law school at night. He had helped arrest a drunken Celia Mylonas who claimed her neighbor deserved killing for sleeping with Celia's husband. The whole matter was settled quickly with a plea. Mike had never observed or tried a first-degree murder case in his years in private practice or as prosecutor.

Now he was responsible and he knew this was a murder that would create a lot of press. Boswick was the city manager not some stranger but a person known to everyone in town. He had grown up here and married a local girl. His daughter was performing at the concert right about the time he was killed.

Mike, up for election next year, knew that a loss in Horace's case could be a disaster. The voters wouldn't care that he had faithfully upheld justice as prosecutor for two terms. His steady service would be forgotten if he didn't convict Dick's murderer.

He turned from staring out the window to see Sheriff Bill Nicholson and Detective Dan Dunlap come in the door of his office.

Both large men who played on competing football teams in high school, they filled up Mike's office.

"Right on time," Mike said, motioning them toward the conference table that took up half the office. The offices in the old courthouse were large, with fireplaces for warmth and bookcases for books. The five-foot high windows were a perfect balance to the twelve-foot ceilings. The eight-foot conference table with its big heavy oak arm chairs fit nicely along one wall. Bill and Dan sat on the long side.

"I want a complete update on the Boswick case," said Mike, sitting ramrod straight at the head of the table, "Have you found the gun?"

"No," said Sheriff Nicholson. "We are searching the area. We sent the .22 caliber pistol we took from Appleworth's house to the lab, but I don't think it's the gun. It didn't smell like it had been shot lately."

"Appleworth is a competitive shooter, a life member of the National Rifle Association—I'm sure he knew enough to clean it after he used it to kill Dick," said Mike, leaning forward and staring at the Sheriff. "But you know that."

"We don't know that and it didn't smell like cleaning lubricant either," said Bill.

"We won't get the report from the State Police Lab for a couple of weeks," said Dan Dunlap.

Mike frowned. "That's not soon enough. We have a probable cause hearing coming up and I intend to nail this case down before that hearing. Call and put a rush on the results."

"Two weeks is a 'rush,' Dan said. "I called in a favor. We might have it before the hearing, but I agree with Bill, I don't think it's the gun that killed Dick."

"We'll see," said Mike. "Do we have the fingerprint matches back yet?"

"No, we just sent Horace's booking prints over. We got the prints off the desk in Dick's office. Andy, the custodian, had just polished it when Dick came in around 7:30. Dick sent him packing so he didn't clean the rest of the office. There are dozens of fingerprints in that room and they all have to run through AFIS."

Dan paused and looked through his notes. He knew Mike was anxious for a conviction and he wanted to be accurate.

Finding the right page, he read out loud, "Andy left Dick's office and went to clean the bathrooms and empty the trash cans like he always did. He isn't sure when Horace arrived but he did hear Dick and Horace arguing. He said Horace sounded really mad. He didn't hear anyone else but he was running the vacuum cleaner and couldn't hear much anyway. He left about 8:30. He walked past the building toward town to meet his wife who was enjoying the concert. He thought he heard noise that sounded like a firecracker. He couldn't say for sure where it came from—but he thought it could have come from the building. Maybe."

"His recollection of the sound coincides with the coroner's estimate of the time of death," said Bill.

"Horace admitted he was in the building," said Mike. "And he admitted he argued with Dick. That's motive in my book."

"Is Horace left-handed?" asked Dan. "The coroner also said that the burn marks on Dick's neck indicate that he was shot by a left-handed person."

"Well, if he isn't, he could have switched hands to confuse us," said Mike.

Bill nodded in agreement. Dan didn't comment.

"We have the security tapes for that night," Bill said. "We can see Horace come in but we don't see him leave. The only people on the tape are Dick, Andy and Horace. We can see Andy leave but not Horace. I'm not sure why. Our computer expert is checking that out."

"We need to nail down the murder weapon," Mike said. "Send out more people to search for it, just in case the one we have is not the one that shot Dick."

"We don't have any officers to spare," Bill said. "But we we'll do what we can."

"I've been hearing some rumblings about Dick's ethics," Dan said, shifting in his chair. "One of my detectives reported that a friend told him he heard Dick took kick-backs on the contracts for work awarded by the City."

"What? Who told you that? I want that person," Mike said, slapping the table. "Why hasn't someone complained? Who got the contract for the most recent job? Get to the bottom of this. We certainly don't want the victim to be put on trial. He was our City Manager for years."

Mike stood up, a signal that the meeting was over. "I have to be in court in few minutes. Keep me posted."

Chapter 6

Alex Jeffries threw his briefcase on the passenger seat of his car. He climbed in the driver's seat, keys in hand and sat looking out at the courthouse parking lot. It was long after five o'clock. Most of the cars were gone. He would be late for dinner with his mother, Mabel. He turned the key and was soon out of the parking lot and pulling into the driveway of the two story Victorian house that had been his home since he was a boy. He bought the house from his parents after he graduated from law school. His parents spent their retirement years traveling around the country hauling the fifth wheel that was their home like a pair of turtles carrying their shell. When his father died suddenly, Alex flew to Florida to drive his mother back to Michigan.

His mother moved into his old room, insisting he keep the master bedroom.

"I won't be here that long," she said in her gentle way. "I may go to Arizona. Your dad and I made some friends there."

That was three years ago and Mabel was still sleeping in his old room. She became involved with several organizations in the community, avoided Michigan winters with her annual trips to Arizona, took care of his house, and generally, unless she thought he needed her advice, stayed out of Alex's life. The arrangement was working well. Alex didn't have to worry about the house and Mabel was free to come and go as she pleased.

Lately, however, Alex noticed that she was asking about his love life more than usual. Alex had never married, didn't think he wanted to be married, and was content with his usual female companions, all of whom were busy creating careers. Mabel had a different view.

He parked the car, closed the garage door—someday he would get an automatic door opener—opened the side door and followed his nose into the kitchen.

"Long day in court?" asked Mabel. "Wash your hands, dinner is ready."

Alex sniffed. "It smells like meatloaf."

"It is and lucky for us it is because it gets better with time." Mabel took the loaf pan out of the oven, placing it carefully on the trivet on the table in the corner of the kitchen. She put a baked potato on each of their plates. The salad came next and dinner was ready.

Alex cut each of them a slice of meatloaf and sat down.

Mabel took off her apron hanging it on the hook on the back of the pantry door joining Alex at the table.

"I saw Kitty Gallagher at the Zoo today," she said. "She was there with a group of students from the Academy. They were meeting with Dr. Fletcher, our veterinarian. I guess some of them think they want to be vets."

"She told me that you rescued Penny from the reporters the other night at the courthouse."

"It was nothing. Penny represents Horace Appleworth and the reporters were insistent she give them a statement. She didn't want to do that so we went out the back door and avoided them."

"That was nice of you, dear. And how was Penny?" Mabel said looking at him innocently.

Alex sighed. He knew where this conversation was going. Kitty Gallagher and his mother were plotting. They believed that the two of them were a perfect match. He wasn't about to tell his mother that he was thinking about Penny.

"Mom, I'm sure Penny does not need you and her mother arranging her dating life. She's quite capable of handling that on her own.'

"Well, maybe so, but I really think it is time that you settled down. I can't take care of this house forever, you know."

Alex looked at his petite mother with her wavy, snow-white hair who handled the education animals at the zoo easily, explaining to the children that the bearded dragon was not as fierce as he looked. He was constantly amazed at her abilities.

"Mom, I know you'll be around for a long time. And I can take care of myself. I do when you are off to Arizona in the winter. I'll admit I eat out more often and no one makes brownies as well as you do. Speaking of which, do we have any today?"

"Yes, but you're just trying to change the subject. I like Penny and her family and I hope you too will connect, but I won't interfere," she said, looking at Alex with a soft smile.

"Right," said Alex, clearing their plates.

"Just so you know," said his mother getting the brownies. "Coffee?"

Later that evening, Alex sat in one of the four Adirondack chairs placed carefully among the potted plants his mother tended every day on the porch that wrapped around the house. He liked the plants, but he knew that he would not have the time or the patience to care for them the way his mother did.

He watched the children in the neighborhood ride their bikes up and down the sidewalk. Parents, their youngest in strollers, walked by.

"Evening, Alex," said Mr. Humphrey. He was taking his little Shetland sheepdog, Toby, for his nightly stroll. Toby turned up the walk and came up on the porch. Mr. Humphrey followed.

"I guess Toby wants to visit."

"Please, have a seat, Mr. Humphrey," said Alex.

"You can call me Ethan, you know."

Alex shook his head, "No, I don't think I can do that. You were my social studies teacher in high school, you coached the debate team, and you are my mother's contemporary. I don't think I can change old habits."

Ethan laughed, "So be it. But know that, if you are able, you can call me Ethan."

Mabel came out the door. "Ethan, how nice to see you," she said. "How about a cold glass of ice tea?"

Ethan nodded. Mabel went back in the house returning shortly with the tea. She also brought a tray of brownies.

"These are really good," Ethan said. "I bet they would win a prize at the County fair."

"They did, a few years ago," she said.

Alex watched this exchange. His mother was beaming. Mr. Humphrey was sitting tall and relishing the attention from Mabel.

What was going on here? Mr. Humphrey had lived in the house two doors down for as long, maybe longer than the Jeffries had owned their home. Alex couldn't remember when Mrs. Humphrey died but it didn't seem like it was that long ago.

Suddenly he realized that both his mother and Mr. Humphrey were staring at him.

"Dear, Ethan asked if you knew anything about the murder of Dick Boswick. Everyone is talking about it, you know," said Mabel.

Alex shook his head, coming back to the conversation. "I don't know much but I did hear that the police arrested Horace Appleworth and are sure they have their man."

"Penny Johnson is representing him," said Mabel.

"I'm glad Penny is representing him," said Mr. Humphrey. "She was on the debate team too. She sure knows how to argue."

The conversation continued. Alex sat and listened to the two of them talk about the affairs of Midvale Corners and its people. He became aware that his mother and Mr. Humphrey had known each other a long time and that he was not needed on the porch. He quietly left, his mother smiling good night. He went to sit inside to read a brief for a case he had the next day. He stared at the words without seeing them. His mind kept wandering to Ethan and his mother and then to Penny. He felt change was in the air making him too distracted to concentrate on the intricacies of the law. After a time, he gave up and went to bed.

Chapter 7

Penny rolled over and looked at the Big Ben wind up clock on her bedside table. It was 4:45 a.m. on Wednesday morning. The last time she looked at the Big Ben, it was 3:30. And the time before that, it was 1:30.

J. D. padded over from his special mat in the corner of her bedroom. He put his head on the covers. Penny patted the spot beside her. J.D. jumped up, turned around his usual three times to beat down the grass that might be on the bed and made a nest.

Penny snuggled down intent on getting another hour or two of sleep. She listened to the loud tick-tock of the clock, which had been on her nightstand since her father gave it to her for her tenth birthday. She and David had argued about the clock. He wasn't sure he could sleep with the loud ticking. His clock radio gave the news or, if one wanted, sounds of nature could fill the room, blocking out the sounds of the street coming through the windows of their tiny apartment in Ann Arbor, MI where they lived the three years he was at University of Michigan law.

She remembered how hard it was for him to study—the living room was the only spot in the apartment—Penny sat in the tiny kitchen, listened to the radio, working on her lesson plans. She was teaching first grade. David clerked for a law firm and they survived.

When David graduated, he found a position clerking for Judge Brown, an appeals court judge. Their lives were improving. They moved to a bigger apartment. Penny, as they planned, started law school part time. They were busy, planning for their future.

All those plans disappeared one evening in May. Penny was thinking about dinner and planning to spend the evening studying civil procedure. Then the phone rang and the words "I'm afraid there's been an accident" changed everything. Penny rushed to the hospital. Her parents and David's parents arrived early in the morning. David was on life support. His car had been t-boned at the intersection. His little car was no match for the cement truck that hit him.

He died the next afternoon. Penny was grateful that she didn't have to make the decision to take him off life support. He made the decision for her and slipped out of this world.

Penny threw her long legs over the side of the bed and stood up.

"I give up. Let's go for a short run, J.D. Maybe that will make me feel better. I have to meet with Horace this afternoon. I think Ryan is coming, too."

J.D., still on the bed, raised his head and looked at Penny. She put on her running clothes, grabbed his lead and attached it to his collar. He got up slowly, jumped down and stretched.

They headed out the door. The sun was just barely rising over the horizon. The sky was cloudless. She saw the red streaking through the trees. There wasn't much dew. The days were dry in the August heat. It felt like they would have another hot day.

Penny jogged down the driveway, turned right and headed down the block. Few houses had lights on. Most were silent, sleeping in the coolness of the morning.

Penny ran until most of the houses had lights on. The town was coming to life

"Hi, Penny," said a male voice. "Having a run?"

Penny nodded and waved at Walter Petry, the local doctor and medical examiner for the county, who was walking toward his car, coffee in hand. He stopped.

"I should have Boswick's autopsy report for you late this afternoon," he said.

Penny bent over, catching her breath. J.D. was hardly winded. She waved at Walter, nodded and smiled. She jogged toward her tiny house. She thought about her day. She had court hearings and research to do; her long day was about to begin.

Penny dressed for court, ate some Raisin Bran deciding to get her coffee at the office. Althea's coffee was superb. Her's was not.

Penny grabbed her briefcase off the chair by the kitchen door. "Come on, J.D. We need to get to work."

Four turns and a few minutes later Penny and J.D. walked into the office. Althea greeted them with a nod, the phone tucked into her shoulder, while she wrote notes on the yellow legal pad.

"Thanks, so much Emma," she said. "I do appreciate your efforts and I know Jimmy's sister will be pleased. Penny can help her with the paper work, I'm sure."

Penny nodded. She went into her office and reached for Jimmy's file, ready to take notes.

"Emma says there is a spot in group home over in Chesterville. She believes Jimmy will qualify. Do you think the Judge will agree to let him go there?

"I'm sure of it. Judge Hancock is getting tired of seeing Jimmy come before him. He wants him settled as much as Ginger does. We all know that jail is not the right place for him."

"Betty Harrison called first thing this morning. She wants an appointment. It seems that she has been charged with contempt of court for using her phone in the courthouse. She was on a jury and called home to check on the baby-sitter. Can you imagine? I told her I would call her back with a time when she could come in."

"Oh, my goodness, poor Betty. I should be back by noon. Horace and Ryan are coming in around 3 pm. I want to have some time to look at the reports and the law before they come in. We might get the autopsy report sometime today. Try to fit her in."

Penny headed back to the office. Her day, successful so far, was not over.

Althea was pounding the keyboard of her computer when Penny walked into the office. Penny smiled—Althea learned to type on a manual typewriter--she didn't believe the letters would appear on her monitor if she didn't press down firmly. Penny kept a spare keyboard in the drawer. It was only a matter of time before Althea would wear this one out.

"The judge agreed to let Jimmy go home with Ginger and Ginger agreed to keep him for a while. She wants to investigate the group home. She doesn't want him in danger."

"It will be hard to her," said Althea. "She raised him, but it is time for him to be more independent. Betty Harrison, the client with the contempt problem, is coming in tomorrow morning at ten. I put it on your calendar."

"Good," said Penny, "I need time to get ready for Horace and Ryan."

Penny went to the small kitchen, poured a cup delicious smelling coffee. "Do I smell cinnamon?"

"Yes, just a tish," answered Althea.

Penny returned to her office after the hearing for Jimmy where it was agreed he would live in a group home. J.D., who had been sleeping under Althea's desk, followed her. Penny gave J.D. several pats on the head, telling him he was a good boy and then sat down pulling the thick file on her desk, labeled People v Appleworth. Looking at it, she knew it was going to get thicker before the trial, fatter than any file she'd ever had. She sat down slowly. JD returned to his bed with a sigh.

Horace and Ryan arrived precisely at 3 o'clock.

"We brought cookies," said Ryan. "We knew you would need a pick me up and it is almost tea time."

They sat down at the small conference table.

Penny came to the table with the file. "I received the autopsy report from Walter Petry. It says that Dick was shot in the back of the head, right where the head is attached to your spine. There were two bullet holes."

Penny read from the report 'soot and stippling were observed around the entry wounds. Stippling or tattooing, happens when gunpowder particles are driven into the skin creating hemorrhages in a spotted pattern.'

"See," said Penny, slowly placed the pictures of Dick's neck on the table, "look at the picture, at that dark circle around the bullet holes. On one side of his neck it looks like the skin is torn in a triangular pattern."

Ryan, who had seen worse at the trauma center, stared at the pictures. He held one up. "It looks like the bullets went into the left side of the neck. Did they find the bullets?"

"It says here that one bullet was found lodged in Dick's brain. The other went right through and was across the room. They dug it out of the wall and sent it for identification."

"Dan said they found two shell casings on the floor to the left of the victim. They were .22 caliber casings. He's waiting for the lab report, which may be able to tell what type of gun was used."

"Dr. Petry thinks that the person who shot Dick was left-handed since the bullets entered from the left."

Horace, who been avoiding the pictures, looked up. Eyes wide, he stared from one to the other. He was pale.

"I'm left-handed," he said. The room became silent.

"Yes, but you shoot and play golf with your right hand," said Ryan, brightening up. "Remember, that time the range officer was annoyed with you because when you shot your pistol left-handed in that match last summer, your shells kept hitting the guy next to you? And that guy complained and so you changed your shooting stance."

"Oh, I do remember that," said Horace. "I play golf right-handed because left-handed clubs are hard to find. Thanks, Ryan. But the point is—I can shoot with either hand."

Ryan patted Horace's arm.

"The police took all my guns," said Horace, shaking his head. "I had a .22 caliber pistol, a deer rifle, a shotgun. They took all the ammunition. They even took my hunting bow and the arrows. Why? Dick was not shot with an arrow."

"They will send your pistol to the lab to determine if it was the murder weapon."

"It most assuredly wasn't," said Horace. "I haven't shot it since the pistol match three weeks ago."

"Mike, the prosecutor, will be anxious to determine if that's the gun that killed Dick. He will rush the reports if he can. He will want to put the reports in evidence at the probable cause hearing," Penny said. "He seems to believe that he has Dick's killer and is not asking the police to investigate further."

"This is strange," she continued, reading from the report. "Horace, did you see any money on Dick's desk? It says here that two new one hundred-dollar bills were found under his head. They were covered with blood."

"He didn't have any money out when I saw him," Horace said. "He was standing and we were yelling at each other. I would have noticed a couple of hundred-dollar bills. He was still standing when I left."

"The report states that they found your prints on the desk and around the office."

"Well, that's not surprising. I told them I was there, but I didn't shoot him."

"Horace, what were the two of you arguing about?"

Horace shifted, reaching down to adjust the tether. Shifting again, he said,

"The City had just put out an RFP for the renovation of the interior of the courthouse. It's a big and complicated job. They want to keep it architecturally accurate. There are only three of us in the area that still bid on that kind of work. Fiona Houlis, she runs her family's company, Houlis Lumber and Victor Miller of Miller Construction. Victor, Fiona and I are usually the ones that submit an RFP. There are some other smaller companies but they don't bid on the really big jobs."

"The winner of the bid was going to be announced the Friday. After Dick was killed. I heard that it was going to go to Victor Miller. And I also heard that Victor paid a kickback to Dick. I've heard that before, but I am pretty sure now that this time it was true."

"What I don't understand is how killing Dick would change anything," said Ryan.

"The prosecutor will argue that it did change things," said Penny. "The commissioners decided to hold off on awarding the contract until the mystery of Dick's death is solved. He will argue that you killed him to delay the contract and that you could influence the commissioners to give you the job," said Penny. "Isn't one of your relatives a commissioner?"

"You must mean Ralph Langdon. He's a shirttail relative of my mother's. He wouldn't help me. He doesn't approve of my lifestyle. And he can't stand Ryan. He claims that when Ryan sewed him up after he cut his arm with his chain saw, Ryan did a poor job and it left a nasty scar."

Ryan shook his head. "He was lucky he kept the use of his arm. A millimeter deeper and he could have lost it. I worked on that arm for hours."

"The long and the short of it is that he would never think of helping me," Horace said.

"That won't stop the prosecutor from using that argument to establish motive," Penny said. "In order to prove first degree murder, he has to prove both that you killed Dick and that you went there intending to kill him. Remember that at the probable cause hearing, he only has to prove that maybe you killed Dick and maybe you intended to."

Horace stared at the floor. "It doesn't look good."

"Horace, I want you to think carefully about that night and try to remember if anyone saw you leave the office. The film from the security camera shows you entering, but doesn't show you leaving, and, it doesn't show anyone else other than you, Dick, and Andy."

"Ryan was working ER that night so I decided to go the concert. The high school band was playing. I found a spot, set up my camp chair. I saw Dick and Sally across the square. Then I saw Dick leave and I followed him."

"Why did you follow him?"

"I was mad about the contract and I wanted to see if I could get him to admit that he took kick-backs in exchange for awarding the jobs. I know that was stupid. There was no way he would admit that to me. I told the police that."

"I know, I read it in the report," Penny pointed to the report on her desk.

"Anyway, we argued. I accused him and naturally he denied it. I left before I hit him. He's, was, an arrogant...you know."

"What door did you go out?'

"I went out the front door."

"Did you see the security camera?"

"I don't think so. Wait," he paused, stood and walked over to the window. Turning back to Penny, he continued,

"I do remember looking up and the camera was a weird angle. Not pointed at the door but off to the side. Then I left. Dick followed me. I think he locked the door after me but I'm not sure. I thought about going back to the concert, but decided I needed to cool down. I went the other way. I walked around the town for a few blocks.'

"Which blocks? Maybe someone saw you. Think carefully," Penny said.

"Oh, I don't know. Do you have a map of the town? Maybe I can figure it out."

Penny got up, went to the door of her office.

Althea looked up.

"Do we have a map of Midvale Corners," asked Penny.

"Yes," said Althea, "I'll get it."

Moments later she appeared at the door. Penny, who had returned to the table, Ryan and Horace looked up. Althea had the map and a yellow legal pad in her hands.

She handed the map to Horace.

"I'll write down your route," she said, pulling the cap off a highlighter. The smell of ink wafted through the room. "Kyle can check it out tomorrow."

Horace smiled his thanks. He studied the map. Pointing, he said, "The City offices are on Oak. I turned left out the door and went down Oak toward the railroad tracks. I crossed over the tracks and went north up Kiwanis toward Laylin Park. I think I turned north on Summit. Maybe I got as far as Rogers. But I know at some point I decided to head on back to the concert to get my chair. I couldn't hear the music anymore. I figured it was over. I walked down back to the Courthouse—not sure what route I took. I found my chair, folded it up and headed to the car. That's it. I don't remember seeing anyone. Everyone was gone. But I was thinking about how mad I was. My company would do a much better job than Victor's."

"Did you get all that?" Penny asked Althea.

"Got it," said Althea, sitting back.

"Do you remember the time?

"Not too sure about that either. The concert started about seven o'clock. I saw Dick leave about the time the concert was getting ready to start. I waited a bit then decided to follow him. It took some time to get to the office, I don't know, maybe ten-fifteen minutes or so. He went around to the back. There is a back door to his office. I started to follow him, but then he came and fiddled with the front door. After he left, I went and tried it. It was open so I went in. We argued and I left. I don't know what time. All I know is that the concert was over and everyone was gone when I got back to the courthouse."

"Good, Horace. I think we've done enough for today," Penny said. "I'm sure we will have more reports in the next few days. I'll send copies and call you if I need you."

"What should we do?" asked Ryan, standing, his brow furrowed with concern. "We can't do nothing."

"For the time being, gentlemen," said Penny, looking sternly at each in turn, "that is exactly what you do. Nothing. Go about your regular business as if all was well. We don't want to raise suspicion."

They both nodded. "Okay," said Ryan, exhaling his frustration. Gathering up their things, they walked toward the door. J.D. followed them, sitting quietly as they left the office. Percy managed to leap through the open door. He headed toward the windowsill in Penny's office. The late afternoon sun was streaming in. It was a perfect spot for a cat to sit. He jumped up on the sill and began a serious wash, starting with the base of his tail.

"Percy, that's not polite," Althea said. "You could at least say hello before getting down to business."

Althea looked at Penny. "Do you want me to call Kyle so he can get started on finding someone who saw Horace that night? He must be close by since Percy is here."

"Yes, we really need to find an alibi witness for Horace. So far, the prosecutor's case looks really good—at least for the probable cause hearing. We still don't have the reports on the fingerprints or the gun—those might make a difference."

Penny stretched. She saw J.D. standing, staring at her. "I know; you need to go for a walk. Let's go. We can walk around the courthouse—maybe I'll get an idea or two that can help Horace."

Chapter 8

Sheriff Bill Nicholson's phone was ringing when he came into his office shortly after one on Thursday afternoon.

"Sheriff Nicholson, this is Wendy Morgan. Me and Georgie and Sam Unger were walking along the railroad tracks in back of the city offices and we found a gun. I thought I should call you. I didn't want the little kids to get it."

"What? Where? Did you touch it?"

"Well, we moved it a little to get a better picture."

"Picture with what?"

"Well, duh, with my cell phone," said Wendy, using the tone teenagers use when exasperated at the lack of awareness of adults. "Then we up loaded it on my Facebook page. I'm getting a lot of likes. I can text it to you. What's your number? It's really cool, but I thought you might want to come get it. We don't want anyone to get hurt."

Sheriff Nicholson gave Wendy the e-mail address. A few seconds later Wendy's picture appeared. He saw a small pistol nestled in the weeds by the railroad track.

"Wendy, tell me exactly where you are. Officer Dunlap and I'll be right there. Don't touch that gun again."

"Dunlap," he yelled across the room, "we need to go get this gun."

Dan Dunlap lumbered up out of his chair and looked across the squad room toward the Sheriff. Puzzled, he thought "What gun?"

The two men walked along the railroad track. After a short distance they saw the kids jumping up and down and yelling. Bill saw Wendy. Some of the kids were poking at something in the weeds.

"Leave that gun alone," yelled Dan.

The two boys backed off.

"See," said one of the boys pointing. "It's right there. Is it loaded? Did somebody get shot? Who does it belong to?"

Bill ignored their questions. He looked across the park that ran by the tracks. He could see a couple of his officers driving toward him. He motioned them to park at the top of the embankment near the location.

Dan moved the two boys and Wendy out of the way. He pulled out a small notebook. "Now, tell me exactly what happened."

Wendy looked at the boys who were suddenly silent.

"We were walking along the tracks looking for stuff. You know, sometimes stuff falls off the train. Anyway, Georgie had a stick and he was hitting the bushes. I don't know why—boys do dumb stuff like that."

"It's not dumb," said Georgie. "Look what we found. I poked at it and then I saw something metal looking. And after I moved the bushes, I saw it was a gun."

"I said, 'Let's take a picture of it and put it on Facebook,' explained Wendy. "I'm the only one whose phone has a camera. Do you think it's the gun that killed that man?"

"I don't know," said Dan, wondering the same thing as he was taking notes in the little notebook he carried everywhere.

"Hey, dude, will we have to testify? Will there be a trial?"

"What trial? We don't know yet who this gun belongs too. You guys go on your way. I have your names and phone numbers. Tell your folks I'll be in touch."

The kids slowly walked away, talking excitedly about their discovery.

Sheriff Nicholson was directing the recovery of the pistol. The crime scene investigator, Nancy Randal, was fresh out of officer training and ready to use her new skills. She carefully blocked off the area with yellow crime scene tape, then took photographs while walking the grid, covering all of the area.

"This pistol looks pretty old, Sheriff,' she said staring down at it lying in the weeds. "It's a semi-automatic. The grip looks like wood, not plastic and it has gouges in it—like someone scratched it with a sharp instrument. We can tell more when we get it back to the lab."

Nancy drew on a pair of latex gloves. She pulled a pencil out of her pocket, leaned over, and stuck the pencil in the barrel of the pistol, picking it up slowly. Another officer held open an evidence bag. She let the pistol slide off the pencil into the bag, sealed it shut, and labeled it. She then placed it in box to be taken to the lab.

"Look carefully for footprints or other evidence—any scraps of paper, cigarette butts, anything that might lead us to the owner," said Bill.

The team looked carefully around the area. After an hour, they stood in circle shaking their heads. They didn't find anything that could suggest where the pistol came from.

"It looks to me like someone threw the pistol into those tall weeds. The kids said they moved it to get a better look so we don't know where it was originally," said Dan. He picked up the bag holding the pistol out of the box. "It's old, but I think we can find a registration number. Has anyone called to report a missing pistol?"

When no one answered he figured the answer was no.

Nancy took notes on all she had done. She packed up her crime scene gear, placing it in the trunk of the patrol car sitting at the top of the small rise from the ditch next to the railroad tracks. She left the scene on her way to the crime lab.

Dan and Bill walked together toward the Sheriff's department.

"What's Facebook?" asked Bill. His skills with the computer were limited to reading e-mail and sending messages. "And how do we get to it? I don't want that picture up there. Or do I?"

Dan explained what he knew about Facebook but from the confused look on Bill's face, it was clear he didn't understand.

"I asked Wendy to bring in her computer," said Dan. "I want her to show Carl, our resident IT guru, her page, what's on it, and more importantly, who has commented on the picture of the pistol. She called her Dad, and they are coming in after he gets off work. He wasn't too happy about it."

Wendy, clutching her laptop computer to her chest, and her father, Oscar, arrived at the police station promptly at 5:30.

"I don't want my daughter messed up in any crime scene," Mr. Morgan said. "I don't want her to get hurt. I already told her that I'm taking that cell phone down to the store and have them disable the camera. There will be no more picture taking."

"I understand," said Dan, leading them back to Carl's small cubicle. Wendy slowly handed Carl her computer. He plugged it in, booted it up and motioned for her to sit down.

"Please find your Facebook home page," said Carl.

"Wow, look at all the comments I got with the picture of the gun," Wendy said. "I've never had so many."

Carl looked over her shoulder at the page—he saw the pistol lying in the weeds, with Georgie holding the weeds away from it with a stick so Wendy could get a better picture.

"Wendy, do you know all the people that wrote on your wall?" Carl asked.

"Of course, I know them; they're my friends."

"Look closely. We may want to contact them and ask them if they know anything about the pistol."

"See the trouble that phone got you into," said her father.

"Daddy, I'm sure none of my friends know anything about that pistol."

Sheriff Nicholson looked at the computer with the picture of the pistol and the long list of comments. If the pistol was connected with a crime, did the fact it was put out on the Internet affect the use of pistol in trial if there was one. He didn't know.

"I'm going to call the prosecutor. I need his advice on what we should do. Do we leave the picture up there or remove it—can you remove it?"

"Of course, see the little button that says 'remove', you click on the picture and click on remove and it will go away. It's real easy," Wendy said. "Do you want me to take it off?" Her hand moved the mouse. The arrow moved toward the picture.

"Don't," said Dan and the Sheriff at the same time. She stopped.

"Can you leave your computer here for a couple of days," Dan asked.

"No, I'd be lost without it." Wendy, grabbing it off the desk, looking horrified.

"Of course, she can," her father said, prying it out of her hands. "No trouble at all. We want to help in any way we can."

"Dad, no," she reached for it again.

"Yes, you can. Now do you need us any longer? It's time to get home for supper."

Dan and Bill thanked them for coming in. Wendy trailed behind her father. She looked back dismayed. Carl was already at work on her keyboard.

"What's he doing with my computer?"

The door to the squad room closed. They were gone.

Bill Nicholson was already on the phone when Dan arrived the next morning at eight. He motioned Dan over to chair across from his desk.

"Yes, I understand, Mike. The gun is already at the lab. It was in the dirt and is old, but the lab guy thinks he can locate the serial number. It may be so old, it doesn't have one, but if so we will have to deal with that."

"Okay, we'll do that," he said. He hung up the phone.

"Mike is not happy," said Dan.

"No, he is not. He's afraid that having the gun on Facebook will cause problems but he's not sure how. He wants the gun identified immediately. The press has been calling and he's getting antsy."

"We got the results back from Horace's pistol," said Dan. He put on his reading glasses, found the second page of the report.

"Examiner shot a bullet from the suspect's gun into the bullet recovery tank. The retrieved bullet was compared to the bullet taken from the victim. Examination under the comparison microscope showed that both bullets were .22 calibre. However, using the FBI's General Rifling Characteristics File, he determined that the bullet taken from the victim was shot from a Colt automatic pistol. The suspect Horace Appleworth's pistol is a Remington. It is my opinion that the pistol taken from the suspect is not the murder weapon."

"Mike's not going to be happy about that," said Bill. "He doesn't want to start over looking for suspects."

"No, but the good news is that the pistol the kids found is a Colt. Do you think that could be murder weapon? The location is right. If the killer left from the back of the city offices after shooting Dick, he could have walked through the park by the railroad tracks and thrown the gun down the embankment," said Dan.

"I suppose Horace could have done that," said Bill.

"I'm not sure Horace is our killer," said Dan.

"Well, Mike is," Bill answered. "We'll see what the report on that gun reveals."

"I'm going to go see if Carl's found anything on Wendy's computer. I wonder if there are any interesting comments on her Facebook page." Dan left Bill's office.

He found Carl staring at the Facebook page.

"I can't believe some of the things these kids put on the Internet. Do their parents know what they are doing? Some of them post pictures that are almost porn." Carl said, shaking his head.

"In answer to your question, no, there hasn't been too much interest in the gun. It seems our younger generation has a short attention span. They are on to new and different experiences. I have the addresses of all the people who commented on Wendy's wall if you want them."

"Yes, I do," said Dan. "I think I'll give them a call to see if they know anything. If you don't get any more comments today, then we can return the computer to Wendy. I am sure she will be happy to have it back."

Dan headed for the coffee pot. He would need lots of coffee. He had a list of twenty-five people to call. It promised to be a long day.

"Hey, Dad," yelled Sammie Rahn to his dad, Jake. "Come look at this gun that Wendy Morgan found. She took a picture of it with her phone and put it on Facebook.

"What gun?" said Jake coming into his son's bedroom. "What are you talking about?'

"It looks like that old pistol you had. Look at the handle—it has those same funny scratches on it that yours had.'

Jake leaned over his son's shoulder and looked closely at the picture on Wendy's Facebook page.

"Naw, that's not mine."

"I don't know Dad, it sure looks like it." Switching gears, Sammie asked, "Can I go to the movies with the guys tonight?"

A long conversation followed during which it was determined which guys, who was driving, which movie, time, and place. Jake agreed to take the boys to the theater in the mall if one of the other parents would pick them up.

"Thanks, Dad, I'll go call Tyler. His dad's usually good for a ride."

When Sammie was out of the room, Jake highlighted the picture of the pistol, hit print and waited for the print to appear in the printer. He wanted to look at it more closely. He had an uneasy feeling about that pistol.

Chapter 9

Penny, Horace, and Ryan came through security at the district court the next morning at precisely 8:00. Penny looked around the large reception area. Mike and Dan were in a far corner of the room, their heads together. She led Horace and Ryan to one of the benches that lined the walls and the center of the room.

"Stay here, I'll go talk to Mike. I think we're first on the docket."

"I don't testify, do I?" asked Horace.

"No, the prosecutor will put on his witnesses. This is not the time for you to testify."

Penny approached Mike and Dan. Dan had a report in his hand.

"Dan has another report for you," said Mike. "After you read it, we will see if you still want to have the hearing today. You might want to talk to your client about a plea."

Dan handed her the report. He didn't say a word.

Penny, clutching the report, walked back to Horace and Ryan.

"What's wrong?" asked Ryan.

"I'll tell you in a minute."

Penny read the report. She read about Wendy and her friends finding the pistol by the railroad tracks. She read about how the CSI Randal took pictures (attached) and put the pistol in an evidence bag. She learned that the pistol had been moved by Georgie Unger, age 12, photographed by Wendy and put on Facebook. She read that the lab concluded that the pistol was the weapon that killed Dick. And she learned that the crime lab was able to find the true owner of the pistol and his name was Horace Appleworth.

Now Penny understood Mike's big smile. She understood Dan's non-communication. What she didn't understand was how this pistol could be registered to Horace Appleworth.

She turned to Horace. "Do you or did you ever own a Colt .22 calibre pistol?"

"No, why?"

"Because the police found one behind the city offices, by the railroad tracks. They determined it is the gun that killed Dick. And they claim it is registered to you."

"To me? No." Horace's body slumped; holding his hands, palm up in front of him, he said, "The police have all my guns."

"They will try to enter this report in evidence today. I'll not agree. We will argue. I may win, but I doubt it. This weakens our case."

Penny led her flustered client into the courtroom.

"Is your client ready to plead guilty," Mike asked when Penny came up to the defense table to left of the Judge's bench.

"No, and I'll not stipulate to this report. I hope you have the lab technician here."

"We do and he is ready to testify."

"All rise," said the Bailiff. Judge Hancock came through the door behind the bench. He sat down. "You may be seated."

Penny stood, put her appearance on the record and sat down. Mike would start the hearing with his first witness, the investigating officer who arrived first on the scene. He testified that he was sent to the city offices by a 911 call from Sally Boswick. Once there he found Dick Boswick lying on his desk in a pool of blood. He secured the site and waited for the Crime Scene Investigators.

Penny took notes automatically. She noticed her hand shook a little. The news of the pistol, a pistol connected to her client, shattered most of her argument. The cases in her briefcase would stay in her brief case. Judge Hancock would never hear her well-planned argument.

Horace moved the yellow legal pad she gave him to write questions on in front of her. He wrote, "OMG—am I going back to jail?"

Penny shook her head and went back to listening. "Your witness," said Mike. She didn't need to cross-examine this witness because he was there merely to set the time and place of the original call to the station.

Penny listened to the testimony of Andy Clinton who heard Horace arguing with Dick. Next was Walter Petry who told the judge that, in his opinion, Dick's death was a homicide, not a suicide. Dan Dunlap was the last to testify.

Referring to his notes, Dan said, "After I learned from Andy Clinton that Horace had been at the city offices and had argued with the deceased, I went to his house to interview him. He let me in and said he would be glad to talk to me. We sat in his living room. He admitted that he argued with the deceased but insisted Mr. Boswick was alive when he left. He wasn't sure what time he left."

"Did you arrest him?"

"No, not at that moment. Based on what we learned later, we went back in the morning, read him his rights and arrested him."

Penny knew from the report that Dan had reviewed the security tape and saw Horace and no one else in the offices that night and that was what led to his arrest. She decided to let his testimony rest as it was, Judge Hancock didn't need to hear about the security tapes. She could argue about them later.

The last witness called was Sheriff Bill Nicholson.

"Sheriff, did you receive a call from a Wendy Morgan the afternoon of Thursday, September, 8th?"

"Yes"

Bill described his conversation with Wendy, which led to the discovery of the pistol in the weeds by the railroad tracks in back of the city offices. "We bagged and tagged the pistol and sent it off to the State Police crime lab to be identified, if possible."

"Sheriff Nicholson, is it true that Wendy Morgan took a picture of the pistol with her cell phone?" asked Penny, as she stood to begin her cross-examination.

"What did she do with that picture?"

"She put it on her Facebook page on the Internet?"

"She did what?" asked Judge Hancock. He looked at Sheriff Nicholson. "She sent the picture to her Facebook page? From her cell phone? How do you do that? Did she say why?"

"Yes, your honor, she did. She told us she wanted to show her friends the 'cool thing' they found."

Judge Hancock shook his head in puzzlement.

"Is the picture still up on her Facebook page?" Penny asked, when she was sure the Judge was done questioning the Sheriff.

"No, we asked her to remove it on Friday—it was only up for 24 hours."

"Did Wendy's friends comment on the picture?"

"Yes, there were 25 comments. We are in the process of contacting those people."

"I am assuming that list will be made available to the defense."

"Yes."

Penny had no more questions for the Sheriff. She made a note to be sure to request the list of names from the prosecutor.

Mike Pritchard called his last witness, the lab technician who had filed the report on the Colt 22 pistol found by Wendy and friends.

The lab technician's testimony followed the report Penny had before her.

"Were you able to identify the owner of the Pistol." Mike asked.

"Yes, we were able to tentatively identify the owner. It is Horace Appleworth."

Mike looked pleased. He sat down. "Your witness," he said.

Penny led the technician through the process used to identify Horace's ownership of the pistol.

"We entered a description of the pistol into the state's databank of registrations. We got three hits, but this pistol is unique because the wooden handle has letters carved into it. They look like RAA. Only one pistol matched that description. It was a pistol registered by Horace Appleworth twenty years ago. We found no subsequent sale or exchange of ownership."

"Thank you, Officer," said Penny. She sat down.

"Any witnesses, Ms. Johnson," Judge Hancock asked.

"No, your honor."

"Your honor," Mike said, "the state has shown that on or about Thursday, August 20th at 9 pm, Dick Boswick was murdered in his office in the city office building at 147 Alexander, Midvale Corners, that he was killed by two bullet shots to the head from a .22 caliber pistol, that Horace Appleworth was at the offices, was heard to argue with Mr. Boswick. It was also established that the pistol used to kill Mr. Boswick is owned by Horace Appleworth.

"Therefore, the state asks that Horace Appleworth be bound over to the Circuit Court to tried for the murder of Dick Boswick. We also ask that Mr. Appleworth's bond be revoked and that he be immediately returned to jail to await his trial."

Penny stood. "Your honor, there is no denying that Dick Boswick was shot in the back of the head, that those shots killed him and that someone fired those shots. My client admits that he spoke with Mr. Boswick at his office that night but denies that he had anything to do with Mr. Boswick's death. The pistol that was found could belong to anyone. Scratches on the handle do not rise to the level of positive identification."

"We ask that Horace Appleworth not be bound over for the murder of Dick Boswick."

Judge Hancock reviewed the evidence presented that day. He said, "After a review of the evidence, I believe that there is ample evidence to show that Dick Boswick was killed by being shot twice in the back of the head and I believe there is enough to establish that there is probable cause to believe Horace Appleworth committed the murder. I, therefore, will send this matter on to Judge Sanford in the Circuit Court, where it will be set for trial."

"As to bond, I believe the prosecutor has asked that bond be revoked. Any comments, Ms. Johnson?"

"Yes, Your Honor. My client denies committing this crime. We will prove his innocence at trial. My client assures the court that he will appear for all hearings required in this matter. My client has been a resident of Midvale Corners for over twenty years; he has a home and a business here. He has no prior record. The court has set a high bond, which has been posted. My client is wearing a tether and is following the directions of the court. We ask that bond be continued."

"Your honor," Mike said. "This is a heinous crime. This man cold-bloodedly killed another human being, we are rightfully concerned about the protection of the public from…"

"Yes, yes, Mr. Pritchard, I hear you. Bond will remain the same. Mr. Appleworth, this is a privilege I am giving you. Please do not disappoint me."

Horace stood quickly. "No, your honor, I'll not disappoint you."

J.D. got up from his bed in the corner of Penny's office. He stretched and yawned. He padded through Althea's office to the door leading to the hall.

"Is Penny coming? Can you hear her?" Althea looked up from her computer. J.D. stood, nose to the edge of door, snuffling and wagging his tail.

Penny opened the door. She saw four eyes staring at her. J. D's happy to see her; Althea's expectant for the news of Horace's hearing.

"I need coffee," said Penny. She walked across the room that doubled as Althea's office and the reception area. She dumped her briefcase stuffed with reports and the much researched but unused cases on the table in the corner of her office. She sat down heavily in her desk chair. Althea brought her coffee. J. D. put his head in her lap.

"The good news is that Horace is still out on bond. The bad news is that he is charged with first degree murder."

"Oh, my," Althea said, sitting in the client's chair across from Penny. "You were so confident there wasn't enough evidence. What happened?"

"Wendy Morgan and her friends happened. They found a 22-caliber pistol in the weeds by the railroad track." Penny told Althea the story of the pistol and its notoriety on Wendy's Facebook page.

"And, the lab tech claims it matches a pistol registered to Horace twenty years ago. Horace claims it's not his. I don't know what to believe. I did discover that about 25 people saw the picture of the pistol and commented on it."

"Do we know who they are? Maybe one of them is the killer."

"We are getting a list of names from the Prosecutor."

Percy walked into the room. After giving JD a quick sniff, he jumped up on Penny's desk.

"Where is Kyle?" asked Penny. She rubbed the top of Percy's head and was thanked with a loud purr.

"Here I am," Kyle said. He pulled over a chair and sat down next to Althea. "I heard Horace is formally charged with the murder of Dick Boswick."

"Bad news sure travels fast in a small town," Penny said. "Yes, and now I need your help on several matters. Did you hear that the police found a pistol or rather Wendy…?"

"Yes, and I saw it. My sister's boy sent me the link. He thought it was really cool."

"Sheriff Nicholson has a list of 25 other kids who thought it was cool. When he sends it over, can you check each one of them out? It is possible those kids know more about the pistol. I'll research the law but I don't know it being on Facebook makes the evidence less reliable. I also want to know why the police think the gun is registered to Horace. I'll get him in here to explain it but see what you can find out."

"Horace doesn't have an alibi—or at least he doesn't remember seeing anyone the night of the murder. He gave us a good description of where he was after he left the offices. I know it was the night of the weekly concerts and everyone was at the courthouse square listening to the band, but maybe someone saw him walking by."

"I typed up my notes," Althea said. She handed Kyle a copy including a map of Midvale Corners. Kyle, who had been taking his own notes in the small spiral notebook he carried with him, took Althea's notes, folded them and stuck them in his notebook.

Penny looked at her two friends and colleagues. She smiled, glad for their help and confidence in her abilities. She didn't believe that Horace was the type to kill someone, but what if he did? And if he didn't, was she the one to keep him out of prison for the rest of his life?

As if reading her thoughts, Althea said, "Don't you worry, we will discover the real killer."

Kyle nodded.

"We need to look more closely at Dick Boswick. What he was doing the last few days before his death and whether he was corrupt and having an affair. Either one could cause someone to want to murder him. What does the prosecutor think was Horace's' motive for this murder?" he asked.

"He thinks that Horace was so angry that he did not get the last contract that he killed Dick thinking the bidding would start again and he would have a chance," Penny answered, stretching, trying to get rid of the tension in her neck and shoulders.

"Horace was not the only one bidding. I'll look into the other people who were interested."

"Thanks, guys," said Penny, with a wan smile. The trio broke up, each going off to take on the matter of the People v. Appleworth.

Chapter 10

At precisely 6:00 pm on Wednesday, Althea walked into the bookstore on Main Street for the meeting of the Midvale Corners Literary and Investigatory Society. Rose, Mary, and Arney were scheduled to arrive at 6:30.

"Your usual latte?" asked the young man behind the counter.

Althea nodded. She tried but could not remember the young man's name. She knew he was related to the Frasier's, but his name would not come to her. She would ask Rose, she knew everyone. She smiled her thanks, took the latte and found a seat at their table.

After a sip of the warm, foamy, latte, Althea leaned back in her chair. The shop was empty at this dinner hour, but she knew people would arrive in a while to enjoy a drink, sit in the tables in front and chat with their friends. Midvale Corners was not a large town and everyone seemed to know each other. They all liked to take a walk in the waning September evening and stop at the bookstore for a treat.

"We're here," said Rose, coming up to the table. "Arney drove by and picked us up. He will be here in a minute. He was looking for change for the meter. He doesn't want to get a parking ticket. I told him that he didn't need to worry because parking is free after seven and none of Sheriff Bill's men are out to find people who park at the meters too long. But you know how he is."

"Shall I get the coffees," asked Mary coming up behind Rose. "I think I know what everyone wants—oh, you already have yours, I see."

Mary returned shortly with the coffees for everyone. She had a small plate of cookies. "Belinda wants us to try these. I got your double latte, Arney." She set the coffees and cookies on the table and settled into a chair. Rose and Arney sat down. All three turned to Althea, leaning forward expectantly.

Althea took some time to explain what had happened in court.

"The prosecutor and the police are convinced that Horace is the murderer. Especially now that they've found the pistol—well, the kids found the pistol—and took a picture of it—with a cell phone."

"My phone can take pictures," said Rose. "I didn't think I would use it, but it's really fun. I take pictures of the events at the library and then load them on our website."

"My goodness, Rose, I didn't know you were so, so, technologically adept," said Mary. "I just use my phone to call people."

"Me, too," said Arney. "I don't have time for all that techno stuff."

"Well," said Althea, bringing the group back to her. "Wendy sent the picture to her Facebook page and it was seen by her friends who then sent it on to their friends so it got lots of exposure. And the worst of it is that the lab believes the pistol belongs to Horace. Kyle is checking on the 25 people who saw it and made a comment. Now, what have you all found out since our last meeting?"

"I'll go first," said Mary, pulling a sheet of paper out of her purse. After consulting it, she said, "Fiona Houlis and Victor Miller have been into the offices several times. I have the dates. They are both asking about the bids, when they are going to be opened again, whether they should be filing a new proposal. Victor keeps asking what happened to his bid. He is furious because he is sure he was awarded the job, but now the commissioners are dragging their heels. Fiona seems relieved that the bidding is going to be opened again."

"She told anyone who would listen that her company was the best and would do the best job. They both have been in several times. Frankly, we are getting tired of all their grumbling. Don't they realize that a man has been killed?" Mary shook her head, reaching for her coffee.

"I don't think they care," said Rose. "It's old news to them, I bet. I have some news to add. Sally Boswick goes to my church. She and Jane both come. It is so sad."

"Anyway, as you know, I help with the flowers for the alter. One of the ladies said she heard that Dick was having an affair with Polly Langstrom who works at The Depot restaurant. I wondered about that so after church when we went there for breakfast, I made sure we sat in her section."

"Polly waited on us. She looked really upset, so I asked her what was wrong. I know her younger sister—she is in one of my young reader book clubs at the library—she had mentioned that she saw Polly crying and when she asked her why, Polly wouldn't say."

"Anyway, Polly didn't answer me right away, then she said she had to call our local travel agency and cancel her vacation. I asked where she was going and she said she had plans to go on a cruise."

"I asked why she had to cancel and she said her friend couldn't go all of a sudden. I wonder who that friend is? Could it be Dick Boswick?"

"Sally's been a little short with Polly's mother, who comes to our church. I wonder if Sally suspects what her husband was up to."

"How can we find out?" asked Althea. "Jealousy can be a powerful motive for murder."

"Not sure, but will keep my eyes open," said Rose, nodding her head, her beige felt fedora staying in place as if it dared to move from its rakish angle.

The ladies turned to Arney, who sat up, ran his thumb and forefinger down the knife-edge crease in his light wool trousers, learned forward, tented his hands and said, "I talked to Greg, the accountant for the city. He confirmed that the city is asking for new bids for the job. He said he had heard rumors that Dick was taking kickbacks from the bidders and the ones that paid got the contract. He hasn't found any proof of that, but he is aware of the problem. He also heard that Victor was nosing around the Sheriff's department, trying to find out how the investigation is going. Remember, Penny told us they found a couple of hundred-dollar bills at the murder scene—they were under Dick's head. If Victor was the winning bid, then maybe that money is his and maybe he wants it back."

"The other good news is that the attorney for Dick Boswick's estate is a client of mine. He has asked me to help him sort out Dick's bank records. He said they were in a bit of a mess. I haven't received everything yet but I should get them soon. We might be able to learn something from those records. If Dick was taking money under the table, where is it? He must have it someplace. I wonder if Sally knows where it is."

"It seems, said Althea, "we have more questions than we do answers. I think it is safe to say that Dick was having an affair. I don't know that we can be sure that Sally knew but maybe someone will know. And there is good reason to believe he was corrupt. We know that Fiona and Victor are looking for business. I wonder if Horace will bid on the job. Can people have accused of murder bid? I'll ask Penny. And if he doesn't bid, does that make him look guiltier?"

"Arney, I know some of the information you have is privileged, but some of it is a matter of public record. And you might get a clue to help us confirm that Dick was taking kick-backs."

"I'll do what I can," said Arney standing up, leaning on his cane.

The group cleaned up their table, gathered up their belongings and went out the door. The bookstore was beginning to fill up. Students with laptops came in looking for a place to study, away from home, and with their friends. Althea wondered how much studying got done when they all congregated together.

"Keep me posted," she said to her friends as they got in Arney's car."

"We will, don't worry. We should have news soon."

Arney carefully backed his car out of the parking space. Fortunately, everyone in the city knew how hard it was to back out of the parking spaces that lined Elm Street. There were few accidents among the locals. Occasionally, the folks who came to court were impatient and caused some problems for the Sheriff.

Althea headed on home. She knew in her bones that Horace was innocent. She was also sure her friends would be able to come up with some evidence to help Penny prove her case. It was simply a matter of time.

Chapter 11

The parking lot of St. Aloysius Church was almost full when Kyle pulled in. He found a spot on the grass at the far corner. The whole town had turned out for Dick Boswick's funeral. He walked to the church, nodding to people he knew.

Coming through the reception area, the sweet scent of the masses of flowers assailed his nose. That smell, lovely in nature, was not so lovely in death. Kyle shuddered, wondering who walked over his grave.

"Kyle, will you sign the registration book. It will be nice for Sally to look at later. It's so lovely that all these people came to the funeral." Kyle nodded at Rose who was stationed near the door of the church and seemed to be in charge of directing traffic. He signed the book, glancing as he did so at the list of names. There were pages and pages of them.

"About fifty people have arrived so far," said Rose sensing his question.

Kyle wanted to sit in the back of the sanctuary where he could easily observe the people in the audience. When he entered the room, he was surprised to see that the only empty pews were in the back. He found a spot and looked around.

He saw Sally and Jane Boswick sitting in the front pew. Sally held her head high as if to dare anyone to say anything bad about her husband. Jane, sitting next to Sally, was dabbing her eyes, trying not to look at her father's casket.

Fiona Houlis was sitting directly behind Sally. Sitting next to her was a dark-haired, thin man. They were talking quietly. Kyle wondered who he was. Seated at the end of the same row was Victor Miller. He was easy to spot since his head was way above the crowd.

Kyle remembered that he was a tall, large man who had played basketball in high school. Kyle thought he had been suspended from the team for some reason. He made a note in his little notebook to check that out.

He noticed Dan Dunlap sitting a few rows away. It was common for a detective to appear at the funeral of a murder victim. Often the murderer could be found in the crowd. Kyle had the same suspicion. He wondered—did Dan think that they had the wrong man; that the real killer was still out there?

Kyle continued looking. He saw the city commissioners, the mayor, the assistant manager and all the staff. He heard they closed the city offices for the funeral.

The congregation became quiet as Pastor Grimes entered and came to the front of the alter. He stood quietly in front of the flower-draped casket. He paused for a moment waiting for quiet then he began the service.

The Pastor knew the limits of his audience. He spoke of Dick's accomplishments, his lovely wife and daughter and of how he would be missed. His words were meant to ease the pain of the grieving family, which included Dick's parents and his two brothers.

When it was time the pallbearers came forward, stood on either side of the casket and escorted it to the hearse to make its trip to the cemetery.

Sally and Jane came down the aisle led by the Pastor. The rest of the family followed. Kyle stood with the others, waiting to proceed out of the church. He heard the woman behind him, "Did you see Polly Langstrom over there? What is she doing here? I heard she was having an affair with Dick."

"I heard that, too," said her friend.

The group of people started to move. Kyle heard no more.

Once outside, the people went to their cars to drive the short trip to the cemetery. Kyle followed the cars. He wanted to see who made the trip to the graveside ceremony.

Kyle stood to one side looking at the crowd. He noticed that the man who had sat next to Fiona was there, but he couldn't see Fiona. He wondered who that man was. He saw Dan off to one side also observing the crowd.

Kyle moved over to where Dan stood. He could see that Dan was watching the stranger also.

"Do you know who that is?" he asked Dan.

"His name is Luther Rahn. He works for Fiona Houlis."

"Why is he here?"

"Don't know about that," said Dan. "I didn't know he knew Dick. Maybe Fiona told him to come. I wonder where she went--back to the office? Why not take Luther with her?"

Kyle wondered the same thing. He made a note of Luther's name wondering about Luther's interest in the funeral of a man he apparently didn't know.

Luther Rahn was already in the office when Fiona Hollis arrived at 8:30 on Tuesday morning. He was standing by the coffee maker, cream carton in one hand, mug in the other, waiting for the fresh coffee. The work crew Luther managed was not due in until ten. They had a re-model to do.

Fiona strode across the small reception area. She was a tall woman with blond hair that needed a touch up. Years of managing construction crews in a man's world had hardened her. She could take on the best of them and win. She went into her office, put her briefcase on her desk and came back out with coffee cup in hand.

Filling her cup, she said, "I want to talk to you. Follow me."

Luther poured his coffee, stirred in some sugar and went into her office.

Even though they were alone in the office, Fiona shut the door.

"Victor Miller called. He wanted to know if I had heard anything about a lot of money at the crime scene. He was interested in what I knew, which is nothing. Have you heard anything?"

Luther shook his head.

"Well, if Victor Miller was bribing Boswick to get that deal, he wouldn't admit it and he couldn't ask the cops."

"Maybe the cops took it."

"I haven't heard anything," said Fiona. "But, maybe they did,

"You still owe me some money," said Luther, frowning. "How about you pay up."

"I'll pay you tomorrow."

"Tomorrow. I'm not waiting, Fiona." He grabbed Fiona's arm, pulling her close to him. She flinched, pulling away. Luther tightened his grip.

"I mean it, Fiona, I won't wait long." He pushed her away and stomped out of her office. Fiona sat in chair, staring. She reached into her bag and pulled out her phone. Punching in some numbers, she waited.

Hearing, "What do you want?"

"Hello to you too. I need more money. Luther's making trouble," Fiona said.

"What kind of trouble?"

"Threatening kind of trouble."

"And, money will help? How much?"

"$30,000. You have it and it's what we agreed to."

There was silence.

"Are you there?" Fiona asked.

"Okay. Meet me at the usual place in a couple of hours."

"Good."

Fiona hung up, put her phone in her purse and leaned back, staring into space.

Chapter 12

Penny returned to her office right after a hectic morning in court. She wanted to sit down, eat her yoghurt at her desk, give JD a pat on the head and relax. Althea had other plans. As soon as Penny came in the door, Althea took her briefcase and her raincoat. Then she handed Penny a stack of phone messages.

"Horace has called four times. He insists he needs to talk to you right away. I told him to come in at 1:30. You have time to eat your yoghurt and take JD for a walk before he comes in."

Penny nodded. She went into the kitchen, opened the little student fridge stuffed under the counter and found her yoghurt.

"I didn't think Judge Hancock would ever finish up. He was in rare form. He felt a need to give everyone that came before him a tongue-lashing. I certainly don't know what that was about."

Penny sat at her small, round conference table eating her yoghurt. She looked through her messages deciding that most could be returned after she met with Horace. Kyle was to report on his progress around 2:30 so she would have time for Horace before Kyle.

"Come on, JD, let's go for a walk." JD got up, wagging his tail. Penny snapped on his lead and they were off.

They went down the stairs, out the door and headed to the courthouse lawn. Penny liked to walk around the courthouse to see how matters in Midvale Corners were progressing. She crossed the street and while JD inspected a tree he had not seen since morning, she noticed that the fabric store was having a sale on yard goods.

She and JD proceeded across the courthouse lawn. The roses and flowers she couldn't identify were still in bloom. It was September. Some of the trees were started to change color. It was a little early for that, but Penny liked the fall season.

Penny returned to her office. She enjoyed the break from her law practice. She had barely gotten to her chair behind her desk when Horace appeared. Crossing the reception area, he came into Penny's office.

"I am so glad you are here," he said, standing over her desk. "I wanted you to know that I know about the pistol. It probably is registered to me."

He plopped down in the client chair across from Penny.

Penny looked at her client. She waited.

"Ryan went to Wendy's Facebook page and downloaded the picture for me. Then he used Photoshop to enhance it and make it clearer. I could see the initials on the handle. They were mine. I did that in my teens."

"It is the pistol I inherited from my father in 1986 after he died. He bought the pistol in 1976. I learned to shoot with that pistol. When the laws changed, even though it was old, I didn't have to but I registered it anyway."

"How did it come to be connected with a crime?" Penny asked.

"Ryan doesn't like guns and after we got together, I promised to get rid of some of them. I kept my hunting rifle because Ryan loves deer meat, but he doesn't like to admit that I shot the deer. He wants to think that it came from Kroger's. Anyway, I went to a gun show and sold all of the guns I didn't need. That old pistol of my Dad's was one of them."

"Then all we have to do is find the person you sold it to. Who was it?"

"That's just it. I can't remember. It was a gun show. People were milling around, showing weapons, trading and selling."

"I didn't get the name of the gentleman who bought it and I didn't bother to register the sale. I figured the buyer would."

"Where was the gun show? Do you think this person is a local?'

"It was at the Fairgrounds outside of town. I didn't know the guy and I don't remember what he looked like. He was about my age, I think, but I don't know for sure. I've been thinking and thinking. Who would have thought this gun would end up shooting someone? It looks bad, doesn't it?"

"Yes, Horace, it does look bad."

Horace rubbed his head as if his hand could pull the memory out of his brain. He had lost weight and his pants hung around his waist. It was clear to Penny that her client was not doing well.

"Is Ryan giving you something to help you sleep? You don't look well. You need to keep up your strength."

"Yes, he is and it helps a little. What happens next?"

"I am working on a motion to suppress the pistol and one to move the trial to another county. I am concerned you may not get a fair trial here. The judge may or may grant my motions and this will take some time. In the meantime, try not to worry too much."

Penny walked her client to the door. Horace tried to smile but it was a weak effort. He closed the door quietly as he left.

Penny turned to Althea. "I don't know if he is going to make it. This whole thing is hard on him."

"I suspect he's stronger than you think," said Althea. "And Ryan will care for him."

Penny went back in her office and booted up her computer. It was time to work on that Motion. If she could keep the pistol out of the trial, she might have a chance to win this case.

Althea was already in the office when Penny and JD arrived at 8 am on Thursday morning. After the usual morning greetings, Althea said, "I'll get the coffee started and then run to the bookstore for some pastries. I could smell them baking when I walked past on my way in. Any particular flavor you want?"

"Anything with cinnamon."

Althea left. Penny paced smelling the brewing coffee. She was pleased with her little practice. It was growing. She managed to meet her expenses every month. She still had some insurance money left so she knew she could survive for a while longer. But the practice had to grow a little faster or she would run out. She hoped that a win in Horace's case would boost her career. But she also knew that a loss would be devastating to her and to Horace.

Althea returned with a wonderful smelling box of goodies. She found a plate, set the sweet rolls on it, placing them on the small conference table. Penny poured a cup of coffee, doctored it with cream and sugar and sat at the table. She was about to take a bite of frosting topped cinnamon roll when the door opened.

"It smells wonderful in here," Kyle said. Percy scurried in before the door closed. He rubbed his head under JD's nose and then jumped up on the windowsill.

Kyle found his favorite mug, the one with the maize and blue logo, poured some coffee and joined Penny. "I have some news," he said, his mouth full of sticky-bun.

"Good news, I hope," said Penny.

"Depends, some good, some not so good. First of all, I went to Boswick's funeral. It was an interesting collection of people. He must have known everyone in town. I saw your father there. And, Dan Dunlap was there."

"Why?"

"Police often go to the funeral of the victim. They know that it is likely that the murderer will show up. I think Dunlap is not convinced that Horace killed Dick. I saw Polly Langstrom. She was crying. The ladies behind me said they thought Dick was having an affair with her. They were a little upset that she was there. They thought it was 'unseemly.'"

"I also heard that Dick was having an affair," said Althea joining them. "Where there's smoke there's fire, they say."

"Jealousy could be a strong motivator for murder, said Kyle. "I wonder if Sally knew about or suspected her husband was having an affair. Victor Miller and Fiona Houlis were there, too. Fiona was sitting right behind Sally and was consoling her. I didn't know they were friends.'

"Oh, my, yes," said Althea. "They've been close since grade school. They were in each other's weddings."

"Interesting," said Kyle. "There was a man with Fiona I didn't recognize. They were talking but didn't seem overly friendly. I went to the cemetery after the service and he was there, too. Dunlap was watching the guy, too so I asked him if he knew his name. He did. His name is Luther Rahn. He's on parole for a bank robbery conviction. Dan thinks he could be a relative of Fiona's

"My buddies at the police department gave me a copy of the fingerprint results from the crime scene. They found Horace's' fingerprints on the desk, which is not surprising. He admits that he was there. Andy Clinton, the maintenance engineer, was cleaning Dick's desk when Dick arrived so there weren't many prints on it.

Horace's and Dick's have been identified so far. There were others that they are running through CODIS.

"They also found a partial print on one of the two spent shells they found on the floor. They are not being too successful in identifying it. The good news is that they haven't connected that partial print to Horace."

Penny told Kyle about Horace's connection to the pistol.

"What can we do to find the true owner of the pistol?" she asked.

"I'm not sure," said Kyle. "I can ask around. One advantage to having the pistol on Facebook is that the owner may recognize it. But I doubt that person will come forward.

The group split up. Kyle rinsed and dried his mug. Althea went back to answering the phones, which had been ringing a lot lately. Many of the calls were from reporters wanting a scoop on Horace's story. Althea, a retired school secretary who knew how to say no to unruly children or demanding parents, was adept at keeping them away from the office and Penny.

Penny picked up the picture of the pistol that Horace left with her. To her untrained eye, the pistol looked so old that it was a wonder it didn't blow apart when it was shot. Using a magnifying glass, she could see the letters HAA on the wooden butt of the pistol. The initials stood for Horace Andrew Appleworth.

She read the fingerprint report to see if there was any mention of prints on the pistol. No, it had been wiped clean. She went back to her computer research of the evidence rules. Around 1:30, Althea poked her head in the door.

"You need to go get some lunch and JD needs some fresh air," she said.

"You're right, I'll take him for a walk and stop by the deli to pick up a sandwich," Penny answered.

She grabbed a jacket from the hall tree, snapped the lead on JD and out the door they went. After a trip around the square, Penny tied him to the doggy post outside the deli and went in to get a sandwich.

She stood looking at the menu trying to decide between number three --turkey, ham, provolone and special sauce or number four-- roast beef, cheddar, lettuce and tomato with special sauce.

"Taking a little lunch break?" asked a familiar voice.

Penny looked up. She noticed for the first time that Alex's eyes had little flicks of gold in them or maybe it was a reflection from the glass case holding rolls of salami, roast beef, cheeses and wonderful looking salads.

"Yes, it's time for lunch," Penny said, thinking that sounded dumb.

"How about joining me at a table outside the book store?' Alex asked.

Penny agreed. She placed her order, deciding on the number three. Alex ordered the number four. They went to the cooler for drinks. Penny grabbed a TC root beer. Alex pulled out an ice tea.

"Here are your sandwiches," said Ray, son of Belinda, who was in charge of the Deli. "Penny, I know you're representing Horace. I don't think he's a killer."

"Let's hope the jury sees it that way," said Penny.

After they paid for the sandwiches, they went outside, collected JD and found an empty table. JD sniffed Alex, gave his stamp of approval, then settled under the table to wait for any scraps that might come his way.

"I just came from court," Alex said. "I had a drunk driving case out there. I don't think we'll go to trial on this one. There's not much wiggle room, my client is going to have to accept his punishment."

"I thought you only did civil work," said Penny.

"This client is the son of one of our bigger clients. I'm doing this as a favor. I would much rather be working on a good medical malpractice or a product liability case. How's Horace's case coming along?"

"We're making progress but I know we'll have to go to trial, which is a big task and I've never handled a murder trial."

"I am sure you will do an excellent job," said Alex taking a bite of his sandwich, which had arrived. He chewed reflectively. He looked at Penny. She looked great even with a few worry lines around her eyes. He knew she was working hard on Horace's case. And, though he had never been in private practice, others had told him how hard it was to get a practice started. And a murder case took a lot of time and energy.

"You need to take a break from all that hard work. How about dinner Saturday night?" he found himself asking.

Penny's head jerked up. She looked at Alex. She paused.

"Okay. That would be nice."

Alex smiled.

"Shall I pick you up at seven?"

Penny nodded. They finished their lunch, separating, each going back to the world of law.

During the short walk back to her office, Penny found it hard to think about Horace. She kept thinking about how tall and muscular Alex was. He moved with litheness that she admired. His hazel eyes dominated a face that she knew would captivate a jury. He had a presence that inspired trust. She wondered if she had the same presence.

"I wonder what gym he goes to," she said to JD.

Arney was at their table in the bookstore when Althea arrived at 7:00. Rose and Mary came in behind her.

After ordering their coffees, and a few of Belinda's peanut butter cookies, Althea called the Midvale Corners Literary and Investigatory Society to order.

She began by bringing them up to speed on what Kyle had reported earlier that day. After listening carefully, Mary said, "I checked around and learned that the only contract submitted to the commissioners for the renovation job was to Victor Miller, which seems strange to me. I was sure Fiona and Horace had submitted bids so when everyone was out at lunch I searched Dick's desk. Stuffed way back in a drawer I found their bids. Horace was the lowest bid and seemed to be on better terms. Fiona was a bit higher but not by much. I can't understand why it was going to be offered to Victor Miller. Unless, of course, the rumor about Dick taking kickbacks is true and Victor gave a bribe to Dick. And if he did, when did he do it? And where is the money?"

"Good questions," said Rose. "We need to do more research. I'm sure we can find out if we put our heads together. I learned that Dick was having an affair with Polly. My husband, he's retired, you know, has breakfast at The Depot every morning. He and his friends eat at Polly's station. She has been down lately. When they asked why, she said she had to cancel a vacation because her boyfriend died. She told them that she was thinking of leaving town, that she was tired of Midvale Corners and that maybe she would move to Alaska."

"Alaska. Why Alaska?" asked Arney.

"She said she liked Sarah Palin and it looked like a good place to be"

"I wonder," Rose said, "How much Sally, Dick's wife, knows."

The three pondered the question with no answer.

Arney spoke up, "I have been working on Dick's estate for his attorney. So far everything looks pretty normal. Even though his records are a bit of a jumble, they seem complete. I do wonder, however, how he could afford the Corvette. It appears to be paid for. I'll keep looking. I have to be careful, because of the issues of confidentiality, but it's hard to take that too seriously when a Horace's life is at stake."

"I also looked into the Fiona's records. They are public, because she has had contracts with the city. She isn't doing too well. I have a strong feeling she needed the contract with the city to stay out of bankruptcy court."

"We have many unanswered questions," said Althea. "Let's keep digging. Can we meet again in a week?"

All agreed, collecting their belongings, they put away their dirty cups and cookie plate, and left the bookstore. The evening was fall-like. Many of the trees around the square had colored leaves. The air was crisper than it had been in August. The folks on the street moved a little quicker. The dogs on their leashes were a little more interested in the other dogs on their leashes.

Chapter 13

Penny stood in her walk-in closet staring at her clothes. I don't have anything for dinner with a man. I have court clothes, running clothes and sweats but nothing to wear on a date. Is this a date? I hope not. Well, maybe I hope so.

Penny pulled out a dress she hadn't worn in a long time. It was still in the cleaner's bag. It was a black light-weight wool short-sleeved sheath dress she bought before David died.

"I paid way too much for this dress," she said to JD. "I think I paid over $200 on sale and that was half price."

She put it on and stood in front of the mirror of the antique penny scale she had in the corner of her bedroom. She and David bought it from an antique dealer in Indiana. She turned around and was pleased that the dress still fit. It was short but not too short, was dressy but not too dressy. She didn't want to look like she was trying too hard.

She found her black sling-back heels and a big clunky black and silver necklace that looked good with the dress. Her small black clutch and the grey shawl she brought back from Argentina completed the outfit. She went back in front of the mirror. She was pleased with what she saw.

Her doorbell rang. JD padded over to the door. Penny opened it to see Alex smiling at her. He was dressed in tan slacks, navy blazer and white silk t-shirt. JD gave him a sniff and went over to his bed. He knew he would be alone for a while.

Penny in her heels was almost eye to eye with Alex, but at 6'4" he still looked down at her. She smiled.

"I'm ready," she said.

"So, I see," Alex.

"I thought we would go to O'Toole's downtown. I don't think we will run into clients or parents there. I hope that's okay with you."

"I love their coffee," said Penny. "I don't know how they make it, but it is wonderful."

Penny turned and looked at JD. She said her usual words, "You stay here and take care of the house, I'll be back,"

Penny and Alex walked out into the September evening. She turned and locked the door. Alex's black Mercedes Benz was sitting in the driveway of Penny's small house. Alex opened the passenger door; she slid in, smelling the leather. Penny was her father's daughter--she loved cars, particularly well-designed models like this ten-year-old Mercedes.

"This car is a different than my pink Escort," she said. "I never did understand why Maureen painted it pink."

Alex laughed. "I remember when she drove it into the school parking lot. We thought it was cool." Alex and Maureen, Penny's older sister had been in the same class in high school.

"Well, it's not so cool, now, and I'm not in high school anymore," Penny laughed.

"No, you're most certainly not," Alex looked over at Penny and smiled.

When they arrived at the restaurant, Alex pulled in front and gave his keys to the valet.

"Treat her carefully," he said to the young man admiring the gleaming black car who knew that the powerful engine would be a joy to drive.

"Yes, sir, but you're taking the fun out of it. I'll park it where it won't get dinged."

When they were seated, the Wine Steward arrived with a long list of the available wines. Penny watched as Alex looked through the list. After studying carefully, he looked up.

"A red or a white?" he asked.

After agreeing on a red, they ordered dinner. Alex decided on the venison over squash, Penny opted for the grilled salmon. While waiting for dinner, they talked about the law and lawyers.

"Why is it that when lawyers get together, they talk law and other lawyers? Don't we know anything else?' asked Penny.

Alex laughed. "I think it is because we love the law. You have to love it in order to practice it. Okay, change of topic, how about those

Wolverines?" Both Penny and Alex came from a long line of University of Michigan graduates and were Michigan grads themselves.

"I have season tickets," said Alex, "but it has been a hard to sit through some of those games."

Penny nodded. "My dad says they will be better next year. A new coach and a freshman team makes it hard to win many games against more experienced teams."

The waiter appeared with their meals. They ate and talked about people they knew in common.

Penny was surprised how much she was enjoying being with Alex. He was an interesting person. She discovered that he had worked abroad for a year after law school.

"I was in London. I did an internship in the Royal Court of Appeal. It was enlightening."

"I visited the British courts," said Penny. "I liked the robes and wigs and the old courtrooms. The red-robed judges in their long-eared wigs can be quite intimidating."

Alex laughed, "The barristers seem to be able to handle them."

The waiter removed their plates.

"Dessert?" He asked. They agreed that coffee would be dessert enough,

When they came out of the restaurant, Alex suggested a stroll to look in store windows after dinner. Penny agreed. He offered and she accepted his arm. They strolled and talked. Coming back to the restaurant, Alex gave his ticket to the young man.

"I took good care of her," he said, accepting the generous tip Alex slid into his hand. He ran off to get the car.

Penny slid into the passenger seat. She watched Alex walk around the car, looking carefully for any possible marks. He got in the car and they were off. Penny was uncertain what would happen when they got to her door. Would Alex want a kiss? Did she want him to kiss her? She didn't know. She thought a kiss might be cheating on her husband, but her logical brain disagreed. David would want her to move on. She stared straight ahead, her hands clenched in her lap.

While Penny mulled that over, Alex drove in silence wondering what would happen at the door. He decided that he would let Penny lead. He remembered Penny from high school--she was a freshman when he was a senior. He remembered her as an awkward, gawking girl who played sports. The woman sitting next to him was not that girl.

They arrived at Penny's home. Alex walked her to the door. She unlocked the door and opened it.

Looking up at Alex, she said "I had a…"

JD had other ideas. He pushed the door open with his big nose and, coming out on the small porch, he sat between them.

"I think my dog needs some attention," laughed Penny. She reached inside the door for JD's leash hanging on a hook ready for a walk.

Alex laughed also. "I can see that," he said. "I'll be on my way."

Alex left and Penny and JD started their turn around the yard. JD did not seem in any hurry to take care of business.

"You did that on purpose," said Penny aloud to the big dog. "Well thank you, it did lighten the mood. I don't know what I wanted. But I did have a pleasant evening. And he is quite nice."

Penny and JD went into the house to sleep what remained of the night. She slept well.

Penny, laden down with two briefcases, a purse, a bag with her lunch and JD's leash in her hands, paused at the door of her office around noon on a bright October Friday morning. As she stood still, trying to figure out which items to place on the floor to free a hand, the door opened.

"Come in," said Althea, "You don't have enough hands. Do you want me to take something?"

"I don't know what that would be," Penny laughed. "I'm all twisted up in this stuff. She walked to her desk, placing it all in a heap on the one clear space.

"Busy day in court yesterday, I see," said Althea.

She opened the briefcases to pull out the files. She would take each file; make note of the next court date, putting it on the master calendar on the computer and the big calendar on the wall. She would take no chances that Penny would miss a court date.

"I'll straighten these up," she said. She hauled an armload of files to her desk.

"It was a long day," Penny said. "There is a report in there from Mike. They found some fibers at the murder scene. So far, they haven't matched them to anyone. They have the clothes Horace was wearing when he was arrested and they don't match those. Now their theory is that Horace hid the clothes he was wearing. They want permission to search his house again. They already searched it once. I'm tempted to make them go to the judge for a warrant, but I need to talk to Horace."

"Shall I get him on the phone?" asked Althea.

"No, I'll call him later. Kyle should be here shortly. I want to hear what, if anything, he has learned."

Penny found her mug, went to the small kitchen and poured some coffee. She was settling at the small conference table when Kyle and Percy came through the door. Percy marched across the room, tail in the air, to greet JD. They gave each other a good sniff and then settled in a pile on JD's bed.

"I have some news," Kyle said. "But I need some of Althea's coffee first." He got his mug, poured the coffee and sat down at the table next to Penny. Althea joined them.

Penny and Althea looked at him expectantly.

"I spoke to Polly Langstrom. I've known her for a long time. I told her my suspicions about her connection with Dick. She confirmed the affair." Kyle pulled out his notebook, flipped thru the pages and stopped.

"Dick and I have been together for a long time" he read. "We met at the restaurant. He came in for lunch. We talked and things just went on from there. He was so easy to talk too. We met out of town where no one would see us. He hated that we couldn't go out in public but I understood. He was so nice. He gave me lovely jewelry."

"I asked her how long this had been going on? She said for three years."

"And Sally didn't know?" asked Althea. "That's hard to believe."

"Polly says she didn't, but I wonder," answered Kyle. "She told me that she and Dick were planning on going on a cruise in January after the holidays. He bought the tickets in her name and gave them to her. She still has them, but she cancelled the trip. They planned to go on the Oasis of the Sea, that new monster ship that Royal Caribbean has been advertising. She was wearing a ring that looked pretty expensive to me."

"Where did Dick get the money?" Penny asked.

"I asked. Polly didn't know. She seemed to think he was paid a lot for his City Manager job. I learned he was earning about $70,000 a year, which sounds like a lot to Polly compared to her waitress salary, but it isn't that much. Polly is really distressed--she seems to have loved the guy. She thinks Sally found out and killed him."

"Dick told Polly that Sally was a cold woman who would never divorce him. But that may have been a line to keep Polly happy. But she believes it."

"Could Polly have killed Dick?"

"I don't think so. And she has an alibi. She was working that night at the restaurant. I checked with her co-workers and they confirmed she was there the whole shift. The evening dinner crowd was small so the waiters had time to joke and talk. They clearly remembered Polly being there."

"Sounds like we can cross Polly off our list of suspects. Sally still looks interesting. We are checking that idea out," Althea said.

"You mean the Midvale Corners Literary and Investigatory Society is on the case?" Kyle asked.

Althea nodded. Kyle smiled approvingly.

"Don't let Dan Dunlap find out," he said. "he's still a little miffed about the Society's success with the last case."

"What has the group discovered?" asked Penny, laughing at the thought of Dan's discomfiture.

"Things are a bit amorphous so far," Althea said. "We heard about Dick's affair, too. Rose's church ladies were talking about it. I'm glad it's been confirmed. I am also pleased that Polly had nothing to do with the killing. She is a nice girl, a bit naïve, but she means well. Sally is a determined woman, according to Rose. It is her opinion she would let nothing break up her family. I think we keep her as a suspect."

"I want to learn more about Victor Miller and Fiona Houlis," said Kyle. "They might have motives."

"Mary learned that Victor's bid was the only one Dick planned to present to the commissioners. She did a little snooping and found the bids from Horace and Fiona. I have copies of them. Horace was the lowest with better terms than the other two. Fiona was a bit lower than Victor, too. It makes one wonder why Victor got the nod from

Dick. It's been decided to start the bidding over now that Dick is dead."

"Unfortunately, that fact creates a motive for both Horace and Fiona. And we have no evidence that Fiona was anywhere near the concert or the city offices that night," Penny said.

"I know," said Althea. Both women looked at Kyle who was searching his notebook. When he found a blank page, he looked up.

"Oh, can I see those bids? I'll review them and then I'll pay Fiona Houlis a visit. I am curious about her. We believe that Horace didn't murder Dick so that leaves Victor, Fiona and Sally. We have too many suspects. I want to narrow the field."

Althea stood. She walked to her desk, picked up the reports, came back. After handing them to Kyle, she said, "Mary gave copies of these to the police so they know about them, but she said they didn't seem too interested."

"That doesn't surprise me," said Penny.

Kyle moved toward the door. "Percy, are you coming?" he asked the big cat. Percy stood stretched and moved toward the door. Kyle waited until the cat crossed the threshold then followed him out the door.

"I'll be in touch," Kyle said closing the door.

Althea and Penny went back to work, soon both women were deep in thought and quiet reigned in the office.

Around 3 o'clock, Althea poked her head in Penny's office. "Did you want to talk to Horace?" she asked.

Penny looked up. "Yes, I'll call him now. The day is getting away from me."

"Horace? Penny Johnson here."

"Have they dismissed the charges?" Horace asked in a half joking, half hopeful tone of voice.

"No, Horace, I'm sorry, they haven't. They found some fibers at the scene and they want to search your house again to see if you have any clothes or other fibers that match the ones they found. According to the report they were rayon fibers."

"Oh, good grief, I would never wear rayon," his voice deepened. "Nor would Ryan. And we wouldn't have rayon in the house. We only have natural fibers. Nothing artificial, absolutely not. If I say no to the search, what happens?"

"They go to the judge and get a warrant. And they will be able to get a warrant. But it is up to you."

"Oh, let them come over, I have nothing to hide," said Horace.

"Will do. I'll call Detective Dunlap. And call you back."

Dan Dunlap and Penny agreed to meet at Horace's house at 4 o'clock. Penny called Horace with the news.

"I'm going to leave now," she said to Althea. Penny snapped a leash on JD, picked up her briefcase and left the office. She hurried to the car. JD jumped in and they were off. Horace lived on Peachtree Lane, a short drive from Penny's office. She turned off Columbia onto Peachtree. In her rearview mirror, she saw Dan's car and two black and whites right behind her.

"I knew they would arrive early," she said. She parked her car in Horace's driveway. Horace opened the door. His two dogs, Mutt, a Bichon Mix, and Jeff, a beige miniature poodle, were at his feet.

"They're here," Penny said. "You'd better put the dogs out in the yard. They will get in the way."

Horace picked up both dogs, came out the door and walked around the house to the back. He set the dogs in the yard and came back to Penny who was talking to Dan and the two men and one woman in uniform. Horace opened the door to let them into the house.

Dan led the way into the house.

"Horace, let's go into the back yard and let the officers do their job. I'll get JD. He needs to stretch his legs."

While the dogs greeted each other in their usual way, Penny and Horace sat around the table on the patio.

"I hope they don't make a mess," Horace said. "I called Ryan and told him they were coming. He wanted to come home but he said the emergency room was full—a three car pile-up on I94. How long will this take?" Horace stood and paced. He couldn't sit still.

"As long as it takes," Penny said. "Sit down and have some of the ice tea Althea sent with me. It is some calming herbal tea. She knew you would be upset. Her house was searched when they found her Harry under her front porch. She's still upset about it."

Penny pulled a thermos of tea, two glasses and a small Tupperware box of cookies. "The cookies are from Romano's."

Taking the lid off the Tupperware, the scent of chocolate and peanut butter brought the dogs over for a sniff.

"Please thank Althea for me," said Horace sitting down and reaching for a peanut butter cookie. "I'll be so glad when this is all over. I have a business to run and a life to live."

"They are opening the bidding for the contract again. Are you submitting a proposal?"

"Yes, I was working on it when you called. It is due at the end of the week. Victor Miller and Fiona and I'll each submit a bid. Victor's mad because Dick told him he had the job, but it's only fair that we re-do the bidding."

After a while, Dan poked his head out the door. "We're done here. We'll be on our way. Here is a list of what we took." He handed the list to Penny.

Penny escorted Dan out the door while Horace looked at the mess of his house. "I have to get this all cleaned up before Ryan comes home. He'll be so upset."

Penny came back to the living room of the old Victorian house. The twelve-foot walls were painted a soft green with white trim and a Persian rug on the random plank floor complemented the walls. Off in one corner, Horace looked in dismay at the small hole in the corner of the carpet. Looking at the off-white drapes, he found a corner missing.

"Did they have to do that?" he said. We'll have to re-do this whole room when all this is over. I wonder what else they took?"

Penny looked at the list. "Some clothes and a couple of towels."

Horace sat down on the deep red couch. He looked up at Penny for a moment, his eyes moist. He put his head in his hands. Penny sat next to him. The dogs were lying on the floor at their feet. After a quiet moment, Horace stood. "I'm okay now. You don't need to stay."

"I'll call you with the results of the report," she said. Penny retrieved the thermos, called JD, and they were out the door and on their way home. She was concerned about Horace, but she knew Ryan would take care of him.

Chapter 14

P ercy," Kyle said, "Get off my bladder." Percy moved off Kyle, pleased he had been able to awaken his human. His dish was empty, and he wanted to take a turn around the yard. It was time to be up and out by his cat reckoning.

Kyle rolled over and looked at the clock. It said 6:00. He sat up and stretched. "It's still dark out," he grumbled. He took care of his bladder, pulled on a pair of sweats, started the coffee, filled Percy's dish, and headed out the door for a short run. He stretched then jogged off down the block. Percy was touring the yard to discover any activity that took place during the night.

Five miles later, sweaty and lungs percolating nicely, Kyle returned home. Opening the door, the smell of coffee brewing assailed his nose. Percy followed him into the house, heading straight for his bowl. After a quick shower, Kyle sat at the kitchen table eating some Raisin Bran. This was the day he planned to visit Fiona Houlis' business. His cop's instinct told him something was going on there.

Kyle pulled into the parking lot of the one-story building that housed the offices of Houlis Construction. He knew Fiona's father had started the business forty years ago. After the old man died, Fiona, who had worked with her dad, took over. Her two brothers were not interested in construction, Fiona had some knowledge of the business, and they agreed she could run it. Up until the recent recession, Fiona had done well. Now, like the other businesses in town, she was struggling.

Kyle parked his car and got out. There were lights on in the building, which sat at the corner of Anderson and Park. Across the street was a long, low building that was the lumberyard. He could smell the wood and heard the saw. A truck was backed up to the loading dock and its owner was stacking the bed of the truck with the cut wood. Kyle went over to talk to the workers. He found the door and followed the sound of the saw.

"That about does it," said the short, stocky man at the saw.

"Thanks, Charlie," said the customer on his way out. Kyle went over to Charlie.

"Hi, Kyle, need some wood cut?"

"Not today, my days of renovation are over for a while. I'm investigating the murder of Dick Boswick for Penny Johnson, who is representing Horace Appleworth. Can I ask you some questions?"

"Sure, but I know nothing about the murder. I don't believe Horace killed him, but you never know. Business has been down lately and competition for city contracts is fierce. Fiona was downright put out when she didn't get the contract. I think she was glad that the bidding was being opened again. She isn't the businessman her father was, but she's tough."

"If business is down, why did she hire that Luther Rahn?" said a female voice. A dark-haired woman joined them, carrying a clipboard. There was a frown on her square, freckled face. She handed Charlie an invoice. "Meryl's coming in. He needs this wood cut ASAP."

Charlie left to get the wood. The woman turned to Kyle. "I'm Yolanda. You probably don't remember, but we were in high school together. You were two grades ahead of me. Didn't you play basketball?"

Kyle laughed, "Yes, but not well. When did Fiona hire Luther?'

"About six months ago. Don't see why we needed him. I've been running this yard for years. I think he's a shirttail relative. I heard he just got out of prison. Maybe she felt an obligation. They spend a lot of time together—not sure what that's about—but, of course, it's none of my business. I did wonder, though, if things had cooled down. They have been arguing a lot lately."

Kyle made some notes in his notebook. He wrote a big question mark next Luther's name.

A phone rang. The woman reached to the holster by her side and pulled out her phone. Listening to the call, she turned and walked away. She mouthed a goodbye to Kyle. Kyle continued on into the lumberyard in search of more information. He found a huge, black man by the wood chipper. He was busy feeding short ends of lumber, not good for anything except mulch, into the machine.

"You a cop?" the man asked, turning away from his task and looking at Kyle. "You have a cop look about you. I ain't done nothing illegal. Least not as far as I know."

"I was a cop. Now I'm a private investigator. I'm investigating the murder of Dick Boswick."

"Don't know the dude and don't know about no murder. I have work to do." He returned to his task stuffing the wood into the chipper.

"Thanks for your time," said Kyle, putting his notebook away and walking toward the loading dock.

"Who are you and why are you bothering my employees?" said a deep, rasping female voice. Kyle turned to the sound. He saw a woman marching toward him. She came within a few feet of Kyle and stopped. "Well?"

Kyle handed her a card, explaining he was working for an attorney investigating the murder of Dick Boswick.

"I'm Fiona Houlis. I own this company. My employees are paid to work and they don't know anything about Boswick's murder," Fiona said, staring at the card. "You must be working for Penny Johnson. I'm sorry for Horace, but I have a business to run so I want you out of here."

Kyle decided there was nothing to be gained from arguing with her. He walked over to the lip of the loading dock, jumped down, and went to his car. Fiona followed. She watched Kyle get in the car and drive away. Kyle looked in the rearview mirror—she was still standing there when he turned the corner to go back to his office.

After a busy morning in the district court, Penny drove to the coffee shop down the road from the courthouse. She entered; the rich coffee smell sweeping over her. She got her usual latte and a bagel, found a small corner table, and sat down. She stared out the window, twisting one long, stray strand of hair that had fallen out of the neat bun at the base of her neck.

"You look deep in thought," said a deep male voice. Penny looked up to see Alex smiling at her. "Can I join you?"

Penny nodded. Alex put his briefcase next to Penny's on the extra chair and sat down.

"A penny for Penny's thoughts?" he said.

Penny laughed, her eyes twinkling, "I was mulling over the idiosyncrasies of the law. It is indeed strange at times."

"I agree. By the way, I may have some information for you," Alex said. "Mabel, my mother, knows Jake Rahn. I'm not sure how, I think they were on a committee together. Anyway, she ran into him at the supermarket. He was asking about the murder case. People sometimes talk to her because they think she knows about the law."

"My mom gets that, too. I'm not sure why they think that. Proximity to lawyers and judges, I guess."

Alex continued, "Jake was interested in the gun that was found. He read about it in the paper. His son, Sammie, saw it on his Facebook page and showed it to Jake. He thinks it might be a gun he had. Jake thought he might recognize the handle—it had carving on. He told her he checked to see if his pistol was there, and it wasn't, but he doesn't want to go to the police because he never registered it. He's afraid he might be accused of murder."

Penny listened, her eyes wide.

"That's great news. I'll call him—no, maybe to start, I'll ask Kyle to talk to him. I think they know each other. I don't want to spook him. Give your mom a hug for me."

Penny got quiet for a moment. She looked at Alex. "I enjoyed dinner the other night. Thanks for the lovely evening."

Alex ran his hand through his shaggy, brown hair. He looked over at her, smiling. He was torn between the desire to ask her out again and the feeling he could be falling for her. He compromised.

"The bar association awards dinner is next week. Are you going?" Penny nodded. "Would you like to ride with me?"

"Sure," Penny said casually, thinking that would be fine. It wasn't a second date; it was simply a ride to the dinner. She wasn't ready for second dates. Or third dates for that matter.

They finished their coffee and left the coffee shop, each on their way to a busy day at their respective offices.

Althea and JD greeted Penny when she returned to the office.

"You seem happy," Althea observed. "You have a glow about you."

Penny blushed, something she hadn't done since high school. She bent over to give JD, who was sitting at her feet, some attention. She rubbed his head, smiling at him. He gave her a doggy smile back.

"I had a busy day in court," she said.

"Mmmhmm," Althea said, taking the files from Penny's briefcase. Althea took the files to log them into their case management system.

"I need to call Kyle. Alex told me he heard that Jake Rahn might have information about the pistol."

At that moment, Percy came in through the opening door. Kyle poked his head in. "Do you have a minute?" he asked.

"Just the person I wanted to see," said Penny.

After filling their favorite mugs with some of Althea's coffee, Kyle sat in the client chair, across from the huge walnut desk Penny had inherited from her father. Penny sat in her leather chair. Percy was on the windowsill behind Penny, watching the people on the street below. JD, after several turns around his bed, settled down for an afternoon nap.

"You know Jake Rahn, don't you?" Penny asked. Kyle nodded.

"Well, Mabel, Alex Jeffries' mother, told Alex she ran into Jake at the grocery store, and he was telling her that he thought the pistol the police found might be his. He saw it on Facebook and thought he recognized the handle. He told Mabel he checked and his wasn't there. He doesn't want to go to the police, so he thought maybe Mabel could casually ask Alex what to do. Can you talk to him? I'm afraid if I talk to him, he will deny everything."

"Penny," Althea said, standing in the doorway. "Sorry to interrupt. Fiona Houlis is on the phone. She insists on talking to you."

Penny looked at Kyle with a questioning look. Kyle shrugged his shoulders and shook his head.

Penny answered the phone.

"Penny, this is Fiona Houlis. I know you are representing Horace Appleworth and that Kyle Laverty is working on the case. I want you to tell him to stay away from my offices. He had my employees all upset. It is hard enough to run a business in this recession without some ex-cop coming around harassing my people."

"I'm sure he didn't mean to upset your employees," Penny began.

"Well, he did. I don't want him coming around anymore. Do you understand? No more visits. If he comes around again, I'll call the police and tell them he is trespassing."

With that Fiona banged the phone down so loud, Penny pulled her phone from her ear.

"Fiona sounds upset," said Kyle.

Penny shook her head. "Yes, indeed she is."

Kyle laughed, "I did talk to three of her employees." Kyle pulled his notebook out of his pocket and searched to find the page.

Kyle told her of his conversations with Charlie, the woodcutter, and Yolanda. He mentioned Yolanda's anger with Fiona for bringing Luther on, and her assumption of an affair gone wrong between Luther and Fiona. He mentioned Charlie's comment that Fiona was tough, which was confirmed when she sent Kyle packing.

"Interesting," Penny said. "Do you think Luther and Fiona were having a fling? What about Jake? Could you get Jake to come in and talk to me? I would like to know if he recognizes that pistol. Do you have a picture of it? If not, ask Althea, we downloaded one from the Facebook page."

"I'll try. I'll stop by to talk to him tonight. And, to answer your question, I don't think Luther and Fiona were having a 'fling.' They didn't seem too friendly at Dick's funeral."

Kyle stood. "I'll let you know if I'm successful with Jake."

Kyle and Percy left the office. Penny stood, stretched and reached for JD's leash. "Let's go for a walk," she said to the dog. They left and went out into the warm October afternoon. The streets of the city were quieter, now that school was in session, and the teens were no longer trying to ride their skateboards and bikes through the people walking. Penny and JD walked around the courthouse. Penny noticed the large, round, cement planters were filled with chrysanthemums in beautiful fall colors. She decided to buy a couple small mums for her porch on her way home. The local market had a small nursery and she needed some eggs, anyway.

Back at the office, Penny sorted through her mail, then began some research into a new case. The courthouse clock struck five o'clock. Althea and Penny straightened the office. Penny decided to go visit her parents—her mom called and said they were having a baked chicken—which sounded good.

Althea was off to book club. "Is it book club or are you guys discussing Horace's case?" asked Penny.

Althea laughed. "I'll let you know. We do have a book to discuss."

The two women locked up and left for the day.

Later that evening, Althea, Rose, Mary, and Arney sat around their favorite table at the bookstore. Their book discussion completed, they pushed the books to one side. It was time for reports.

Althea told them of Kyle's investigation of Fiona's business and her reaction.

"I'm not surprised," said Arney. "I know she's in trouble financially. I learned she's having trouble-making payroll. No one knows of any job she has in the works. She was banking on getting the renovation contract."

"I know she sent in a bid," said Mary. "I saw her bring it in and give it to the assistant manager who, by the way, has been made acting city manager by the commissioners. He will hold the job until they find a new one. I guess the job will be posted soon. The staff is pulling for him to get the job."

Rose nibbled a cookie. After a moment, she turned to Mary and asked.

"Would he kill Dick to get the job?"

"Good heavens, no," Mary said, her eyes wide, "He is too meek to kill anyone—but he can be firm—I'm not saying he's a wimp."

"Anymore news, Arney?" Althea asked, turning toward him.

"Yes, I learned that Victor withdrew about thirty thousand dollars from the bank the afternoon of Dick's death. I won't say how I came across that information, but I am sure of my source. And the money has not been returned. If Dick was taking kickbacks, then perhaps Victor paid him that night. But where did the money go?"

"I can tell you there is nothing in the police report about money being found—wait, I remember they did report finding two one hundred-dollar bills under Dick's head. But that was all," said Althea.

"Maybe that is why Victor has been snooping around, asking about the contracts. He was the one Dick recommended for the job. And he's been asking about what was found at the crime scene. If he left money there with Dick, where did it go?" Mary asked.

"If there was money there, it is safe to assume the real killer took it," said Althea.

"Has anyone been flashing a lot of money lately?" asked Arney. The ladies all shook their heads, no.

"We will keep our eyes open," Althea said.

"My niece, Mildred," said Rose, "who is in my Saturday reading group had an interesting bit of information. She told us the night of the concert, she had to go to the bathroom and she won't use Portolets. They're 'too unsanitary,' she said."

Althea nodded and smiled. "That sounds like Mildred."

"She lives near the city offices, so she and her dad were going past them on their way to her house. They cut through the yard in back of the offices. They saw a man come out of the back door and go off toward the river and the railroad tracks. She and her dad went up to the door, thinking they could get in, so she could use the restroom there.

"Mildred said the door was locked and she was quite put out about it. 'That man got to use the potty, he should have waited and let us in,' she said.

"I asked her what the man looked like, and she said, 'he looked like a man.' It may have been too dark to see. He didn't appear to have seen Mildred and her dad. I asked her if her dad knew the man and she said she didn't think so. I don't know if her dad reported the incident to the police."

"There's nothing about it in the police report. That could have been the real killer," Althea said, leaning forward, her eyes intense. "Mildred and her dad could have been in danger. I'll tell Penny. She'll want to get Kyle on it right away. That's great news. Thanks, Rose."

Rose beamed. She loved solving these mysteries in the town. She was an avid reader of crime but being involved in real life murder was such fun.

The bookstore clerks were closing up for the night. Rose, Mary, Arney, and Althea cleaned up their table, gathered up their belongings, and headed for the door.

On the sidewalk, they parted, agreeing to meet again in a few days.

We have made a lot of progress, Althea thought as she walked to her car. Mildred's information is a big help—if it is true—and I think it is. Mildred is a smart and observant little girl. She reminds me of Penny when she was that age. We need to get Kyle to work on this new information. I'll tell Penny first thing tomorrow.

The next morning the two women arrived at the office door at the same time. JD sat patiently while Althea unlocked and opened the door. Ignoring the usual pleasantries, Althea said, "I have some news or rather the Society has a lot to report. I'll make the coffee first."

"Hmm, sounds interesting," said Penny. She went into her office. Sitting in her big leather chair, she pulled out her criminal procedure book from the corner of the desk and began reading. She wanted to find a way to keep the gun out of the trial. So far it didn't look promising.

When Althea announced the coffee was ready, Penny found her favorite Biltmore Estate mug, poured some coffee, and went to the small round table in the corner of her office. Althea joined her.

Althea began her report with the information from Rose about Mildred and Randy seeing someone coming out of the city offices that night. She told Penny about Victor and his money withdrawal and about Fiona's money problems.

"Do we know if Randy told the police what he saw?' asked Penny. "This is great news. Randy and Mildred may have seen the real killer. I wonder if Victor was bribing Dick—there hasn't been any proof Dick took kickbacks—merely rumor and innuendo. I'll see if Kyle is in. I want to know if he talked to Jake and he needs this information."

Penny got up and went to the outside door. JD padded after her. She opened the door, walked a short distance and came to Kyle's office. The door said Kyle E. Laverty, Private Investigator. The black, block letters were carefully centered on the frosted glass top half of the door. Penny smiled. She remembered the day the sign maker came to put the name on the door. Kyle had beamed while he watched the man work. He was proud of his growing business.

She opened the door to find Kyle sitting at his desk, phone at his ear, writing on a yellow legal pad. He motioned Penny to a chair. When she sat down, Percy jumped in her lap.

"You're putting on weight," she said to the big, gray cat, scratching the top of his head.

Kyle put down the phone. "I know he is, he must be getting ready for winter. Every fall he puts on an extra pound. I have some news for you."

"And I for you, but you go first."

"Okay." Kyle reached for his notebook, flipped some pages, and came to the spot he was looking for. "Jake Rahn is pretty sure the gun is his. He is terrified of going to the police and wants to talk to you first. He vehemently denies killing Dick. He doesn't have any motive, and he barely knew the man, so I believe him. He said he'd call you."

"Fantastic news, but then how did the gun end being the one that killed Dick? The police will want to know that, and Jake could be in for some unpleasant questioning."

Kyle nodded.

Penny brought Kyle up to speed on the activities of the Society.

Kyle laughed, "That group is scary—they sure can get information that no one else can. No wonder Dan gets so annoyed with them. He thinks they interfere."

"I, for one, am glad they do. They have an impressive record," said Penny.

"I'll look into this today," said Kyle, "I'll let you know what I find."

"Thanks, come on, JD, we need to go back to our office." She got up and headed for the door.

When she opened the door to her office, Althea was talking to a middle-aged man dressed in jeans and sweatshirt that announced his loyalty to the Detroit Lions. He was sitting on a reception room chair, holding his dirty Lions baseball cap.

"Penny, this is Jake Rahn," Althea said.

Penny turned to look at the man. She held out her hand.

"Mr. Rahn, I am so pleased you came by."

When he shook her hand, she noticed his hand was rough. His handshake was firm, but she could sense the tension.

"I didn't want to," said Jake in gravelly voice that sounded like it had smoked too many cigarettes. "But it is the right thing to do."

"You believe the pistol is yours?" Penny asked, after they both settled in her office.

"Well, it sure looks like the one I bought at a gun show a few years back. I bought it because it was an old Remington. I collect old pistols, not to shoot; I have a target pistol for that. This one had something carved in the handle."

"When my son, Sammie, showed me the pistol on Facebook, it looked familiar, I checked and my pistol is missing."

"Do you remember who you bought it from?"

"No, not really, I was more interested in the pistol than in the dude selling it. I don't even remember what he looked like."

"Did you register it?"

"No need, as far as I'm concerned. I didn't intend to shoot it. That registration business is stupid. We have a right to keep and bear arms, according to the Constitution, you know."

"Yes, Mr. Rahn, I know," Penny said, not wanting to get into a political discussion about guns. "Would you be willing to talk to Detective Dunlap at the sheriff's office about what you know? We can ask him to show us the pistol; that way you could be sure whether it is yours."

"I don't want to—what if they think I killed Dick?"

"Did you have any reason to want him dead?"

"I didn't even know the man; I have worked on city projects but for the construction company that got the job. Never worked directly for the city."

"I'm sure it will be fine," Penny said. "I'll call Dan right now."

Penny placed the call, while Jake sat with his head down staring at the floor, turning the Lions cap in his hands around and around.

"He can meet us right away," said Penny, hanging up the phone. "You can ride with me." Penny was worried Jake might back out and take off.

They went in the front door of the police department. The building, built in the late 50s, was brick. The entry was covered with a large black canopy. Inside the building, the front entry was empty except for Dan Dunlap, who was standing to one side of the long counter. He was talking to the officer on duty. When he heard the door open, he turned.

After introductions, Dan led them to a small, windowless room used for interrogation. Jake hung back a little, his small brown eyes taking in the scene. Dan closed the door to the room. The metal table was bolted to the floor. Four institutional metal chairs were around the table. Penny and Jake sat on one side of the table and Dan on the other. Dan took out his small digital tape recorder,

"We have to tape everything," he said.

"I am here as a friend, not an attorney," said Penny. She then explained how she had learned about Jake's connection to the pistol.

Jake looked around the room. "I want you to know I had nothing to do with Boswick's death. I've never spoken to the man. I have worked on city projects. He would come to the site but I didn't speak to him. I'm a finish carpenter," he said, the words rushing out of his mouth.

Dan leaned back in his chair. "And a good one," he said. "You did some work on my aunt's house. I think you put a new mantel over the fireplace. She lives on Barnes in two-story, green house. The new mantel was beautiful."

Jake looked up. He smiled. "I remember that job. It was a bitch, I mean hard, to do. But I liked the end result."

"So did my aunt. Tell me how you came to have the pistol," Dan said.

Jake told Dan about buying the pistol as a collector's item. "I figured since I didn't plan to shoot it, I didn't have to register it, so I didn't."

"Did you ever shoot it?"

"I took it out to the range, you know the one in the back of the fairgrounds. I shot a few shots but it wasn't dependable. I'm a pretty good shot, but it was never that accurate. I kept it clean, though."

"Where did you keep it?"

"In my gun case, which is locked. I keep the key in a drawer in the marble-topped chest in the hall. When my son, Sammie, showed me a picture of the gun on Facebook, I thought it looked like mine. I went to check and mine was missing."

Dan reached into the box on the floor and pulled out the plastic evidence bag that held the pistol. He slipped on some latex gloves and took the pistol out. He laid it on the table.

"Could you turn it over?" Jake asked.

Dan turned the pistol over. It was possible to see the scratches on the wooden butt of the pistol.

"Yep, that looks like mine," said Jake. After a moment, he turned to Penny. "Am I in trouble?"

"No, Jake, you're not. I am sure Detective Dunlap knows you had nothing to do with the murder. Isn't that right, Detective?"

Dan nodded. "How did this gun come to be used in a crime? That is the question. Jake, where were you the night of the murder?"

"I was at the concert in front of the courthouse. I was with my wife, Hilda, and our neighbors, the Spencer's. After the concert, we went to get ice cream at Tom's Creamery, then we walked home."

"You know I'll want to talk to them," Dan said.

Jake nodded. His mouth was pressed into a straight line, his brow furrowed.

"Who has access to your house?"

"Well, really about anybody," Jake said. "My wife is a cook for the school and is gone until around 1:30 in the afternoon. Sammie's in school. He has football practice until six when I pick him up. Like most people in Midvale Corners, we don't always lock our doors."

"Do you have any idea when the pistol went missing?"

"No, I don't."

'Who has been in your house, besides the immediate family?"

"We had a neighborhood block party in late August. It was mostly in front of my house. A lot of people went in the house to get stuff or use the bathroom. My sister and her husband were there, Luther, my nephew and…Oh, I know, Hilda's mom, Hilda's aunt—her mother's sister—but she's in her 80s, I don't think she had anything to do with the pistol. She was a crack shot in her day but hasn't shot in years."

"I'll need names and addresses for these folks," said Dan.

"Are they in trouble?" Jake asked.

"No, but they might have seen something. Luther, your nephew, wasn't he in prison?" Dan asked.

"Yes, but he's straight now. He's working."

"Do you know where he's working?"

"Sure, he works at the lumberyard owned by the Houlis family."

Dan gave Jake a pad of paper and asked him to write down the names of people who had access to his house.

Jake bent over the paper. He wrote each name carefully.

"My writing's not too good. I don't have to write often. I'm better with my tools."

"Take your time," Dan urged. He and Penny sat quietly and waited.

"That's all I can remember," said Jake, pushing the paper toward Dan.

"Thanks," Dan said, standing. He left to make a copy for Penny then led her and Jake out to the lobby of the police station. Dan stood by the glass door and saw them get into Penny's pink car, which shined like a beacon in the parking lot. It's easy to find, he thought.

Penny and Jake parted on the street in front of Penny's office. "I sure hope I'm not in trouble," Jake said. He walked away; shoulders slumped, staring at the cracks in the sidewalk.

Penny went up the stairs to her office. She grabbed her sandwich out of the tiny refrigerator, got her coffee, and sat at her desk to check the morning mail.

"I put the files you'll need for court in your briefcase," Althea said. She put Penny's briefcase on the chair.

"Thanks." Penny finished her lunch, then checked the briefcase for paper and pens. She smiled when she saw her lucky Petoskey stone in its special pocket. She loaded up. On her way to the door, she patted JD on the head.

"I'll take him for a walk," Althea said. "See you later."

Penny left and the office was quiet. JD went to his bed to sleep; Althea went to her desk to work on some pleadings for Penny. Each had a job to do.

Kyle backed his bike out of its parking spot in back of the building. He wanted to talk to Randy Haywood. Since Randy had the best motorcycle shop in town, he rode his BMW, savoring the warm October day.

Pulling into the parking lot of the dealership on Cedar, he saw rows of Harley-Davidsons gleaming in the sunshine. He looked more closely and discovered three BMWs at the end of a row.

Kyle parked his bike, took off his helmet, and put it on the seat. "That's a beaut of a bike," said a dark-haired man with quick blue eyes. "I prefer Harleys myself, but that model BMW does make for a nice ride. Randy Haywood," he held out his hand, "Can I help you? Bike sounds fine, so maybe you want to trade up to a Harley?"

Kyle laughed, "No, I don't think so. This bike and I have logged a lot of miles. You're right. It is a good ride."

Kyle introduced himself. "I'm investigating the Boswick murder, and I'm hoping you can help me."

"Sure, I'll do what I can. You want some coffee?"

"No, I'm coffeed out," Kyle said.

Randy led Kyle inside to a desk in the corner of the showroom. They sat down. Kyle pulled his notebook out of his pocket.

"Do you remember the night of the murder, when you walked past the city offices?"

"I sure do. I had to take Mildred home to potty. She absolutely refuses to use the porta-potties. I can't blame her, they do smell like chemicals, but it's a nuisance. It seems like we're always looking for the right bathroom for Mildred. Anyway, we left the concert and were walking around behind the city offices. We saw a man come out of the building and walk toward the railroad tracks. I didn't see him up close and he seemed to be in a hurry."

"What did you do next?"

"I thought maybe the city building was open because of the concert, so we went up to try the door."

"It was locked and all the lights were out. Mildred was annoyed and so was I. You'd think the building would be open on the night of the concert. We went on home."

"Did you get a good look at the man?'

"Like I told the police, it was dark and I couldn't see much of him. I got the impression he was thin, about average height. He had on dark clothes and the lights of the building weren't on, which seemed a little strange to me."

"What time was it?"

"Not sure, about 8:30 or so. The concert had been going on for a while. Great concert by the way—high school band is pretty good— they've won some awards, I think. Yeah, about 8:30."

"You reported this to the police?"

"Yes, I thought it was my duty to do that. They weren't interested. They acted like I was imposing on them. They took down what I said, but I think they believe they have their murderer."

Randy reached over to pick up the ringing phone.

"I need to take this, I'm alone here this morning. Can you wait?'

Kyle nodded.

"Yes, he wants the Road King Classic in Velvet Black with chrome aluminum wheels, and luggage bag and riding gear. It came to about twenty-three thousand dollars. The guy paid the deposit in cash. I'll wire transfer the money to you in the morning, as soon as the bank opens. Why they hold cash, I don't know, but that's the way it is.

"Yeah, he wants it quick. Good, you'll put it on the truck as soon as you get the money? Can I get a confirmation number?" Randy wrote it down. After hanging up the phone, he turned back to Kyle.

"Big order?" asked Kyle.

"Business has been slow, but this guy came in first thing this morning. He wants the fancy Harley Davidson and he wants it in a hurry. Paid me in cash. Money was weird, though. It was kind of greasy, I don't know what was on it—and some of it had brown spots on it. Guy must have been saving it for a long time."

"Who was the guy? I know most of the bikers around here, so I might know him."

"Luther Rahn," Randy answered. Kyle nodded without comment.

Kyle stood. "Thanks for your time, I better be on my way."

"If you want to trade up to a fancier model or a Harley, give me a call," Randy said. He reached over to the corner of the desk, picked up a business card, and handed it to Kyle.

"Thanks, don't think I'll leave BMW. It's a nice ride."

"We have a complete repair shop, if you ever need work done," Randy said, watching Kyle leave.

Kyle put on his helmet, hopped on the bike and rode away. I think I'll give Luther Rahn a visit, he thought. We can talk bikes. Where did he get the money?

Kyle rode down Cedar, passing the new fancy McDonald's, the strip mall with the Family and Home shop, a dollar store, and the Goodwill. He turned on Columbia, noticing that, as usual, the BP gas was a penny more a gallon than the Speedway across the street. Two blocks of small bungalows went by and he turned right on McRoberts. Houlis Construction and Lumberyard was on the corner. He drove into the parking lot, stopped, and started to get off his bike. He sat back down when he heard a female voice.

"I thought I told you to stay away from here," said Fiona Houlis. She stood with her fists on her hips, glaring at him.

"You did, but I would like to talk to Luther," Kyle said.

"Forget it, he's busy working and doesn't have time to talk to you. Talk about what?"

"I just found out he's a fellow biker, and I wanted to congratulate him on his new bike."

"What new bike? I haven't seen any new bike. Please leave. If you want to talk to him, find him after work. We've got a business to run."

Kyle rode away. It was time for lunch and he was hungry. He turned on Mason Street, pulled into the parking lot of the Depot, a restaurant in the old train station. Kyle knew a lot of the police officers ate there; maybe I'll see Dan Dunlap and I want a hot roast beef sandwich with rich brown gravy and real mashed potatoes. Not good for my heart, but I'll work it off tomorrow.

Kyle parked his bike up close to the old building. He walked to the door of the restaurant, his helmet tucked under his arm. Opening the door, he saw a pile of used books stacked on a bench in one corner of the small vestibule. The sign said "50 cents each." He paused but then moved on, his stomach was growling, letting him know it was time to eat.

Coming through the door to the dining room, he stopped, looking for a table. He saw an arm motioning to him. The arm belonged to Dan, who was sitting in a far corner. Kyle walked to the table.

"Join me," said Dan, a big grin on his round face. "I haven't seen you for a while."

Kyle sat down. "Keep eating, you don't want those nachos to get cold." Kyle ordered his sandwich from the waitress, stirred some cream in the coffee she brought him, and settled back in the booth.

He and Dan had known each other for a long time. They had crossed paths when Dan was with the FBI and Kyle with the CIA. Dan left the FBI, preferring the local sheriff's department. Kyle retired to become a private investigator.

Kyle and Dan caught up on the people they knew in common. Over coffee, Dan asked, "How's the investigation of Boswick's murder going? The sheriff has closed his file, but, between you and me, I'm not convinced that Horace Appleworth is the murderer."

"Neither am I," Kyle said. "I wonder about Boswick's ethics. I heard rumors he took kickbacks from contractors."

"Well, I'm supposedly off the case, but I have been asking around and I agree. He drove that white Corvette, and even if he bought it used, it is still an expensive car to maintain. I know Sally teaches, but she doesn't seem like the type to spend money on fancy cars."

"The other person who is flashing money is Luther Rahn," said Kyle. "For a man right out of prison, where did he get cash for a new Harley?"

"What do you mean?" Dan asked.

Kyle explained his meeting with Randy Haywood and his comments about Luther.

"I went to Houlis Construction to talk to him, but Fiona kicked me off the property. I'll find him later."

"You want some help?" Dan asked.

"Sure, a little pressure might help stir the pot," Kyle said. "It will be like old times when we worked cases together."

"I'll stop by and chat with him. Fiona can't keep me off the property—it is an official investigation."

They finished their lunches and left the restaurant. They took off in opposite directions, Dan in the unmarked gray car, Kyle on his bike.

Dan pulled into the parking lot of Houlis Lumberyard. He climbed out of the car and went into the main building. The room, a combination sales room and office, smelled of freshly cut wood and birdseed. He saw a display of fancy birdhouses and bags of seed.

He approached the L-shaped counter that separated the clerks from the customers.

"Can you tell me where I can find Luther Rahn?" he asked the closest clerk. She told him Luther was across the street in one of the buildings used to store lumber.

"Ask any of the guys there, they should know where he is," she said, smiling up at him.

"Why do you want to see Luther?" asked another female voice.

Turning toward the sound, Dan saw Fiona Houlis.

"Hello, Ms. Houlis, haven't seen you since the last Chamber meeting. I just want to see how Luther is doing. Won't take up much of his time."

Fiona paused. "He's working hard," she said. "I'd appreciate it if you'd let him keep at it." She turned and walked back toward her office, tucked in a corner next to the birdseed.

Dan went out the door and across the street.

The sound of a saw led him to a back corner of the building. "Know where I can find Luther?" he yelled. The big man at the saw stopped and pointed to the back of the building.

"He's back there with a customer, I think."

Dan saw two men talking. He approached but waited until one of them turned to walk away.

"Thanks, Luther, I'll pick up the order tomorrow morning," he said.

After the man left, Luther turned toward Dan. "Can I help you?"

Dan took out his badge and showed it to Luther.

"I haven't done anything wrong," Luther said. "I do my job and keep out of trouble."

"I don't have any complaints," said Dan. "I do have a question, however. I understand you bought a new Harley Davidson motorcycle. I was wondering about that, being as how you just got out of prison."

"You mean, where did I get the money? I don't see how that is any of your business—I could've won the lotto or inherited the money, for all you know. I don't have to explain my actions to you. I'm a free man."

"Yes, you are. I was just curious, being a BMW man myself."

"Well, I like Harleys. If there is nothing else, Officer, I have work to do."

Luther walked away. Dan decided the interview was over. He left the way he came, climbed in his, car and started to pull away. He looked up and saw a woman's face in the small window at one end of the building. It looked like Fiona Houlis.

Dan headed back to the sheriff's office, wondering about Fiona, Luther, and Harleys—if they were connected—and if so, how.

Chapter 15

Fiona turned from the window of her office and went in search of Luther. She found him next to a pile of rough lumber in the far corner of the warehouse.

"Why are Kyle Laverty and Dan Dunlap looking for you? And since when do you ride a Harley?"

Luther turned from counting the boards in the pile. He stared at Fiona.

"Damn, now you made me lose count. Raff needs 100 2 x 4's to frame in a new barn and wants them yesterday. He's coming back in an hour. And I have no idea why they are asking about the Harley. Like I told them, it is none of their business or yours."

"I don't like them coming around and interfering with our work. It's hard enough to get jobs without having people snooping around."

"Don't worry, they won't be back. I sent them packing." Luther turned from Fiona and started counting boards again.

Fiona watched him. He looked like a man busy with work, but she wasn't sure. She thought she saw his hands shake.

"Well, I hope you're right about that."

She strode through the warehouse, looking at the piles of cut wood. She loved the smell of fresh lumber. She looked around pleased with what she saw but worried about the recession. She thought of her conversation with the bank manager who wasn't too interested in extending her line of credit. She knew if she didn't get a big job soon, she might be in a serious cash flow crunch.

Penny looked up from the report she was reading when the outer door to the office opened. Althea came in laden down with bags of candy. "I take it that candy is for Halloween, not for the office."

"Yes, I get a lot of 'trick or treaters' and Halloween is Sunday night. That's only two days away. They were having a sale at Miller's. I couldn't resist. I think I have more than I need if you want some for your house."

"I don't get many customers—the house sits too far back—they go to the main house and then go on their way. But I'll take one bag, just in case. I'll take tootsie pops. They aren't my favorites so maybe I won't eat them all myself."

Althea laughed. She put a bag on the chair in Penny's office. "It's about time for you to go home," she said. "It's been a long week."

Penny stood up and stretched. She had been sitting at her desk all afternoon. "You're right. It is time to go home. We have a new client. Lia called with the appointment. She faxed over the police report. I'll put the file on your desk. It can wait until Monday. The pre-trial is next Thursday. Our client is out on bail. He called while you were gone. He's coming in Monday afternoon around 1 o'clock. I put a note on your desk."

Penny and Althea straightened up the office. They left together. Penny, JD's leash in one hand and her briefcase slung on her shoulder, locked the door. Althea, loaded with her bags of candy, walked to the elevator. Penny and JD walked down the hall to the stairs.

Penny noticed that Kyle's light was on in his office. She opened his door. He looked up and smiled.

"On your way out, I see," he said. "Have a great week-end."

"You, too. Let's meet on Monday afternoon to talk about Horace's case. I've got a feeling we're missing something."

"I'll put it on my phone—how about 3 o'clock?" Kyle grabbed his phone.

Penny reached in her briefcase, which was on the floor and pulled out her calendar.

"Got it," she said, writing a note on Monday, November first.

Penny gathered up her belongings, called to JD who was busy exchanging sniffs with Percy. They took the stairs at the end of the hall, went out the door, and walked toward Penny's car, parked in the lot in back of the building. It was the only car left. It sat in the space right next to the alley that led to the courthouse at one end and Ash Street at the other. Two drive-up mailboxes ready to receive bills, letters, and cards from folks who still used the printed word were opposite the entrance to the lot. Kyle's motorcycle was in its special spot next to the building. Penny opened the driver's car door, tossed her briefcase on the floor of the passenger side, and turned to JD.

"In you go," she said to the big dog. JD stuck his nose in the open door, sniffing. He backed up.

"Get in the car. It's time to go home." Penny said. She pulled on his lead. JD pulled back, dragging Penny away from the car. She looked at him.

"Oh, okay, we'll go for a quick walk, but I think you could wait."

Penny slammed the car door.

"Do we have to walk so fast?" JD was pulling Penny down the alley.

"Heel," she commanded. JD kept pulling.

"What is the matter with you? You know better."

They arrived at the intersection of the alley and the main street of Midvale Corners. JD stopped. Penny looked both ways. There wasn't any traffic. They crossed the street to the sidewalk surrounding the courthouse. Penny paused by the strip of grass between the sidewalk and the street. JD sat next to her.

"I thought you had to go potty. Why are you...?"

Penny stared down the ally. She saw pink metal parts flying through the air. Then she heard an earsplitting blast. Flames shot out from the back end of her car that was just visible from where she stood.

JD started barking. Penny stood stock still unable to move.

"Did you call 911? What happened? Was anybody hurt? Somebody call 911? I did, I have my cell phone. The fire department is on its way. Does anyone have a fire extinguisher?"

The voices around Penny brought her out of her daze. She started back down the alley. She could hear the sirens in the distance. She smelled burning gasoline. She started to move.

"I wouldn't go down there, Penny," said a male voice. Penny turned to the sound. She saw Ethan Humphrey.

"Let the fire department get the fire out first."

"But it was my car, Mr. Humphrey. Why would my car blow up? My briefcase and cell phone are in there—I need them."

"No, you don't," said Ethan. "You need to sit down for a minute. There is a bench over there across the street in front of the bank."

Ethan and Toby, his Shetland sheepdog, led Penny to the bench. Penny sat. JD followed Toby. Both dogs sat down next to the bench. JD was sitting as close to Penny as he could. He put his big head in her lap. She put her hand on his head.

Kyle came running out of the alley, looking up and down the street. When he saw Penny, he ran over to her.

"Oh, thank God, you're alright," he said, looking at Penny closely. "I heard the explosion, but I couldn't get to the car. The fire department arrived. They told me no one was in the car. Are you okay?"

"She's a little shook-up," said Ethan. "Does anyone have any water?" he asked the crowd of people milling around the end of the alley watching the fire trucks and the firemen put out the fire.

A woman stepped forward with a bottle of Evian. "This is fresh," she said. "I haven't even opened it." She handed it to Penny who took it, holding it in her hand.

Penny looked up at Kyle. "Why did my car blow up?"

"The fire fighters will tell us. But, for now, I'm just glad you're okay."

"I had better call my mother. She will hear about this before it's on the news. I'm sure someone has called her already. Can I use your phone?" Penny tried to open the water bottle but her hands wouldn't stop shaking. Kyle took from her to open it when his phone rang.

Penny jumped. Kyle answered. He listened for a minute. "She's right here sitting on the bench at the end of the alley and she's fine. He's fine, too." He handed the phone to Penny. "It's your mother."

"I'm fine, Mother," said Penny not surprised that her mother was on the line. The woman had always been able to find her children no matter where they were. "I don't know what happened. The car just blew up."

"It's funny though," she went on. "JD wouldn't let me get in the car. He insisted we come to the courthouse lawn. I thought he had to go potty, but he didn't, and then the car blew up. Isn't that odd?"

"No, I can stay in my house tonight. Dad's on his way here? Oh, well, he doesn't need to do that. I want to talk to the fireman if I can."

Penny flipped the phone closed and handed it to Kyle.

"Are you okay?" said a voice.

Looking up Penny saw Alex looking down at her. He kneeled down in front of her. He held her hand.

Penny looked at him. "I'm fine—a little shook up but fine. How did you hear about this?'

"It's a small town," Alex said, standing up. "News travels fast. And Ethan called me."

"Althea's here, too," Kyle said.

"Penny, thank goodness you're okay. JD is okay, too." Althea rushed up and gave Penny and JD a hug.

Penny extricated herself from Althea. "I'm fine, Althea. JD's fine, too."

Althea sat next to Penny on the bench.

"I spoke to the fire chief," said Penny's dad, Judge Gallagher, approaching the bench. "He's pretty sure that the car was rigged with a bomb."

"A bomb," said Penny. "Why would anyone do that?"

"Chief Whittaker thinks that's the reason JD wouldn't let you get in the car. He was trained to smell explosives and even though he flunked out--no offense, JD," he said, patting the big dog, "still he knew enough to get away from the car."

"What set the bomb off?" asked Penny.

"He won't know until the fire is completely out and his fire investigators finish their investigation."

"I think we should get some hot coffee in you," said Althea. "You look a little pale."

Ethan got up from his end of the bench. "I better get on home. Toby needs his dinner. I'm glad you're okay," he said.

"Thanks for your help, Ethan," said Penny. Ethan and Toby headed home.

Penny gathered up JD's leash and stood. Her hands still shook. "I could use some coffee. It's too cold to sit outside and they won't let JD into the bookstore. Where should we go?"

"He can come in the store. No one will say anything. After all, he saved your life," said Belinda. She held the door open ushering them all in. "I have some fresh coffee and newly baked cookies--just what you need to calm you all down."

Kyle, Alex, Althea, Judge Gallagher and Penny went into the bookstore. They sat at a large table. JD ambled under the table and curled up by Penny's feet. He sighed.

The clerk, who had been outside watching the excitement, followed them in to take their orders. Even though it was close to closing time for the store, he was willing to stay to hear all the news.

Coffees were served with a plate of cookies, everyone sat silently staring at their coffee.

"If it hadn't been for JD," said Althea. "I hate to think what could have happened."

"He's a hero," Kyle declared. All agreed looking under the table at the sleeping dog.

"I bet he gets his picture in the paper," said Alex.

"We need to talk about the possibility that someone tried to kill Penny," said the Judge, bringing them back to reality.

"Why would anyone want to do that?" asked Penny.

Alex leaned forward to voice his opinion that perhaps Penny's representation of Horace had something to do with it when he saw Kitty Gallagher come sailing in the door.

"I think we can wait to talk about that after Penny has a good night's sleep," said Kitty, pulling up a chair. A look passed between Kitty and her husband. He nodded.

"I guess we can talk about it tomorrow," he said.

Penny smiled at her mother. "Thanks, Mom," she mouthed. She wanted to go home, take a shower and climb into her bed. Talk could wait.

Kyle announced that he would go to Penny's house to be sure it would be safe for her. The rest of the group headed out the door. Alex and the Judge were deep in conversation as Kitty, Penny and JD went out the door.

Penny and her mother were quiet on the short ride home. "Do you want me to come in with you?" asked her Mother.

"No, Mom, I'll be fine. I see Kyle's bike over there. I'm sure he's checked everything out."

Penny found Kyle by the front door. "I don't see any sign that anyone has been here, but I think JD and I'll take a tour of the place."

Penny waited while Kyle and JD walked through the house and yard.

"It looks okay and JD didn't act up."

Penny thanked Kyle and went into her house. She looked around. The small living room looked normal, her family pictures were in their places on the fireplace mantel. The cabinet with the paperweight collection was as before.

JD walked over to his bowl, drank some water and then lay down in his spot by the fireplace with a sigh.

Penny stood in the shower thinking about the events of the day. "Why would anyone try to blow me up?" she asked the water pounding on her back, easing her tense shoulder muscles. She turned off the water, stepped out of the shower, dried off and climbed into her bed. JD came into the bedroom and curled up on his bed in the corner of the room.

Wondering if the explosion had anything to do with the murder of Dick Boswick, she knew it couldn't be Horace. Maybe it was one of her crazy clients. After tossing and turning, she turned on the classical music station and drifted off to sleep.

Chapter 16

After a restless night, Penny rolled out of bed early for a Saturday morning. She stretched only to discover every muscle ached. Glad she suffered no harm but feeling as sore as if she had blown up rather than her car, she climbed out of bed.

Slipping on a pair of jeans and a hoody over her pajamas, she went to the kitchen, ground some fresh coffee beans, and started the coffee. She grabbed JD's leash and called the big dog to her.

"Come on, my hero," she said. "You need a walk."

She snapped on his leash, which he didn't need since he usually obeyed her commands but when she became a lawyer, she swore to uphold the law and the city ordinance said he had to be on a leash. They proceeded out the door; JD following Penny like the dog trainers said all good dogs should do.

Penny and JD took a turn around the block. It was early, and no one was out, a fact that pleased Penny since she was not ready to talk about the last night's events. The sun was rising, the air cool since fall was turning into winter. She smelled the dry leaves stacked in piles on the street waiting for the street cleaners. She knew more would be added as folks raked the last of the leaves out of the flowerbeds. This was about the end of the season for leaf cleanup, which meant she had to do a little raking herself, but first, she needed some breakfast, another hot shower and time to think.

When she turned the corner, she saw her dad's old green Jaguar in the driveway. Her mother was getting out waving a bag at Penny.

"I have breakfast," she said. "I figured you'd be up early."

Penny gave her mother a hug, holding a little longer than usual. She felt like she did when she was little and hurt and her mother fixed everything. The women went into the house and headed for the little kitchen. The scent of fresh coffee greeted them when they walked into the kitchen.

"Why don't you go take a hot shower and I'll get breakfast started?" Kitty said. She pulled eggs, bacon, a coffee cake and some bagels from the bag she had set on the kitchen table and began looking for pans.

"I need to give you some of my pans," she said to Penny's back. She got no response.

"I don't think she heard me," she said to JD who was lying in the doorway to the kitchen. He knew when Kitty was cooking, he best stay out of her way.

A short while later, Penny appeared at the door with clean jeans, a white T, and a red flannel shirt. Her long auburn hair, still wet, was hanging around her face. Maureen thought she looked pale but didn't say anything. Instead she poured her a cup of fresh coffee. Penny poured in the cream and stirred. After breathing in the fresh coffee fumes, she took a taste.

"That's better," she said. "I'm beginning to feel human again."

"You'll feel even better when you finish this, "said Kitty placing a plate of hot scrambled eggs and bacon in front of Penny. She had added what cheese she could find in the refrigerator to the eggs to give them a little boost of taste.

Penny didn't realize how hungry she was until she started eating. Her mother placed a slice of warm coffeecake on her plate, which she quickly consumed.

Kitty sat down to her own cup of coffee. "I have already eaten," she said, 'but I'll have a piece of that coffee cake. I used your grandmother's recipe and it is pretty tasty if I do say so myself."

"Your father is meeting you at your office at 10. Althea and Kyle will be joining us. He has a preliminary report on the car—it's pretty brief but I guess it has some information."

"Did someone tell Maureen that her lovely pink car is no more?" Penny asked. "I know she doesn't need it but still it does have some sentimental value. I feel really bad about it."

"I sent her a text," said her mother. "She knows you had nothing to do with it being blown up and is glad you are okay."

Penny finished her breakfast. The two of them cleaned up the kitchen. Penny didn't have a dishwasher—they fell into the familiar pattern of Mom washing and Penny drying and putting away. The familiar routine calmed Penny. She began to feel more like herself.

That is until she went to get her briefcase and realized it had been blown up, too.

"Oh, my, we will have to get copies of all that stuff, and my laptop was in there too."

"Don't worry, dear, it will be alright. I am sure Althea has copies of all that was in there. She is so efficient."

Maureen, Penny and JD left the house. Penny carefully checked the locks to make sure it was secure.

They climbed into the Jag, heading downtown.

"Dad loves this old car," said Penny. "How did you get him to let you drive it? I hope JD's paws are clean."

"I have my ways," said her mother, smiling.

Penny, Kitty, and JD entered her office to find Althea, Kyle, and her father sitting around the conference table drinking coffee and reading a report. All eyes turned to Penny when she opened the door.

"I'm fine," she said. "You all can stop staring at me now."

Penny and Kitty pulled up a couple of chairs and the others moved to make space for them at the table.

"Here is a preliminary copy of the report on your car," Judge Gallagher said. "From what we know so far, it was no accident. The investigator found the remnants of a crude bomb in what was left of the car. Fire Chief Brimley concluded that when you slammed the door, the car rocked—those struts were old and needed changing, remember, I told you that—at any rate, the car rocked just enough to set the timer on the bomb and it went off shortly after that. It is a blessing that JD dragged you away—you could have been killed or seriously injured."

They looked at JD, sleeping peacefully; Percy curled up next to his tummy. They all smiled at him.

"The question becomes who wants to kill you?" her father asked.

"I have no idea," Penny said. "Some of my clients are a little crazy, but I don't think they want me dead. And I can't think any of them know anything about blowing up cars."

"Well," Kitty said, "I think it has to do with Horace's case. "I think you should call Gordon and ask him to take over—not that I doubt for a moment that you can handle it—but it is too dangerous."

The others nodded. Penny looked around at her family and friends.

"I am not going to do that," she said. "I can defend Horace. Horace wants me as his lawyer and I am not going to let some cowardly idiot scare me away."

Following a long silence, Kyle said, "Okay, let's get started on finding the 'mad' bomber and maybe we will find Dick's killer at the same time. My gut tells me that the bombing of the car and the search for Dick's killer are connected. Somehow, we must have stirred the pot enough to scare the real killer into trying to kill or scare Penny.

"The car or what's left of it has been taken to the police lab. They couldn't get much in the way of footprint evidence, because the fire department was all over the place, but they may be able to find some fingerprints on the parts remaining. I'll contact Dan. He's working with the fire investigators on this."

"I have two problems," Penny said. "I don't have a car and all my notes on Horace's case were in my laptop and briefcase."

"I have copies of all your notes," Althea said. "You probably don't remember but we subscribe to a server that includes storage, so your notes are all stored off-site on the Internet. We can re-construct the file. That is not a problem. I ordered a new laptop computer for you first thing this morning. It will be delivered this afternoon. It will take a little time, but we can get it set up."

"The car is not a problem," her mother said. "You can drive the Jag until you have time to shop for a car."

"The Jag? Are you sure, Dad?" Penny asked, turning toward her father.

"Yes, of course," said the Judge, smiling at his daughter. "It will do until winter. Then you will want a different car—the heater doesn't work that well--but we can fix it, if we need to."

At that moment, the office door opened. A young man with a pierced nose entered holding a package. He stopped when he saw five people turn and stare at him.

"I, I have a package for Penny Johnson from Al's computer store," he mumbled. "My dad said to get here pronto."

Penny stood up, walked over, took the package and signed the form he held out. He thanked her, turned and left without a word.

"I'll take that," Althea said. "I'll have it ready for you in a couple of hours."

She stood, took the package from Penny and walked to her desk. She was ready, in her usual efficient way, to set the computer up for Penny to use.

Kyle stood. "I'll check with Dan and see if he has found anything new." He left, holding the door for Percy, who had to stretch before walking out the door, tail erect.

Penny's folks stood. "I don't like the idea of you being alone," her dad said. "I think you need a body guard. At least temporarily."

"No, I don't," Penny said. "I have JD. He has proven he can take care of me. Besides, I don't think anything more will happen. I am going to spend some time reviewing all my clients, but I don't think the answer lies there."

"Okay," her mother said. "I expect you for dinner tomorrow—around two?"

"Sure," Penny said. "Tomorrow at two."

Her parents left. Penny sat at her desk staring out the window. Someone wanted her scared or worse, dead. But, she decided, it won't work. She was determined to get to the bottom of this.

"Penny," Althea said, "Horace is on the line for you."

After Horace asked how she was and what happened and was she able to continue. Penny assured him yes, indeed, she was willing to continue.

"In fact, I am really mad that someone destroyed Maureen's car and tried to kill me. We will figure this out and you will be fine," she assured her client.

"I hope I mean that," she said to JD, hanging up the phone. "Let's go for a walk."

She snapped on his lead, said good-bye to Althea, head down, typing on the new computer, and went out the door. They stopped to look at the spot where her car had been. She could see that the driveway was pitted but the fire department had cleaned up the scene. There wasn't a bit of her car left and what debris they didn't want was pushed up against the building on one side of the lot. JD sniffed and started to pull Penny away. The smell of fire and cordite was still in the air.

She stood staring, shuddering at the thought that parts of her could have been what they cleaned up. The sun glinted of one of the stones. She stooped over, moved them around with her finger and plucked her lucky Petoskey stone out of the pile. She held it in her hand, smiling. This is a good omen. I'm going to win Horace's case.

Chapter 17

Penny climbed the stairs to her office on Monday morning. She held JD's leash in one hand, her purse on her shoulder. Reaching the second floor, they walked down the hall to her office door. She opened the door slowly. JD, contrary to his training, went in first, looking back at his mistress. Penny didn't correct him.

Althea looked up. "Good morning," she said.

"I'm not so sure," said Penny. "It feels odd to have only my purse and JD. I usually have my hands full. I feel like I'm starting all over."

Penny crossed the room to her office, unhooked JD's leash, hanging it on the doorknob of her office door. She plopped down into her chair. She looked at the new computer sitting on her desk.

Althea followed her, empty coffee cup in hand.

"I'll bring coffee. And, I have news. Do you want the good news or the not so good news first?" she asked.

Penny didn't answer right away then she said, "I think I need the good first, then I'll take the not so good."

"The good news is that I have all the programs and old files on your new computer. It is much faster than your old one. The bomber may have done you a favor by forcing you to improve your technology. You will be able to access the new, fancy IT in the courtroom with this computer. Your old one was a dinosaur." Althea said.

"Also—there is a supplementary report on Horace's case from Dan Dunlap. It's in the envelope on the corner of your desk."

Penny smiled. It would be nice to work with a computer that didn't crash all the time.

"And the not so good news."

"Well, Mike Pritchard called or, as he says," Althea's voice deepened, 'this is Michael Pritchard, Jackson County Prosecutor.' He wants you to call to talk about Horace's case."

Penny nodded. She booted up her new computer. It blazed on, startling her. "Oh, my, you are fast," she said. She picked up the bulky envelope with the report from Dan. She opened it, taking out the report on its official police form. It was typed, making it easier to read than the original, which had been hand-written by the patrol officer. The bad writing and the coffee stains made it hard to read at times.

She sipped Althea's coffee and began to read the report. Ballistics tested the gun found by the railroad tracks determining it was the gun used to kill Dick. And they reaffirmed the gun was registered to Horace Appleworth. The gunshot that killed Dick entered the left side of his head just above the spine. There were powder burns on the head, indicating the shot was fired at close range. The examiner determined the killer was left handed and could have been a pro based on the position of the shot, however, a slug was found in the wall to the right of where the body was found, indicating, it was surmised, the first shot missed.

Horace, Penny knew, was left-handed. But, she also knew that when he shot competitively, he shot right-handed. She also knew he won a lot of the pistol matches, outshooting the police competitors every time. And, they didn't like it that he, a civilian and gay, could so easily beat them.

The report included a hair analysis of the hairs found at the scene, which could not be identified. Also mentioned was an ear print found on the frosted glass part of back door near Dick's office. The ear print was also not identified. Penny made a note to ask Kyle to investigate further if he could.

The analysis of Horace's clothes was good news—no blood was found on the clothes he was wearing that night or on the clothes taken from his house. Given the amount of blood at the scene, it was unusual to not find a trace of blood on the items taken. Penny highlighted this portion of the report to use in the trial.

"Althea," Penny said, "Will you make a copy of this report for Kyle and see if he can come in after lunch so we can discuss things. I want to talk to him before I call Mike. I know he is not calling to dismiss so I may need some ammunition and maybe an adjournment if Kyle needs more time."

She picked up the envelope to throw it away when she noticed another pile of papers stapled together. She pulled out the report. It was also labeled supplementary. The first part was a report by Dan of his conversation with Luther Rahn regarding Luther's new Harley Davidson. The report concluded with a question from Dan— "where did Luther get the $5,000 to make a cash deposit for the Harley?"

There was also a report from the bomb squad regarding Penny's car. They determined an amateur made the bomb. The reporting officer concluded that it was "astounding that it blew up at all."

Just my luck, thought Penny, the jerk that blew up my car was lucky and I wasn't.

"Kyle will be here at two," said Althea, standing in the door. "And I think JD needs to go out—shall I take him?"

Penny nodded, "Thanks." Althea and JD left and the office was quiet. Penny started a list for her meeting with Kyle. She needed him to work fast. The trial would be here before she knew it.

The office door opened promptly at two. Kyle walked in holding a file. Percy followed him. Percy walked across the room, rubbed under JD's chin and jumped up on the windowsill. Kyle walked over to the conference table and set down his file.

Returning from lunch, Penny came in the door, smiling when she saw Kyle. He was busy reading the report Althea had given him. Althea and Penny joined him at the table.

"Looking at this and I'll have to read it more carefully, it looks like I have some work to do. I wonder about the ear print. Why an ear print on the door? I wonder if we can pinpoint when it appeared. I'll check with the cleaning staff. An ear print could mean someone was listening or trying to listen through the door. I wonder if Mildred and her father noticed anyone listening.

"I want to check the hairs found also, but I need time to do all this. Can you get Mike to adjourn the trial so we can test all this evidence?"

"I thought you might need time," Penny said "I have on my list a request for adjournment. The trial is coming up soon. I know the judge wants to clear his docket before the end of the year so it may be difficult."

"I'm sure that car bomb had something to do with Horace's case. I think we should wait for that investigation to be done," said Kyle. "And, I know that Horace is left handed but uses his right hand to shoot, I want to find a witness from his pistol shooting matches to testify. What do you think?"

"Good idea, at least, if nothing else, it would help to raise reasonable doubt," Penny said.

"Okay, I'm off to find some experts and witnesses," Kyle said. He stood up, collected his files and started for the door. Percy followed him and they left.

Althea stood, "Are you ready to call Mike?"

Penny nodded.

"Mike Pritchard," said the male voice. Penny identified herself, a bit startled because he answered his own line. After pleasantries were over, Mike said, "Is Horace ready to plead guilty? I might consider a lesser charge. I'm not saying I will, but maybe.

"I heard about your car blowing up. I am glad you weren't in it at the time, but it was an awful color. It's almost a blessing to the city to have it off the streets. We've been looking at it for years. Are you alright?"

"Thanks for your concern," Penny said, dryly. "I am fine. And, no, Horace is not going to plead guilty for the simple reason that he isn't guilty."

"You defense lawyers always say that. I think you have blinders on when it comes to your clients. We have more than enough evidence to convict him."

"And that's why I'm calling. We got the latest supplementary report about the hair analysis and the ear-print. I want our expert to review those reports and...,"

"I don't think the ear print or the hair analysis has anything to do with this case," Mike interrupted. "I sent those reports over as a courtesy, not as an excuse for more delay, which is what I assume you're looking for. You know the judge won't be happy about that request."

"We don't know the importance of those items, which is why I would like some time to investigate. And, then, there is the issue of the bombing of my car. Horace's case is the only one of my cases serious enough to create that type of response. We need to finish the investigation of that, too.

"If you won't agree to a short adjournment, I guess I'll have to file a motion and set it for a hearing in front of the judge," she added.

"Go ahead, file your motion. I'm betting you'll lose. The judge will agree with me that the bomb has nothing to do with Horace's trial and he wants this finished."

Mike hung up. Penny sat looking at the silent phone. She was not really surprised. She knew Mike believed he had a solid case.

"He doesn't think we have a chance," she said to Althea, who was standing in the doorway looking at her.

"We will see about that," Althea said. "I've called a meeting for tonight. We will find some evidence for you."

Penny smiled.

Althea left after shutting things down for the day.

Penny found her old briefcase from her law school days, loading it with files and her laptop. She had her work cut out for her.

That evening the Society met at their usual table in the bookstore.

"I'm sorry I'm late," said Althea, rushing up to the table.

Her fellow readers and investigators looked at her.

"Not to worry," Mary said. "We got your coffee, take a moment to catch your breath. My goodness, we all have news, but settle a bit first."

"I was late because Dan Dunlap called and asked, ever so nicely, that we stay out of this. He's worried since Penny's car was blown up that we might be in danger."

"Why?" Arney asked. "What does Penny's car incident have to do with Horace? I think it does, but…"

"Dan does too," said Althea. "He implied but didn't say that he didn't agree with Mike Pritchard that the two incidents weren't related. I told him we would be just fine. He sort of growled at me to be very careful."

"Isn't that sweet that he's concerned," said Rose. "He is such a nice man."

"I know that Dan is not happy with the prosecutor," said Mary. "I heard him tell one of the police officers that he thought Mike was rushing to justice. He also said he thought Fiona or Victor had something to do with the whole affair."

After taking a sip of coffee, she went on, "And, I wonder, Fiona has been in the City Offices a lot lately trying to pry information about the progress of the proposals. I think she might have money problems. People are saying that she might be going under if she doesn't get this job."

"That would be a shame, the lumber yard has been in her family a lot of years," Rose said.

"I was thinking today" she continued, "do you remember when I told you about the time Mildred was upset because a man was using the shielded computer—you know the one they use for porn. She is a pretty sharp little girl, if I do say so myself, and she didn't think people should do that when the 'little kids' were in the library."

Althea smiled, "Yes, I remember but ..."

"What I didn't tell you was that when I went over to look, not for prurient interests, but out of curiosity and to ask him to stop when the 'little kids' were in the library, I was surprised to see he was looking up explosives and information about bombs and guns. I was worried that we might have a homegrown terrorist. When he saw me, he clicked off and told me that he wanted to blow a tree stump. Now, I wonder if he was the one that blew up Penny's car."

"Who was he?" Althea asked, peering over her glasses at Rose.

"That's just it. I don't know. He is new to the area or from out of town. I know everyone and he looked kind-of familiar, but..."

"Do we know one of those people who can draw the faces when you describe them—you know, like on Bones or CSI?" Arney asked.

"Well, Ethel is the art teacher at the High School and she's good at faces. Remember how she did caricatures at the church fair? I'll give her a call," Rose said. "And I'll start writing down what I remember."

"You should ask Mildred—she might remember something you don't," Mary suggested.

With that the women turned to Arney who had yet to report.

"Okay, as you know, I am working on Dick's estate for the lawyer. When I went through the bag of bills and receipts from his office, I discovered a receipt for two airline tickets to Florida. The flights were scheduled for the last week of the year. The names on the tickets were Dick Boswick and Polly Langstrom, so I didn't say anything to Sally about them, but she will find out."

"I guess that proves he was having an affair," said Rose, "but I don't think Polly has anything to do with his death. The guys who eat at Big Boy every morning say she has been down since Dick's death. She may be the only one who misses him."

Althea nodded her head, "I don't think Sally shot her husband. She was seen by everyone at the concert at the time he was killed."

"She is spending a lot of money, though," Arney said "And I don't where she's getting it. But I'll have to ask about it, because the government will want its share. I know she bought a Christmas Package tour to Disney in Orlando for the family including grandparents and that cost a pretty penny."

"I wonder if Sally would plot to kill her husband, is she that kind of person and when, if ever, did she discover that Dick was having an affair that everyone in the village seems to have known about?" mused Althea. "And, did she know he was corrupt?"

"Well, first things first," she said, sitting up straighter. "Rose, will you call Ethel and see if she can draw the face of the man you and Mildred saw in the library? We can give it to Kyle to look for."

"I'll try to find out about what Sally knew and when she knew it," said Arney.

Mary agreed to try to discover who was bidding on the restoration and Althea decided to review the police reports again. The group cleaned up the table after agreeing to meet or report back soon.

The next morning when Penny opened the door to her office, she was surprised to find Althea and Kyle already at the conference table, coffee cups in hand, and fresh fruit on the table.

"You two are here early," Penny said. After depositing her briefcase and purse on her desk, she joined them. Althea poured her a cup of coffee from the carafe on the table.

"I wanted Kyle to know what Rose remembered—I told you the Society was meeting last night, didn't I?"

Penny nodded.

"Rose told us some time ago about Mildred, you know little Mildred, Rose's niece, she lives in your neighborhood, Penny." Kyle and Penny smiled yes. Althea proceeded to tell them what Rose had seen.

"Which didn't make a big impression at the time," Althea said, "but with Penny's car being blown up, we decided to investigate further. Rose didn't know the man, but she got a good look at him—so we decided to ask Ethel, the art teacher, to try to draw his face from Rose's description—you know, like on CSI."

Kyle said, "People that do that have special training, Althea, I wonder if – "

"I'm sure Ethel will do just fine," Althea said in her no-nonsense voice. "Rose left a message that she was meeting with her Saturday afternoon. Ethel's glad to help out."

"Okay," he said. "I have been checking into the ear print left on the door window. I spoke with Andy, the cleaning man and he remembers that he cleaned that window earlier in the evening before he began on the offices. He said that he cleans it every day because it gets covered with fingerprints all the time. I recorded our conversation and will type it up this afternoon.

"I sent the ear print and the hair analysis off to my expert. She needed a comparison sample. She explained how to get the ear print so I got one from Horace and some of his hair. She'll compare them and get a report to us ASAP. And, Jake Rahn called."

Kyle opened the little notebook he carried to take notes. Flipping through, he found his spot. "Jake said that he remembered that Horace was one of the people who came to his house before the murder. Jake's wife. Myrtle, wants a new kitchen. Horace was there to give an estimate. After they told Horace what they wanted, they left him there to take measurements because they had to get to a church meeting. Horace was in the house alone for about an hour. He was gone when they came home and Sammie, their son, said he wasn't there when he got home from football practice. He's a great quarterback."

"Who?" asked Penny.

"Sammie Rahn. He's having a good year. He's a junior and already getting looks from the college scouts. I know, that has nothing to do with our case, but Friday nights will be a lot of fun this fall."

"Is Jake sure Horace was there before Dick was killed?" Penny asked.

"I'm afraid he is," Kyle said. "I told him he had to report that information to Dan."

Penny sat quietly, staring out the window. "I wonder," she said. "Is it possible our client is guilty?"

"No," Althea and Kyle said in unison. "He is not guilty, and we'll prove it."

JD raised his head at the sounds. He came over and stuck his head under Penny's hand sitting in her lap.

"I think JD agrees with you," Penny said stroking the big Shepherd's head. "He does this when he thinks I'm upset. I'm okay," she said looking into JD's brown eyes.

Looking up at Kyle, she asked, "Did you find anyone to testify that Horace shoots with his right hand?"

"Yes," said Kyle. "Several of his friends are willing to testify for him. One of them is looking for some pictures showing Horace shooting right handed in a match."

"Well, that's one for our side," Penny said.

"On other matters," Althea said, "We can confirm that Dick was having an affair with Polly. Arney is handling the financials for Dick's estate and he found tickets for a trip to Florida in their names. We don't know if Sally knew about the affair, but I don't see how she couldn't. And we learned that she is taking the whole family to Disney World over Christmas and you know how expensive that is."

"She could've gotten the insurance money," suggested Kyle, "I'm sure he was well-insured."

"Maybe or maybe she was well aware that Dick was taking kick-backs and having an affair. Is that a motive for murder?" Penny mused.

"Could be. People have been killed for less," said Althea, standing up. She collected her notes and coffee cup and moved over to her desk in the other room. Kyle stood, looked around for Percy. "Percy? Where is that cat?" he said. "Did he come in with me?"

At the sound of his name, Percy jumped down out of Penny's desk chair with a thud.

"Now I know why I am always covered with grey cat hair," Penny laughed.

Moving over to her desk to unload her briefcase, she said, "I have to get moving on my motions. I told you, didn't I, that Mike wouldn't agree to an adjournment. I think I'll request a change of venue, too. I'm not sure we can get a fair trial here. We will see what the judge does."

Kyle and Percy left, Althea settled at her desk and Penny sat at her desk, pondering motions and the news of the day.

The weak November sun was streaming in Penny's bedroom window when she woke up on Saturday morning. Her nose was stuffed up and her head ached. I think I'm getting a sinus infection. She stretched to her full 5'10" length. Her toes touched the end of the bed. I need a longer bed. She rolled over on her side, put the covers over her head to keep out the sun and started to go back to sleep.

JD would have none of it. He stuck his cold nose under the covers searching for Penny's cheek. Finding it, he nudged her.

"Go away. Go back to sleep. I don't want to get up. I have a headache and I need a bigger bed." Penny said.

JD pushed harder.

"Oh, Okay. I suppose you have to go out. And, you did save my life."

Penny got out of bed, went over to her closet to look for something to put on over her pajamas. No clean running sweat pants caught her eye. A search of the laundry basket in the corner of her tiny bathroom revealed a pair of red sweat pants. She gave them a cursory glance and a quick sniff. They would do. A purple sweatshirt completed the outfit. She piled her long hair on top of her head, twisting it into a knot and securing it with a hair tie she found in a pocket.

She and JD went to the front door. After unlocking the deadbolt and removing the chain lock her father insisted she install, she grabbed JD's harness. He stood patiently while she pulled it over his head, put his left front leg through the opening, pulled the strap around his belly, and snapped it in place. She grabbed a coat, stuck her feet in her UGS, found the hook on his harness for his lead and opened the door. A cold wind blew in her face.

Looking up she saw thick, grey clouds in the distance. It looks like snow. I'm not ready for snow, I have a headache, I need a longer bed and I can't afford one even if I could find time to get to the bed store, I have an innocent client and I can't find a way to prove it and now, snow. Putting her head down, and against all dog-training advice, she followed JD off the porch and down the driveway to the sidewalk.

She heard the courthouse clock chime. She counted the chimes. Good grief, it's 9 o'clock. No wonder JD had to go potty. JD went about his business. Penny searched in her coat pocket for a plastic bag. Relieved to find an old grocery bag, she cleaned up after JD. They continued their walk around the block.

"Hi, Ms. Johnson, isn't it a lovely day? I think we're going to have snow soon. I can't wait to get my sled out. How are you and JD today? I'm wearing my new winter coat. Do you like it?"

Penny and JD stopped. They both looked at Mildred who seemed to appear out of nowhere.

"Yes, I do," Penny said. "Bright red is a good color for a warm, winter coat. But, aren't you a little too warm? I don't think it's that cold."

"Well, no, it isn't, but don't tell my Mom I said so. She told me not to wear it, but I just couldn't wait. If I keep it unzipped, it's fine."

JD sat patiently while Mildred petted his head and back.

"Do you think the man my Dad and I saw coming out of the City offices that night was the guy who killed Mr. Boswick?" Mildred asked, changing the topic as suddenly as a lightning bolt. "My Dad and I are going to the library this afternoon. Aunt Rose from the library called. She wants us to come in and help her describe the man to Ms. Ethel who is going to draw a picture of him from our words. I'm not sure how that works, but that's what we're going to do. Do you think that will help?"

"I'm sure it will. Thanks for your help."

Mildred reached in her pocket, took out a cell phone, found the text message and turned toward her house. "My Mom wants me," she said. "Goodbye, JD. Goodbye, Ms. Johnson."

Mildred skipped down the sidewalk, her long legs, encased in pink and green stripped tights, almost a blur. Penny smiled.

She's a bright, slightly weird child of the twenty-first century, Penny thought. I never had a cell phone to call me home. Mom yelled as loud as she could and we came running.

Her thoughts turned to the idea of the local art teacher being a sketch artist. I sure hope it works.

The phone was ringing when Penny and JD came in the front door. Picking up the phone, she heard her mother say, "Of course, you can fix it on Sunday."

"Mom?" Penny said. "Who are you talking too?"

"Hi, sweetie. Your father. I want him to fix that loose door panel on the Jag. It's not safe for you to drive it that way. Can you bring it over sometime later today? He can work on it in the morning. I'll come get you tomorrow—we can have a nice dinner—and your car will be fixed."

"Does Dad know all this?" Penny asked.

"Yes, he's standing here, nodding his head."

Penny heard a shuffle noise and then her father said, "I'm sure I can fix it in an hour or so. I bought the special tools and screws I need over the Internet. Here's your mother."

Penny and her mother arranged to meet later that afternoon. After her usual breakfast of yoghurt and blueberries, Penny took care of her Saturday morning chores and then was off to her office to check mail and tend to those things best done without interruptions.

"We've been invited to the Gallagher's for dinner this afternoon," Mabel said to her son, Alex, reading the Sunday paper at the dining room table.

"What's the occasion?" he asked his mother looking up from the article on the latest antique car show.

"No reason, really, Kitty and I want to talk about the Wine and Stein Fundraiser for the Zoo. She's on the committee," Mabel said casually. "Oh, and we have to pick up Penny on the way. She's expecting us shortly before two. The Judge has her car. He is doing some work on that old Jag."

"That 'old Jag' is a beautiful car and what are you and Kitty up to? You can talk about the committee work any time. I am quite capable of taking care of my own dating life," Alex said.

"I can see that," his mother said dryly.

Alex smiled to himself. He didn't want his mother to know that he was pleased with the plan. He thought about Penny more than he expected he would. He hadn't called her because he knew how busy she was with a murder trial coming up. But this could prove to be a pleasant non-threatening interlude. Finishing the paper, he went upstairs to get ready for the afternoon.

Promptly at 1:55, Alex and his mother pulled into Penny's driveway. Alex smiled at Penny when she opened the door. She returned his smile.

"You stay here and take care of the house," she told JD, closing the front door behind her. "He can stay home," she said in response to

Alex's questioning look. "We took a long walk this morning and he's ready for a nap."

Alex held the car door for Penny. She and Mabel said their hellos and they were off to the Gallagher's.

When they pulled into the driveway, they saw Judge Gallagher standing next to the green Jag. He was rubbing the knuckles of his left hand. They couldn't quite hear the words coming out of his mouth but from the frown and the head shaking they decided that was just as well. Mabel and Penny got out of the car and walked to the front door. Alex walked over to the Judge.

"You are just the person I need," Judge Gallagher said. "I can't hold the door panel in place and put the screws in at the same time. The screws a bit large and need some push to get them in."

Alex nodded, moving to the side of the door. He reached one hand inside the rolled down window and the other on the outside. Bracing the door against his knee and using both hands to hold the interior panel, the door was stable.

"Does that scrape hurt?" Alex asked looking at the Judge's bloody knuckles.

"Not too much. I'll take care of it when we finish this."

"Did you see that the Spring Antique Car show will be part of the Automobile Show in Detroit? You should enter this car. It's in beautiful shape and it was manufactured by the Brits, not by Ford or TaTa in India. Those Jags are pretend Jags in my opinion."

Judge Gallagher laughed. "I'm sure the folks that buy the modern Jag would not want to think that their cars were 'pretend Jags.' And I bet they are happy their cars run reliably. The old ones—particularly this model—need lots of TLC. If Penny has a car by then, I'll think about entering it."

"I'll be glad to help you get it ready," Alex said.

"Dinner's ready," Penny said, coming around the corner of the garage. Her mother hated that the garage was not attached to the house. She didn't like making the walk from the garage to the house when loaded down with groceries. The Judge liked the garage right where it was. It could hold three cars, had its own furnace, banks of electrical outlets, and its own water supply. He could stay out there happily working on his old cars for hours at a time.

"Good, I just put in the last screw. That should hold it," Judge Gallagher said, putting the tools in their proper places in the tool chest. He and Alex followed Penny into the house.

"What happened to your hand," Kitty said, looking at the scraped knuckles. "I'll get the Neosporin—wash it good. Does it need a Band-Aid?"

"No, it's stopped bleeding and the antibacterial cream will take care of it," said the Judge taking the tube from his wife.

The group went into the dining room where Kitty instructed all where to sit. She sat at the foot of the table, near the kitchen door, the Judge was at the head, Alex and Penny on one side and Mabel and Rob, Penny's younger brother who happened to stop by in time for dinner, on the other side.

"My wife and kids are visiting her parents up North," he said by way of explanation to Alex who hadn't known he was there. "Mom was kind enough to invite me for a good meal. I've been eating out all week—I had forgotten how tough it is to be a bachelor."

"Alex wouldn't know, but he should listen, I won't be around forever," Mabel said. "I keep…"

"Would you like sweet or mashed potatoes, Mabel," interrupted Penny, who was helping her father put food on the plates. "The roast looks wonderful, Mom."

Conversation turned to events in Midvale Corners. Kitty's rule that no business was to be discussed during dinner kept things light and cheerful.

"We have apple crisp for desert," Kitty announced when everyone's plate was empty. All agreed that a small piece of pie would be perfect. Penny and Mabel helped Kitty clear the table. Dessert and coffee served, the conversation turned to the election and murder trials.

"How's the campaign, Dad," asked Rob.

"I think I'll be fine. There are three spots open and four people running—Alph Munson and incumbents—it would be hard to lose," he said laughing then turning serious. "I'm more concerned about who is trying to harm Penny. That bomb was frightening. Thank goodness JD was on the ball. Dan says they are still investigating."

"Mike, the prosecutor, doesn't think the blowing up of my car and Horace's case are connected, but Kyle and I disagree. I'm sure there is a connection somewhere but we just don't know where," Penny said.

"I certainly hope you're being careful," said her mother. "If they tried once, they might try again. Whomever 'they' are."

"Of course, I'm being careful. I let JD inspect when he wants. I would hate for someone to blow up Dad's car."

"I'm more concerned with someone trying to blow up my daughter," said the Judge. "I can get another car but I can't get another daughter."

"How is the murder case?" Alex asked. "Can I help?"

"We're making progress," Penny said. "Kyle is investigating some leads. The Midvale Corners Literary and Investigatory Society is at work and I'm working on motions. I would like to get the trial adjourned until we know more about the bomb, but Mike is not cooperating."

"You know I'll help with the motions if you need it. I have used all kinds of pre-trial motions in my practice. Your motion for change of venue might bear fruit. I don't know how you'll get an unbiased jury in this town. Everyone knew Dick and whether they liked him or not, they still might have an opinion. And not everyone approves of Horace's lifestyle. Judge Sanford might be more than happy to send this matter off to another judge to deal with."

"I was thinking along those lines," Penny answered.

Kitty rose to clear the table and Penny and Mabel followed suit. Soon the table was cleared, foodstuffs put away, with portions for Rob and Penny wrapped in foil to be taken home to enjoy later, the dishes rinsed and in the dishwasher.

The time came to go home. Rob grabbed the bigger of the packages, gave his mother and Penny a peck on the cheek and went out the door. Penny started gathering her things to go home. She said her goodbyes. Mabel and Alex followed her out the door.

"I'll wait in the car if you and Alex want to talk," Mabel said.

Penny and Alex laughed at her not-so-subtle matchmaking.

"I'm sorry, Penny," Alex said. "My mom can be a bit pushy."

"As can mine," Penny said. "You notice that there wasn't any talk about the Zoo fundraiser even though that was supposed to be the reason we were at the same table."

"I noticed. I did mean it, if you need some ideas for pre-trial motions, I'll be glad to send them over. I have your e-mail.

"Thanks," Penny said, opening the car door. Alex came over to close the door after she swung her long legs into the car. He closed the door carefully so as not to loosen the door panel, smiled, waved good-bye and went over to join his mother in his car.

Penny watched him. She caught a whiff of the aftershave he wore. She wondered what it was—it smelled spicy. She liked the way he walked. He carried himself with confidence. And the old leather jacket accented his still slim waist. He might be approaching middle age, she thought, but it is easy to see that he works out and takes care of himself.

Alex backed his car out of the driveway. Mabel waved good-bye. Penny backed out and headed the other direction.

"When are you going to see Penny again?" Mabel asked.

"Mom, Penny is working hard on defending Horace, she doesn't have time for social activity now."

"All the more reason to call her. She needs a break once in a while. It would help clear her mind, which could give her a new perspective."

Alex nodded. His mother might be right. Penny could use a release from the trial prep. While he used the gym as a release from the stress of a busy law practice, maybe a movie or a coffee would be good. He realized that he was looking forward to their next meeting.

Chapter 18

"Good morning," Penny said to blue-eyed, blonde receptionist guarding the sixth-floor offices of the Swanson, Mitchell and Cross, located in downtown Culver City. "I'm here to see Gordon Swanson."

"I'll tell him you're here," she answered.

Penny thought she looked a little too fresh and perky for a cold, cloudy, November, Monday morning.

At a few minutes after nine, Gordon walked into the reception area. He smiled at Penny, his teeth white against his tan face. Penny suspected he bleached his teeth and spent some time in the tanning bed at the gym but that small vanity didn't matter—he was a well renowned criminal defense attorney and long-time friend of her father. As a matter of fact, they started a practice together when they were fresh out of University of Michigan law school.

Gordon led Penny down a hallway to a conference room. "I'm in the midst of a trial, my office is a mess, so we'll meet in here," he said opening the door to a large room with tall windows overlooking the city. The oval shaped conference table was almost bigger than Penny's office. Twelve chairs were tucked neatly around the oak surface. A carafe of coffee was sitting on the sideboard.

"Would you like some coffee?"

Penny, who never refused coffee, nodded. After the coffees were poured and they were settled at one end of the table, Gordon said, "Now, how can I help with Horace's case?"

"My theory of the case is simply that Horace didn't kill Dick. So far, all the evidence is against him, but after someone blew up my car, I became convinced that Horace was not the killer. Mike doesn't believe the bomb and Dick's murder have anything to do with each other, but I don't think I have any clients who want to blow me up. Kyle and I are convinced that the bombing is related."

"I want to delay the trial until we can get the bombing sorted out. Dan Dunlap agrees with me, but he won't say so out-loud. Mike won't agree to an adjournment so I am preparing a motion asking the Judge. I'm not sure that will work, but I can try."

"I'm also asking for a change of venue to move the trial to another county. I'm not sure Horace can get a fair trial here."

"I agree," said Gordon, "I'm not sure he can either. On your motion for a change of venue, you might ask for a visiting judge if the court won't go for a geographic change," suggested Gordon. "If that doesn't work, then I would also ask that the qualifying of the jury be done individually in the Judge's chambers. That way you might be able to discover which of the jurors is biased. They will sometimes be a bit more forthcoming if they aren't answering in an open courtroom."

"That's a great idea," Penny said, taking notes on her usual yellow legal pad. "If the judge denies the other requests, he will probably go for the third. It might take more time, but it could help with the prejudice problem."

"How do I handle the press? I get questions every day and I don't have a ready answer."

"I have two answers. In the early stages, when I don't have a clear idea what my legal theory is going to be, I tell them I want to 'try the case in the courtroom not in the court of public opinion.' Once I have a legal theory or defense, I give them that sound bite. My belief is that if I can't explain succinctly to a reporter the theory of my case, how can I explain it to a judge or a jury? That seems to work for me."

"Have you received the list of witnesses the prosecution intends to call? I would suggest that you ask Kyle to interview them. He might find a new avenue of investigation to pursue."

Gordon continued to explain his method of trial preparation. Penny took notes as fast as she could. At first, she was overwhelmed with the task ahead of her, but gradually she began to realize that she understood what he was saying and had thought of many of his suggestions herself.

"Remember that a murder trial is like a marathon—you'll notice that as the date gets closer you get frantic, right up to the time when you start questioning the jury. At that point, you're off and running.

You jog through your opening statement, speed up as the questioning of witnesses and evidence is introduced, and then, before you know it, it's time to stop and give your closing argument. Get lots of rest. Know your facts cold, have the Court Rules and the Rules of Evidence at your fingertips, and you'll do a great job."

Penny paused in her writing, staring out the window, motionless. Gordon waited and then asked,

"Any more questions?" pulling Penny away from her thoughts.

"No. Thanks so much. This has really been helpful."

Penny stood, stuffing her legal pad in her briefcase. She followed Gordon out the door and into the reception area. Gordon turned, smiled, and shook her hand. "If you have any more questions, don't hesitate to call—day or night—I'm glad to help."

They parted, Gordon going through the door to his office, Penny hopping through the elevator doors, which opened immediately when she punched the button. Penny left the building, found the green Jag where she left it in a corner of the parking lot, climbed in and headed back to Midvale Corners.

An hour later, Penny opened the door to her office. JD padded over greeting her with a nudge on the hand. Penny looked at Althea questioningly.

"I stopped by your house and picked him up. I knew you wouldn't have time this morning."

"Thank you—I'm sure JD would rather be here than at home."

Penny crossed the small reception area, went into her office, put her briefcase on her desk, and turned back to Althea.

"Gordon was helpful. He gave me great ideas for pre-trial motions to file."

"Which you will have to file soon--we got a notice that the pre-trial conference is set for November 17th and today is the 9th. The motions will have to be filed by tomorrow. I have your draft. Can we finalize it by tomorrow?"

Penny smiled and nodded yes. "I worked on them this week-end. Gordon agreed with my request for a change of venue. I just have to add another request and tweak it a little."

Penny went into her office, pulled out her notes, booted up her new computer, and began to compose the final touches to the document. She planned to file it electronically with the court and the prosecutor's office no later than the next morning.

Time passed quickly. Sometime after noon, Penny felt eyes staring at her. She looked up to see JD standing in the doorway to her office looking from his lead hanging on the doorknob to Penny and back again. She smiled at the big dog, stood up and moved over to grab the lead and attached it to his harness.

"Do you want a sandwich from the Deli?" she asked Althea. "I can pick it up on our way back from our walk. I think I'll get the veggie wrap. I think I need veggies after the big roast beef dinner at my parents' house yesterday."

Althea, who usually brought her lunch every-day, shook her head, no. She favored the ploughman's lunch of sharp cheese, hard salami, a small roll and fruit that she discovered when eating in the pubs of London on her last long trip abroad.

"Kyle called to say he would be here around two o'clock," Althea said. "Maybe you can get a treat at the bakery for a snack?"

"Will do," Penny said. She and JD headed out the door.

Later that afternoon, Kyle, Althea and Penny sat at the conference table. Their favorite mugs filled with fresh coffee, newly baked chocolate chip cookies in hand, they were ready to go to work.

"Dan Dunlap called me this morning," Kyle said starting the meeting. "He faxed over the latest information about the bomb in Penny's car. They gave me a list of what they found, which included gunpowder and pieces of a trigger drive. I can try to trace where they were bought, but they are pretty common items. He also said they might be able to get a fingerprint off some of the bottom of Penny's car—the pieces are small—but he thinks they can use some special techniques to get some prints."

"What about the art teacher AKA sketch artist?" Penny asked, turning to Althea. "Did she have any luck?"

"We'll know by tomorrow. She and Rose are meeting again tonight after the library closes."

"I hope we can recognize him," Kyle said. "We need a break in this case. Dan did say that he's been trying to convince Mike to adjourn the trial until he finishes the investigation of the bombing, but Mike is resisting. Unless you can get the judge to agree with you, Penny, I'm afraid we'll just have to go along on what we have so far."

"And, what do we have?" Penny asked, pushing away from the table. She stood up and began to pace. "I know in my heart that Horace didn't kill Dick. But, so far, I can't prove it, and Mike has all the evidence he needs to convict Horace. I know it's all circumstantial but people have spent a life in prison on circumstantial evidence.

"And I'm worried about Horace. Ryan has him on some pills for depression, but he isn't eating and doesn't sleep well, which has Ryan worried."

Althea and Kyle looked at each other. They were worried too, but they didn't want Penny to know that.

"We'll know more when I have the test results from our expert on the ear print and the hair. I'll bet they don't match Horace. I'll interview everyone that had access to Jake's house—someone took that gun from his gun cabinet—someone who knew where Jake kept the key."

"Oh, please," Penny said, "the key was on the top of the cabinet. Anyone could have found it there."

"I know but I also know it wasn't Horace."

"And, Ethel will come up with a sketch of that man," Althea said. "And I know we will find someone who saw Horace that night when he was walking around the village. I just know it."

Althea stood and starting clearing the coffee cups and the empty cookie plate. Penny came over to help.

"Thanks," she said. "I needed to hear that. I am truly grateful for your help. I'll go back to my motions."

"And we'll go back to our investigation," Kyle said. He and Percy, who had been sitting on the window ledge observing the humans talking, went out the door, closing it carefully behind them.

Around 5 o'clock, Penny came out of her office. "I put my motions in Dropbox," she said to Althea. "Would you look them over in the morning—I don't want any spelling or grammar errors—you know all those funny rules."

Althea laughed, "I guess the fact I loved studying grammar in school is now being put to good use. I don't know all the legal terminology, but I can check the spelling and grammar."

"Thanks," Penny said. "I want to file it in the morning so I can move on to the next step. Not sure what that will be right now, but I know I have to move on."

Althea and Penny were performing the closing down tasks for the day when suddenly the fax came to life.

"Good grief," Althea said, reading the document. "You've been appointed to represent a woman who was found living in her car with 15 cats. I can't imagine where they were or what the car smelled like."

"How could she get herself and 15 cats in a car?" Penny mused. "Where is she now and where are the cats?"

Althea kept reading the police report that was attached to the Notice of Appointment. "The cats are at the animal shelter. It seems they are fine. She is in the jail for the night because the shelter was full. She sounds like one of those 'hoarder' people. And, she's homeless, too."

Penny looked at the Notice. She had to be in court for the arraignment on Friday. She read that her client had been charged with animal cruelty.

"I need to meet with her. There is more to this than we see here."

"I agree, but you can't do anything about it now. Save it for the morning," Althea said.

"You're right. I'll look into it tomorrow."

Penny grabbed her criminal law book. JD came over ready to be on his way home. She snapped on his lead and went out the door. Althea followed, checking the locks to make sure all was safe. The ladies parted at the bottom of the steps, each going their respective ways.

The next evening promptly at 7 o'clock, Althea, Mary, Rose and Arney sat at their table in the back of the bookstore. Althea was filling them in on Penny's day with the 'cat lady.'

"She appeared at our door promptly at 9 o'clock this morning demanding that Penny get her cats back. She couldn't seem to understand why anyone would care where she kept her cats. Penny spent over an hour with her. The strangest thing was JD. He liked her right away and lay by her feet the whole time she was there."

"Was Penny able to help?" Mary asked.

"A little," Althea said. "We found her a bed in the shelter and Penny explained that we had to go through the court process before she could even think about getting her cats back. I think she understood."

"After she left we filed the motions for a change of venue in Horace's case. Penny's concerned that Horace will not be able to get a fair trial here. This modern world—we filed them all electronically, even sending copies to Mike through e-mail. No more paper and stamps. It is more efficient."

"Well, to the business at hand. I hope we have some good news to report—Penny is discouraged and Horace is so depressed Ryan has him on medication."

Rose reached down in her bag and pulled out an envelope. "I have the sketches that Ethel came up with. Mildred and I met with her last Saturday. Mildred was a big help. She sees so much."

Rose pulled two sketches of a man's face out of the envelope. "It really looks like him, I think," she said, laying the sketches on the table.

"He looks familiar to me," Mary exclaimed. "I've seen him." She paused. "I seem to remember he was at the city clerk's office, but it's not clear. Could I get a copy? I'll take it to work and see if the others remember."

"He doesn't look familiar to me," Arney said. "But," he laughed, "I rarely see people. I only see numbers."

"What are the numbers telling you?" Althea asked. "They usually talk to you in ways I'll never understand."

"Well," said Arney, sitting up straighter looking at each of them in turn, "they told me that Victor Miller withdrew over $30,000 from his bank account a day before Dick Boswick was killed."

Mary was the first to react. "The rumors around the office were that Victor was going to be awarded that contract," she exclaimed. "If Dick was taking bribes or kick-backs or whatever you call it, and Victor paid him the money, where did it go?"

"Assuming he was going to pay Dick then I wonder if he paid him that night and the killer got the money." Arney said. "There was no mention of that much money in the police report, only a few hundred-dollar bills were found on Dick's desk. And, if I remember correctly, no fingerprints were found on those bills."

"Victor has been asking a lot of questions about what was found at the crime scene," Mary said. "But he has to be careful. I'm sure he doesn't want anyone to know that he was bribing a government official. Isn't that a crime of some sort?"

"I'm sure so," Althea said. "I'll ask Penny. And I think Kyle should talk to Victor. And I'll see that Kyle gets a copy of this sketch. He might know who this is. Oh, Rose, I have a list of the things they found when they investigated Penny's car bombing."

Althea reached down in her tapestry bag, pushing things aside until she found the envelope she was looking for.

"Here it is." She handed it to Rose.

Rose opened the envelope, took out the list and began reading.

"I don't know. They don't look familiar. I was able to go back on the computer that the man in the sketch was using to find the list of the sites he visited that day. My grandson showed me how to do that. Did you know all those sites are stored in the computer? Well, it does make one think. Do we have any privacy left at all?"

Rose shook her head as she looked through the report.

"Sorry, Althea, I don't see anything that's familiar. Here is a copy of the list of sites from the computer," she said, handing it to Althea. "Maybe Kyle can make sense of it. Oh, did I tell you all that I saw Fiona and Sally at Biff's Barbecue out on Marshall Road? We were out there for a late dinner the other night. They were so absorbed in their conversation that they didn't see us. I didn't know they were such good friends."

"They were best friends in high school. Maybe Fiona is helping the grieving widow. Well, we've made some progress today," said Althea. She stood and reached for the sketch. "Mary, you need a copy of this sketch. Belinda has copier in the back. I'll ask her to make a copy for us. If we find out who he is, that would be a big help. Then maybe we can discover if he had something to do with blowing up Penny's car and if so, why. Kyle has his work cut out for him."

Althea returned with copies, which she gave to each of the three sleuths. After clearing up and collecting their belongings, they moved through the bookstore to the door. When Arney opened the door to let the ladies precede him out to the street, a blast of cold wind blew in.

"I think we're in for some snow. It has held off a long time, but it is November in Michigan," Rose said, pulling her scarf snuggly around her neck. The others nodded. Waving their good-byes, they each hurried to their cars to get out of the cold, November wind.

Chapter 19

Saturday began with the remnants of a snowstorm that had dumped five inches of snow on Midvale Corners and surrounding areas. Because it was the first snowstorm of the winter and was not predicted to bring so much wet snow, the snowplows were moving slowly, cautiously driving around cars parked on the street in violation of the winter rules, which had caught the good citizens of Midvale Corners off guard.

Penny was driving the old Jag cautiously through the streets, following the snowplow where she could.

"It really is beautiful," Penny said to JD, strapped in the back seat. "The bare limbs of the trees look pretty covered with the wet snow."

Penny slowed for a turn onto Ash Street. She felt the back end of the car slide in the slushy street. She held on the steering wheel tightly, trying to remember how to drive a rear-wheel drive car in the snow. Turning into the skid, she straightened the car, and drove around the corner. She turned into the alley behind her building, which was still snow covered, but the car moved through it. She came to the small parking lot in back of her building, which had been plowed. She pulled into her parking space, turned off the engine, and sighed.

"We made it, JD. I'm not sure that I remember why we're here, but we made it."

She got out of the car, grabbed her briefcase and JD's leash. After Penny released his seat belt, JD jumped out of the car. Penny unlocked the rear door. They went into the dimly lit hall heading for the stairs. Up they went to the second floor. JD's good ear pricked up when he heard a familiar 'meow.' Percy came ambling down the hall.

Penny opened the door to her office careful to turn off the new alarm system her father had insisted be installed; she did not want the police coming with guns drawn. Although she objected when the installers arrived, she did feel a little more secure with it in place. Percy and JD followed her into the reception area. Penny went into her office, took off her coat, hanging it on the hall tree in the corner. She walked toward the small kitchen area when suddenly the door opened.

"I brought fresh scones," Althea said bustling in. "I have fresh cream, too. Ours was starting to turn. After I get my coat off, I'll start the coffee."

"What are you doing here?" asked a startled Penny. "You do know its Saturday."

"Of course, I know that, but I also know that Horace is coming in today and I suspect Kyle will be along and I have some things to report. And you know Kyle doesn't like your coffee."

"I know. I don't like my coffee," Penny laughed. "Horace should be here shortly."

No sooner had she said those words than Horace opened the door. Ryan was with him. Kyle followed them into the office.

"Is it okay if Ryan is here?" asked Horace. "He can only stay for a minute or two. He's been up all night. The emergency room was busy last night with the snow and all."

"Of course, he can stay." Penny said.

When the coffee was ready and all had their snack, they assembled around the conference table. Penny thought longingly of Gordon's huge conference room with its view. Oh, well, some day. They were a bit cramped, but it was okay. It felt cozy.

Penny started, saying, "I wanted to tell you where we are on your case and I thought it would be good to do that when the phones weren't ringing. I do have to caution you that the aura of lawyer confidentiality covers you, Horace, Althea and, of course, me, but doesn't extend to Ryan or Kyle so if there is something you want to say that is strictly between you and I, then please wait until they leave."

"Ryan knows as much as I do about all this. Of course, he can stay and hear whatever is said," Horace said, placing his hand on Ryan's arm. "And I suspect Kyle knows more than any of us."

"Now, can I tell you what happened last night that might have a bearing on all this?"

Penny nodded; leaning in to hear what Horace had to say.

"Around five o'clock last evening, I was at home thinking about dinner. Ryan insists I eat so I've become the cook since I can't go anyplace with this thing on my leg," Horace paused, his eyes moistened.

Ryan patted Horace's hand. "It'll be off soon, dear. We'll see to it."

Penny, Althea and Kyle nodded. Althea handed Horace a Kleenex she pulled out of her pocket. "It's a little dusty, but it will help," she said.

J.D. padded over. He put his head on Horace's leg.

After dabbing his eyes, he patted J.D.'s head and looked up.

"I know it will be okay, but it gets hard at times. At any rate," he said, squaring his shoulders and sitting up in his chair, "the doorbell rang. I went to the door, opened it and there was Victor Miller. He was pacing back and forth on our front porch. I held the door open. He strode into the living room. I invited him to sit down suggesting he might want the chair by the fireplace. It is one of those huge chairs and I thought he might be more comfortable. He's a big man, you know. Then I asked if he wanted some tea or coffee. He didn't. He kept pacing."

Penny began to shift in her chair. She knew Horace had to tell the story in his own way that she couldn't rush it but that could be the very reason to keep him off the stand at the trial. She knew she might have trouble reining him in and she wasn't sure how the jury would take Horace's telling of his story.

Kyle sat with his pen poised over the blank yellow legal pad in front of him. Althea leaned back in her chair, held her coffee cup with both hands and waited.

"I know," Horace said, looking up at the group, his eyes dry. "Get on with it, Horace. Ryan says I do go on and on sometimes."

Ryan smiled.

"Okay, Victor accused me of taking his money. I could not figure out what he was talking about. He said I knew Dick Boswick took bribes and that he had given Dick $30,000 that night and it was missing and since I was the one who saw Dick last, I must have it. I don't, you know."

"Arney was right," Althea murmured. She felt the group looking at her. "Oh, we learned at our meeting last night that Victor had taken $30,000 in cash out of one of his savings accounts."

Penny and Kyle looked at Althea.

"I won't ask how he found that out," Kyle said, writing it down on his yellow legal pad.

"What else did Victor say?" Penny asked.

"Well, not much. I did suspect that Dick took bribes, but I don't do business that way. Victor claimed when he left Dick he was alive and counting the money. He said he didn't see me or anyone else when he was there so he assumed I killed Dick, which he didn't much care about, he wanted his money back. He started yelling at me. I yelled right back. I told him, one, I didn't kill Dick, and, two, there was no money on his desk when I saw him so the real killer must have the money."

"He finally left after telling me if he found out I had the money, he would kill me himself and the state wouldn't have the expense of a trial. I think he meant it."

"Do you want me to call someone for protection?" Kyle asked. "I have some acquaintances that can be very effective."

"Not necessary." Ryan said. "We can take care of ourselves. Neither Horace nor I are unfamiliar with violence. We've both had our share of bullying. I've already called to have an alarm system put in the house. I can't be there all the time and Horace is gone most of the day. He still has work to do. Not everyone has abandoned him. The men are coming this afternoon to install it. I paid extra to have it done on the weekend."

With that, Ryan stood, taking the keys to his car out of his pocket. "I need to get some sleep. If this snow continues, the hospital will be busy again tonight."

"I'll give Horace a ride home," Penny said.

Ryan reached the door, turned the knob, holding the door open he said to the group. "I do appreciate what you're doing for Horace. I know all this will turn out well, but...."

"We will solve this," Kyle said. The others nodded in agreement. Ryan left.

Penny told Horace that some of his shooting buddies had come forward willing to testify that he always shot his pistol with his right hand and they were looking hard for some pictures other than the ones of Horace holding the first-place trophies.

Horace's face lit up with a smile. Even his eyes twinkled. "That's great. We know Dick was shot by a lefty."

Penny thought about telling him that Mike, the prosecutor could argue that Horace was normally left-handed and would probably use his left hand when under stress, but decided she liked seeing him happy even if it was for only a minute.

"I think the first thing on my list is to go have a talk with Victor," Kyle said. "Now that we know he was not only at the crime scene but also gave Dick some money, we can put pressure on him."

"Dan Dunlap has to be told of this," Penny said. "He can put more pressure on Victor. After all, he has committed several crimes that I can think of off the top of my head and, as an officer of the court, I have a duty to report crimes."

"Wait until I have had a word with him," Kyle suggested. "Then I can bring Dan up to speed."

Penny nodded.

"Did you get any of the reports back from your expert? You know, the ear print?"

Kyle shook his head. "Not yet," he said.

Althea pulled out Ethel's sketch of the man Rose and Mildred described.

All four of them stared at it for a long time.

"It sort of reminds of Luther Rahn," Kyle said. "He doesn't have as much hair and his nose is a little different, but it could be him."

"Could you get a picture of Luther to show to Rose and Mildred?" Althea asked. "That might jog their memories."

"I thought I would find you here," said a male voice coming from the hallway door.

Penny looked up to see Dan Dunlap walking into the office. He held a large manila envelope in his big hand. After greeting everyone including Horace who looked pale when he saw the police officer that had arrested him.

"I think I have some interesting news," he said after accepting a cup of Althea's delicious coffee. "Remember we took footprint casts from around Penny's car after it blew up and we had some from behind the village offices. Since I think that the two crimes are connected, I compared them. Most of the casts were useless, too many feet and too smudged, but we found a match. One from around Penny's car and one from the offices."

Penny, who had known Dan all her life, gave him a big hug. "Now Mike will have to admit that the two crimes are connected," she said.

"Not so fast," Dan said, extricating himself from Penny, "Mike says it is a coincidence and that the prints probably belong to one of officers who responded to the scene. And he could be right, so I am getting prints from everyone I know who was there. But that could take some time and might not prove anything."

Horace, who had been leaning forward, slumped back in his chair. Penny sighed.

"It's not the end of the world," Dan said. "I'll follow up and I'll get them all."

"I need to get going," Kyle said, "but before I go, Dan, would you take a look at this sketch. Does this guy look familiar to you?"

"Yeah, it sort of looks like that Luther Rahn character. Where did you get this?"

"I'll answer that one," Althea said. "Now, Dan, I know you don't like the Society to snoop, but Rose, the librarian, and Mildred, you know Rose's niece, saw this guy at the library. He was researching chemicals and what looked to them like explosives on the library computer. And he was doing that right before Penny's car blew up."

Althea went on to explain how Ethel had created the sketch. Dan leaned back in his chair with his arms folded across his chest staring at Althea.

"One day you people are going to get yourselves in trouble. If that guy was the killer, he could come after Rose and Mildred. And then you'll see why it is better to have the authorities work these things out," he said, sounding serious but with a twinkle in his eye.

"Oh, pish, posh," said Althea, "we'll be fine. If we need you, we promise to call. We all have cell phones complete with panic buttons. We are not naïve—we know how to be careful."

Dan left with the picture in his big manila envelope. "I'll check this out," he said walking toward the door. He turned the knob, waved good-bye with the hand holding the file and left.

Kyle, Althea, Horace and Penny smiled at each other. "I think he thinks I didn't kill Dick," Horace said breaking the silence.

"And, why didn't you tell him about Victor coming to my house? I saw that look you gave me when I started to talk," he said to Penny.

Penny smiled, glad Horace read her mind, "I want Kyle to talk to Victor first, he might tell Kyle more than he would Dan. Then we can tell Dan."

"Do you need a ride home?" Kyle asked Horace. "I'm going your way."

"No, I need some fresh air," Horace answered. "It's not that far. I'll walk."

The two men left the office. Althea and Penny could hear them clumping down the stairs to the floor below.

"I think Horace feels a little better," Althea said, heading for her desk. "He looked better after Dan came in with some positive news."

"I know it's positive news," Penny said. "But my lawyer brain tells me it's not enough to prove Horace is innocent. Maybe Kyle will get something out of Victor Miller that can help. Maybe he saw something and doesn't know it. Let's close up. All I can do at this point is worry and that doesn't do any good."

J.D. looked up when Penny moved to her desk. When he saw her putting files in her old briefcase, packing up her laptop computer, stuffing some pens in her purse and searching for her keys, he knew it really was time to get up. He got up and stood by the door to the hallway.

Penny hiked her briefcase, computer case and purse up on her shoulder. She took the J.D.'s lead off the doorknob, hooked it on his harness, opened the door and they went into the hall.

Althea followed, turning to set the alarm and lock the door before closing it firmly behind her.

"I don't know why you are taking all that stuff with you," she said. "You need to let your brain rest for a while."

Penny smiled, knowing that she was mostly carrying this for security. It made her feel confident to have it with her, whether she looked at it or not. She and Althea went their respective ways, each with her own thoughts and plans for what remained of the weekend.

While Althea went to the local market for groceries and Penny went home to ponder their next moves, Kyle sought out Victor Miller. He found him at the Best Brewery, a micro-brewery and sports bar in Midvale Corners. Kyle, who had come in to check up on how his alma mater was doing football wise, spotted Victor sitting at the long bar positioned along one wall of the room. He was drinking a beer and staring intently at the big screen high definition television that dominated that corner of the bar. There were huge TV's mounted on all four walls. All were silent with a zipper of words across the bottom edge of the picture.

Kyle crossed the length of the room, heading for the bar. He slid onto the bar stool next to Victor recently vacated by a fan disgusted with his team who announced to one and all that 'he, for one, was sick of losing and he was going home to dig out the driveway and sidewalks.'

Victor looked up, saw Kyle sitting next to him, and nodded hello. "Not your usual Saturday afternoon spot," he said to Kyle.

"Hello to you, too," Kyle said. "You're right it's not, but it is your usual spot and I am looking for you."

"I've got nothing to say to you," Victor said, his lips set in a straight line and his hands clenched around the beer in front of him like it was going to fly away. "I don't know anything."

"How do you know you don't know anything when you don't know what I want to talk to you about?"

"Oh, I know. You're working for the Penny Johnson and she's representing Horace Appleworth who killed Dick, although I don't know why he'd want to do that, and you want to know about what I know, which is nothing."

"Well, let's start with finding a place where we can talk without being heard and we can talk about Horace and your recent visit with him."

"I knew that would get me in trouble," Victor said. The two men got up and moved to a corner booth far from the noise of the bar and the cheering fans.

"Alright, I did go see Horace. I gave that miserable son of a bitch, Dick Boswick, $30,000 dollars the night he was killed."

"In cash? Why?"

"Of course, in cash. Neither of us wanted a paper trail. And you know why. That was Dick's price for giving me the contract to renovate the courthouse. He wanted 10% of the contract price. And, don't look at me that way. I know it was a bribe, but I needed the work. And no, I did not kill Dick. He was alive when I left him. Besides it would make no sense for me to kill him, I was going to get the contract the next day."

"So, you went to see Horace because you thought he had your money," Kyle said.

"Right. But he claimed he didn't and I believe him. I've known Horace for years and he's a pretty straight shooter—well other than being a queer—but for a queer, he's okay."

"Who do you think has your money?"

"Well, I have three choices—the police who were first on the scene, the real murderer, or it's hidden somewhere in that office and I can't get in there because it is a crime scene."

"I can't be positively sure," Kyle said, "but I don't believe the police have it. Dan Dunlap was the lead detective and he is an upfront guy. He didn't say anything about money and it wasn't in his police report. Well, they did find some hundred-dollar bills under Dick's head, but not as much as you're talking about."

"Then it was the killer who took it," Victor said. "And the sad part is, if the money is found, I can't claim it because I think bribing a public official is a crime, isn't it?"

"Most assuredly," said Kyle with a slight smile and little sympathy for a man who thought bribery was simply part of doing business.

"Any idea who might want Boswick dead?" Kyle asked.

"A lot of people. He was a sleaze ball. All the contractors in the area knew what he did, yes, even Horace. I don't know if Horace ever participated but it was only recently he started bidding on public jobs. Usually he rehabbed those big old Victorians on the northwest side of town. But Fiona and I were always bidding on the jobs and so were a few of the smaller outfits."

"Did Fiona pay Dick for work?" Kyle asked, taking a sip of his drink.

"I'm sure she did, but she never said so. And I don't think she has the cojones to kill anyone, but you never know. In these tight economic times, each job means a lot. And don't think Dick didn't know that. He used his position to advantage and I didn't like working that way but I didn't kill him." Victor sat back, his arms crossed.

"I'm sure you didn't or you would have the money and wouldn't have threatened Horace."

"That was just talk and you know it. I don't think I could kill anyone, well, maybe in a war, but not in Midvale Corners. And, you know, Kyle, I don't think Horace could kill anyone either."

"Well, unfortunately, all the evidence points to Horace, but I'll keep digging. What are you going to do about the money? And, at some point, you may find yourself charged with a crime. Too many people suspect what was going on."

"I know, I suppose I should find a lawyer," Victor said, staring at his empty beer. "Do you think Penny would represent me?"

"It may be a conflict of interest," Kyle answered, "but you could talk to her about it. She is a new lawyer, but smart and good at what she does. If she can't help you, I'm sure she can recommend someone."

"I'll think about it," Victor said, sliding out of the booth. "You want another beer?"

"No," Kyle said standing up. "I'm going to head on back to the office. I would recommend you talk to Penny ASAP—you might be in more trouble than you realize."

Victor nodded. The two men went their separate ways, Victor to his usual spot at the bar and Kyle out the door into the wan November sunlight.

Chapter 20

Alex's cell phone came to life at exactly 5:30 am on Monday morning. The University of Michigan fight song rang through the air. Alex groaned then rolled over, his arm reaching for the phone, which was not in its usual spot on the table by his bed. He remembered why; the night before he left the phone on the dresser on the other side of the room. He knew if he reached the phone before he was upright and out of bed, he would go back to sleep. His plan was to go to the gym before he went to court for 'motion day.' All motions, criminal and civil were heard on Mondays at the local court. They would drag on all day, but Judge Sanford expected everyone to be in court and ready at 9:30.

Alex grabbed the phone silencing it. He pulled on his gym shorts, his sweats, and charged down the stairs to the kitchen where he heard Mabel say, sweetly, "Good morning, Dear. You're up early."

His mother was sitting at the kitchen table drinking a cup of tea and reading her latest murder mystery. After determining he didn't want any breakfast, she reminded him that she had to be at the Zoo early because she and Ina, another docent, were off to Rockberry Elementary School with some animals. They would be there all morning.

"I won't be able to fix your breakfast," she said.

"Oh, by the way, Ethan Humphrey is coming to dinner tonight. We will eat at 6:30 promptly."

Alex looked at his mother who looked back at him, her lips pressed together as if she were holding back a smile.

"Really," Alex said, "Do you want me here?"

"Of course, we do, it's just dinner. Why don't you invite Penny? I would love to see her again. I think I'll do a pot roast—that's good for a wintry day, don't you think?"

"Yes, Mom," Alex smiled, leaned over and gave his mother a kiss on the cheek and went out the door, got in his car and was off to the gym.

After his workout, Alex stopped at the small lounge area in the gym for a cup of coffee, some fresh fruit and a bagel.

"Hey, Alex," said his high school friend, Clark, who was sitting at a corner table. Alex joined him. "I saw you and Penny Johnson with your heads close together at the coffee shop. What's up?"

"I don't really know," Alex said. "Our mothers are pushing us. I suspect they want grandchildren. But I'm not sure either of us is ready to settle down."

"Well, my friend, you better get to it. You're not getting any younger. Your bachelor days are numbered, I think."

Alex laughed. "I don't think Penny is ready either, after all, she just opened her practice. Speaking of which, I need to get going. I have to be in court this morning for a couple of motions."

The men left together parting in the parking lot, Alex heading for his black Mercedes, and Clark off to his white BMW.

Alex heard Clark say before he got in his car, "Life is short, my friend, you need to settle down soon."

Alex, looking around the interior of his car thought about marriage, car seats, messy children and dirtier dogs and wondered if he was ready for all that.

"All rise," said the bailiff in a loud voice. Judge Sanford strode into the courtroom from the door in back of his bench, his robe swirling around his feet. He paused by his chair, sat down, the bailiff banged the gavel and announced in his nasally voice, "You may be seated."

Judge Sanford, a short man who raised his chair up as high as it would go in order to see over the bench and kept a foot stool under his desk to rest his feet, a trick he learned from his father who was also a judge and from whom he had inherited his short stature, looked around his court-room taking in the six foot windows with the cedar blinds left by the film company that had been in his court for the better part of a week filming a legal scene for the movie.

He looked out at the crowd sitting on every available space in the gallery. He recognized some as part of the media—a couple of TV people, that uppity reporter from the local paper and the smart aleck from the big city paper down the road. They had never had a kind word to say about him. He didn't need to look at his docket to see what case was of interest to them—it was that Boswick murder—and Horace Appleworth, the alleged killer. From what he had heard, it was possible that Appleworth did the city a favor by killing Boswick who was supposedly corrupt and a philanderer, according the judge's wife and her gossipy friends.

"Bailiff," he said, "Remove those people who are standing and leaning against the back wall. I will not have people standing in my courtroom. And close those blinds, that sun is blinding."

The bailiff moved toward the back of the courtroom, but it was not necessary. The folks standing were already looking for any possible seats or moving toward the door to the hallway, which was between the bar separating the business area of the court from the gallery. Only lawyers and parties or those invited by the judge could go on the business side of the bar. No one could sit in the empty jury box, which at present was full of prisoners waiting for their cases to be called.

"That's better," Judge Sanford said, "I see by my docket that we have some motions filed in the matter of the People v Appleworth. Are the parties ready to proceed? I suspect we can handle this in short order and then the media people can get on to their business. Elvira, call the case."

Alex, who had been sitting with the usual cadre of lawyers in the row of seats by the side wall, saw Penny and Horace moving down the aisle headed for the defense table, placed to the right of the Judge's bench and furthest from the jury. Penny's long black skirt, flared at the bottom, moving gracefully as she walked. Her red and black jacket was snug but Alex thought he could see a small bulge in her left pocket—he suspected it was her lucky Petoskey stone, which she always carried.

"You just never know when you might need a bit of luck," she had told Alex over coffee.

Penny stood by the table, waiting for Mike Pritchard to arrive at the Prosecution table. Horace, his face pale but with his head held high, wore a navy suit, a white shirt and a red tie that appeared striped but if looking closely, you would see that the stripes were really small bears on skateboards, their red scarves flying, stood next to Penny. Penny, in her two-inch black heels, was still a little shorter than Horace.

The door flew open. Mike Pritchard came in, followed by his latest intern, her arms full of files. Mike went to the Prosecutor's table, took the top file off the pile in the intern's arms and turned to the judge.

"Nice of you to join us," Judge Sanford said. "Can we get started now?"

Penny put her briefcase on the floor by her feet, opened it, took out her file, placed it on the table, with her Mont Blanc pen, given to her by her grandmother who still believed in writing letters, by its side.

After Mike and Penny said their names for the record, Mike said, "Yes, your honor, but I believe we are here at Ms. Johnson's request, not mine."

"I am aware of that, Mr. Prosecutor," Judge Sanford said. "As I see it Mrs. Johnson, you are several requests of the court—five, in all, by my count. Is that right?"

Penny stood up when the Judge said her name. "Yes, your honor," she said. "We are asking the court to suppress the pistol found by the railroad tracks, for a short adjournment of the case as a result of the bombing of my car, and to move the trial to another court or in the alternative, request a visiting judge, and for a more aggressive method of qualifying jurors. Would the court like me to address each motion in turn?"

"I can tell you that I'll not grant the motion to move the trial or to request a visiting judge. The pre-trial publicity has been substantial," he paused to glare at the journalists sitting in the front rows of his court, "but I am sure your client can receive a fair trial right here in Midvale Corners and, frankly, I see no reason to remove myself from the case."

"I can also tell that, after reading your argument for an adjournment because your car was destroyed, I'll not allow it. I am sure the car bombing was the result of one of your disgruntled clients and has nothing to do with the Appleworth matter."

Penny, listening intently, was not so sure since most of her clients were petty thieves or eccentrics, not bombers. Horace's case was the only violent case on her personal docket.

"This trial will begin on December 14th as it is scheduled. The court does not look kindly upon obstructionist or delaying techniques, Ms. Johnson. We will keep things moving along."

"I am willing to hear your argument about the pistol. Please proceed."

Penny found her notes for her suppression argument, tossing the sheets for the motions already decided to the side.

"Your honor, we are asking the court to suppress the pistol found by the police by the railroad tracks on the basis of suggestiveness. As the court may know, the pistol was found by some young people by the railroad tracks. They admitted they poked at the pistol with a stick moving it around so they could take a picture of it, which they did and then sent the picture to all their friends by posting it to Facebook on the Internet.

"Are you arguing chain of custody problems, here?" interrupted the Judge, "Because if you are, I'm not seeing it."

"Yes, we are, your honor. The pistol was all over the Internet, seen by hundreds if not thousands of persons. Anyone could have planted it there to make my client look guilty. We ask that the court suppress the pistol."

"Your honor," Mike said, rising slowly to his feet, "that is a spurious argument. We have established the chain of custody from the time that Sheriff Nicholson came upon the scene at the behest of young people. From that moment all procedural rules were followed and Ms. Johnson knows that."

"The prosecution asks that the motion to suppress be denied."

"I agree with the prosecutor," Judge Sanford said. "It will be up to the Jury to decide the importance or relevance of the pistol. That is their domain, not mine."

"Now, have we taken care of all your motions, Ms. Johnson?"

"No, your honor," Penny said. "There is still the matter of selecting an impartial jury. As the court knows, there has been extensive publicity about this case. The victim is the City Manager, well known throughout the community. Horace Appleworth attended school here, is known by almost everyone in our town. There is also the issue of Mr. Appleworth's sexual orientation, which he does not deny, but he knows, from the harassing letters he has received, that there are many in our town that don't approve of his lifestyle. This could easily bias the jury against him."

"I am sure the Prosecutor will agree with me that we want a fair trial. We need to ensure that an impartial jury is selected. We know that jurors don't always answer completely when questioned in open court about their prejudices or what they know about the trial. My request is that we question each prospective juror individually in your chambers under oath. And that Mr. Pritchard and myself be in the room to ask questions of the jurors."

The reporters in the front row leaned forward, writing furiously, Judge Sanford would not let the media bring computers in the courtroom, arguing that the tapping on the keys was distracting to all present. Judge Sanford frowned at Penny, but before he had a chance to rule, Mike Pritchard stood.

"Your honor," Mike said, "I am not disagreeing with Ms. Johnson's suggestion. I, too, want a fair trial and an impartial jury. I believe if we question the jurors individually in private, we will be able to accomplish that purpose."

Judge Sanford pursed his lips, his eyes narrowing. He looked down at his notes then looked up.

"Okay, I grant your motion to individually question the prospective jurors. We will do that in my chambers. I'll ask all questions. The prosecution and the defense are to file their suggested questions with the clerk no later than one week before trial. I want to make it clear that I'll ask the questions. This will not be a fishing expedition or an attempt to influence the jurors one way or the other. Am I making myself clear, counselors?"

Mike and Penny nodded their assent. Penny handed one of the two orders for the jury selection process that she had prepared in advance to the judge. Since she had suspected that Judge Sanford would not let the lawyers ask the questions, she had not included that option in one of them. The clerk took that order to the judge, who read it over carefully, signed it and returned it to Elvira.

"My clerk will make copies at the end of this court session. You may pick them up later today. Now, assuming that has taken care of the People v Appleworth, we will proceed on to the next matter."

"The People versus Sherwood," called the Bailiff, raising his voice over the shuffle of the reporters exiting the courtroom. Penny and

Horace quickly left their spot at the defense table leaving room for the next lawyer and his client.

Penny led Horace out the door. The reporters, knowing they could not approach them in the hall—Judge Sanford had long ago made that abundantly clear—more than one reporter had been fined for contempt when he violated the rule.

Penny stopped by a bench placed by the wall. She put all her papers back in her briefcase, took her Petoskey stone out of her pocket, placing it carefully in an inside pocket of the briefcase. Horace, who was watching, smiled.

"I don't know much about law, but I do know about good luck," he said. "I have on my lucky watch." With that, he pulled back his coat sleeve, pulled up his shirt on his left arm, revealing an antique Mickey Mouse watch.

"My dad gave me this for my twelfth birthday and I have worn it for luck ever since. I'm not so sure your stone or my watch helped us much today."

"On the contrary," Penny said. "It did help. I didn't really think we would win on all those motions, but I had to try and it helped to make Judge Sanford aware that we are serious about having a fair trial. It also helped to make the press aware, too."

"Now we are going to go downstairs. I suspect the reporters will be outside waiting for us. I'll talk to them. You will not. I will tell them that you are innocent and we are sure that with the methods put in place by Judge Sanford you will have fair trial. Ryan's going to meet us with his car and we will get in the car and leave. Do you understand?" Penny asked staring Horace in the eye.

"I get it," Horace said, almost but not quite laughing. This was a side of Penny he had not seen often. The determined lawyer gladiator; he could almost imagine her on her horse challenging all comers.

They went down the marble steps leading to the main floor of the courthouse. Built over one hundred years ago, the building was in need of renovation but still had a bit of its original grandeur. Horace looked at the fading paneled wood, the unpolished marble and the chipped wrought iron and thought about all he could do to restore its beauty if he didn't end up in prison, a sobering thought.

On the main floor, Penny led the way to the main door. The reporters, warned to stay on the sidewalk and away from the door, surged forward, coming as close as they dared.

"Penny, Penny, what do you think? Can you get a fair trial here? How are you going to defend Horace?"

The questions flooded her ears. Penny stopped, turning to the cameras, she said, "We are satisfied that we will have a fair trial and that my client will be found innocent at the end of the day. Now, please excuse us, we have a case to prepare."

She smiled and moved on, the crowd of reporters separating. Horace spotted Ryan's new Lincoln stopping at the curb. He and Penny walked over to the car, got in and Ryan drove them away.

"Don't hover—either one of you," Penny said to Althea and J.D. standing side by side in front of her desk. "I want to get these things out of my briefcase and get settled, then I'll tell you what happened in court."

"We'll wait," Althea said, settling in the client chair across from Penny's desk. "J.D. probably wants a pat on the head, I took him for a walk a few minutes ago so he doesn't need to go out, no matter how sad he looks. I, on the other hand, want to know what happened in court. Do you want a cup of coffee?"

"No, Ryan took us to his country club for lunch. It was delicious and I don't need anything more to drink."

"Judge Sanford hates the press and the courtroom was full of reporters and media types and the usual court watching folks. It's motion day so there are a lot of people and since this Judge doesn't always follow the docket, everyone gets there early to be ready if their case is called out of order. The room was so full, he ordered all the people standing to leave."

"That man has always been cranky," Althea said. "He was that way in high school, we all thought he had a Napoleon complex because he's so short. What happened to your motions?" Althea leaned forward. J.D moved up to a sitting position resting his nose on Penny's desk.

"It wasn't that exciting," Penny said leaning back, her head back looking at the ceiling. Seconds passed. Penny looked at Althea.

"He denied everything except my request that we question the jury in chambers. We have to get him the questions we want asked in a couple of weeks since he won't let us question the jury spontaneously. Mike and I agree that is not right, but we can't change Owen's mind.

We might file an interlocutory appeal on that issue. We decided to think about it over-night."

With a bang that startled both women, the door to Penny's office flew open. Percy flew across the room to rub noses with J.D. Kyle followed quickly behind.

"It is amazing how fast that cat can move when he wants to," Kyle laughed. "I have news."

Kyle placed a fat file on the small empty space at the corner of Penny's desk. He sat down in the second client chair across from Penny. Penny and Althea stared at Kyle

Kyle proceeded to give a report of his conversation with Victor including the fact that Victor might come to Penny to represent him if he is charged with a crime.

"I'll cross the representation bridge when I come to it," Penny said. "I am sure there is a conflict someplace, but I can't worry about that now. What we have to do is find the money. We can be sure Horace doesn't have it. Anyone spending a lot of money lately that we know about?"

"Not really," Kyle answered after a pause. "I remember that Luther Rahn paid a cash deposit for a new, fancy Harley, but I sort of figured that he had stashed that money away from some criminal activity before he went to jail. I think Detective Dan questioned him but didn't get anywhere."

"I don't know why he would want to kill the City Manager—there is no benefit to him with Dick dead as far as I can see," Penny said, her eyes narrowing, her brow furrowed.

"But," Althea commented, "he works for Fiona, doesn't he? And maybe it would benefit her in some way."

Althea and Kyle agreed to do some digging. Penny, realizing that it was after five and she had an appointment with Alex, which she wouldn't call a date, she wasn't ready for dates, stood up suddenly.

"I have to get going," she said. "I have an appointment."

Kyle and Althea looked at her questioningly.

"I'm having dinner with Alex and his mother and Ethan Humphrey. I think Mabel wants us there dispel any notion that inviting Ethan over for dinner is a date."

Kyle and Althea looked at each other with a smile. It seems Penny was not the only female in town that didn't 'date.'

"You go," Althea said, "I'll close up."

Penny grabbed J.D.'s leash, snapped it on, and dashed out the door.

Penny arrived home in time to change out of her court 'uniform,' as Althea called it and into a pair of grey, wool slacks and a crème silk blouse with a deep neckline that she filled with a silver beaded necklace. She added her favorite black velvet vest and slid her feet into a pair of black low-heeled shoes to complete the ensemble.

"What do you think?" she asked J.D. who was watching her turn in front of the mirror. He sensed, as dogs can, that she was excited about something but as it didn't involve treats or walks it was out of his league. He wagged his tail slowly.

"I agree," said Penny. "It's not too dressy—after all, it is dinner at home not in a fancy restaurant—and it is comfortable. Lord knows, I'm into comfort after a busy day." Penny took the knot out of her hair, gave it a brushing and a toss so that it spread around her face with a slight curl.

The doorbell rang just as she finished putting on her lipstick. Startled, she jumped. She didn't know if she was excited about the evening or still a little hyper from the day in court. She opened the door and smiled at Alex.

Alex smiled back.

Helping Penny with her coat he said, "Thanks for doing this. I think my mom has been cooking all day. When I left she was eyeing the dining room table, which looked fine to me, but she was busy debating with herself whether to use the good china."

"She said she didn't want Ethan to get the wrong idea, whatever that might be, and since it was Monday night, the second-best china would do. When I left she was snatching dishes off the table and putting on a different set. They all looked the same to me." Alex looked puzzled.

Penny laughed. "I do understand how she feels. In Mabel's world the 'good china' is only brought out for special dinners and Ethan knows that so she is worried about the impression she is creating."

Penny set the alarm, locked the door and soon they were on their way in Alex's car.

"Penny, I'm so glad you came for dinner," said Mabel when she and Alex came in the front door of the house. Please come into the living room, dinner is about ready. Ethan is already here."

Ethan was sitting in one of the chairs by the fireplace, which was crackling with a small fire. Penny gave her coat to Alex and went into the living room to join Ethan.

Alex came into the room carrying a tray with wine and wine glasses.

Penny and Ethan decided on red wine. Alex poured the wine and they sat back to enjoy the pause in conversation.

Mabel took a sip of wine, then stood and headed for the kitchen. Penny got up to follow. Mabel's kitchen smelled of pot roast and fresh vegetables.

"It smells delicious," Penny said. "Suddenly I realize I'm hungry."

Mabel, who was carefully removing the roast from the oven, smiled.

"Good," she said. "Can you get the salad out of the refrigerator? I'll put the roast and vegetables on the serving plate."

Penny looked in the refrigerator, found a large tossed green salad in a wooden bowl, which she took to the dining room table. She smiled when she saw the Oneida stoneware plates--weekday dishes that were a step up from family, but not the best china. She put the salad at one end of the table, next to the salad tongs already there.

Mabel came in with the roast, the vegetables arranged neatly around the roast on the large platter that matched the stoneware. Mabel stood back, looked at the table carefully checking that all was in order then pleased with what she saw, she smiled.

Penny and Mabel went to the living room to announce dinner and collect their wine glasses.

Alex sat at the head of the table, in front of the roast, Mabel at the foot, Ethan to her right and Penny to her left. Alex picked up the large carving knife to carve the roast. As each plate was passed down to him, he filled it with roast and vegetables. Mabel passed the salad. Once everyone was served, they began to eat.

Conversation was limited as they ate. Mabel beamed, happy that her dinner quests were enjoying the meal. When the roast was no more, the dinner plates cleared, Mabel suggested they return to the living room for coffee and cookies. Soon they were settled, nibbling on Mabel's chocolate chip cookies and drinking their coffee.

"How is your case with Horace going?" asked Ethan. "I don't believe for one minute that he killed Dick Boswick. I know some people don't like it that he and Ryan live together, but that doesn't make him a killer, now does it?"

"No, it doesn't," Penny said. "The case is going along. The biggest problem is that Horace admits he was at Dick's office that night. When he left Dick was fine. Horace was angry so he walked around town before returning to his car. He never went back to the concert. And he doesn't remember seeing anyone."

"That was the night of the concert on the courthouse lawn?" Ethan asked. Penny nodded.

"Toby and I went for a long walk that night. The Chamber of Commerce asked me to take pictures of the village at different times of the day and during each of the seasons. I was shooting pictures for a long time. I don't remember seeing Horace though. But I wasn't paying attention to people around me. I may have seen him."

"Thanks, Ethan, for trying. My PI, Kyle Lafferty is going around interviewing practically everyone in Midvale Comers. I am sure he will find someone who saw Horace that night."

The conversation turned to the Christmas parade and craft show coming up after Thanksgiving. Mabel was pleased that she would be at the Zoo table with the other docents and Ethan was carving some special wooden items for his station.

"I plan to have several wooden salad bowls with salad grabbers. And some of those wooden tongs for getting your toast out of the toaster without getting a shock." he said.

"I love my tongs," Penny said. "I bought them from you a couple of years ago. They are a little burned but I've never gotten a shock."

"Thank you. And thank you Mabel for this wonderful evening," he said rising from his chair. "I must be going. It is getting on 10 and time for Toby's evening walk."

"I am so glad you could come," Mabel said, rising to walk him to the door.

Alex got their coats. Ethan walked down the street to his house. Penny and Alex got in the car to drive the short distance to Penny's house.

Alex pulled in the driveway, went around the car and opened the door for Penny.

"You don't have to walk me to the door," Penny said. "I can manage."

"I'm sure you can," Alex said, "but my mother taught me that I was to make sure to escort my d--- guest, friend, to the door."

They walked the short distance to the porch. Penny pulled her keys out of her coat pocket. She looked up at Alex. He looked at her. After a pause, Penny turned to unlock the door. She opened it to find JD standing in the short hallway, wagging his tail, happy to see his mistress.

Alex laughed. Penny thanked Alex and went into the house. Alex got in his car and drove away. He wasn't sure what had happened but he felt something had and he decided to see Penny again. Maybe his mother was right.

While Penny and Mabel were trying to decide if their dinner with Ethan and Alex were dates, the members of the Society were seated around their favorite table at Romano's Bookstore. Each had their favorite coffee except for Mary who was drinking Chamomile tea.

"I am a bit jittery today. The tea will calm me down," she explained, jiggling the tea bag up and down in the little pot of water. "How did Penny's motions go today?" she asked turning to Althea.

"Penny seemed satisfied, but not happy," Althea said. "The only motion she won was the right to question the jurors in Judge Owen's chambers. But the Judge won't let either Mike or Penny ask the questions. They may file an appeal with the Court of Appeals challenging that decision. Mike does seem to want a fair trial as much as Penny does."

"I don't know about Mike," Mary said. "I heard he and Dan arguing. Dan thinks the bombing of Penny's car is connected to the murder and Mike doesn't. Mike won't spend the extra $1000 to rush the prints found on one of the bomb parts. He doesn't see it as a priority."

"Now I understand why Dan came to the office on Saturday and left reports for Penny and Kyle. He even took a copy of Ethel's sketch and said he will get a picture of Luther Rahn for you, Rose. He thought that the sketch looked like Luther and so did Kyle," Althea said.

"I'll tell Ethel-she'll be pleased that she was able to help," Rose said. "I am sure she would like to see the picture, too, to see how close she came to a live human being."

The women turned to Arney who was always the last to report.

"I don't have much exciting news except to say that Fiona Hollis heard I was looking for work. She called and wants me to come over to straighten out her books. She said she's not much of an accountant and the Board is meeting next week and wants a financial report. I am planning on going over there tomorrow morning. I suspect that the financial records are a mess. I'm not looking forward to that job."

Althea explained that Penny was looking for anyone who might have seen Horace the night of the murder.

"So far no one has come forward, but I'm sure someone saw him and just doesn't know it."

The book lovers and puzzle solvers nodded, each promising to ask and listen in hopes of finding someone to alibi Horace. They cleaned up their table, put on their coats and headed for the door. Pulling their coats close to hold off the November cold, they each headed for their cars.

Chapter 21

Althea arrived at the office on Tuesday morning at 8:30 loaded down with her special coffee that she ground at home. She noticed a note from Pete the Fed Ex man that he had tried to make a registered delivery earlier and if she called his cell phone he would stop by with the envelope. Puzzled she took the note, unlocked the door and went into the office. After setting things down and hanging up her bright red coat, she called Pete. He promised to stop by before he left Midvale Comers.

Penny and JD arrived. Althea looked to see if Penny was acting different after her "meeting" with Alex. She thought she detected a happier note, a little bounce in her step, maybe or a ready smile. Penny had settled at her desk when the phone rang. She answered.

"Mike Pritchard here," said a male voice. "I think we should appeal Sanford's decision on jury selection to the Court of Appeals. I want to be able to question the jury myself. I'm sure you do, too. I'll send a draft over for you to look at-if we can agree, we can e-mail it to the court this afternoon. With electronic filing, these things move faster than ever."

"I look forward to reading it," Penny said. "I agree we need to get it out ASAP, the trial is less than a month away."

Penny didn't want to admit that she had never written an interlocutory appeal to the Court of Appeals, but she had worked on one while in law school so she had some idea what was required. How hard could it be?

Althea appeared at the door. "Pete, the Fed Ex man, is bringing a letter that you have to sign for sometime this afternoon. Will you be here most of the day?"

"Yes, 1 plan to do research on interlocutory appeals and work on trial prep. 1 think I'll start with questions for the jury. Gordon sent over a list of questions he has used in the past. I'm sure they will be a big help."

Penny began by calling Gordon to consult about appeals and to ask whether she could send Victor to him for a consultation since she decided that it would be a conflict of interest for her to represent both Victor and Harold. And, she had enough on her plate with a trial coming up soon.

Gordon was a great help. He advised her on the appeal and agreed to consult with Victor if asked. Penny was relieved. She felt more confident that she would be able to assess the Motion from Mike and had an answer for Victor.

"Victor Miller is on the line for you," Althea announced breaking into Penny's thoughts.

"First, 1 want to say I don't think Horace killed Dick," Victor said after the hellos were said. "And I know 1 didn't do it. But I do think 1 may be charged with something before all of this is done so I need a lawyer."

"1 understand," Penny said, "Kyle mentioned it to me. 1 suggest you call Gordon Swanson. I told him you might call. His phone number is 214-0654."

"Thanks, Penny. If I think of any way I can help Horace, I'll let you know."

Penny went back to work. Althea brought her a sandwich from the deli, which she ate at her desk. She was deep in thought when her e-mail pinged signally a new message. She looked up and saw that it was the Motion from Mike. She opened the e-mail and the attachment noticing Mike's message-"Did you get my package yet?" Penny had no idea what he was talking about so she didn't answer.

After a review of the Motion, she sent it back to Mike with her approval. She doubted the Court of Appeals would grant their motion to ask the questions of the jury; she knew a judge had a right to run his courtroom as he saw fit and the appeals court didn't often intervene. With a sigh she returned to the list of questions for the jury. She knew she would get a list of the panel of prospective jurors a week before the trial, but she also knew that things would be hectic then and she wanted to have the questions prepared for the judge.

After a time, she needed a stretch so she took JD for a walk around the village. When she returned Althea handed her the Fed Ex envelope. Penny took it to her desk. She opened the envelope and out fell a flash drive and a ten-page report. The report was labeled "A New Life."

The writer was Dick Boswick.

What followed were pages of lists of names, dates, a project name and amounts of money. Looking more closely, Penny could see that the dates began about ten years back, starting when Dick first became City Manager. The amount of money by the names was quite small in the beginning, increasing as the dates got closer to the present. She recognized a few of the names as general contractors that worked in the area. She began to realize that here was a list of moneys paid to Dick Boswick that he must have put away someplace.

Flipping through the pages to more recent times, she stopped.

"Oh, no," she gasped, standing so suddenly her old wooden desk chair crashed to the floor, missing the window by a hair.

J.D. jumped up at the sound.

Althea rushed into the room. "What's the matter?"

Penny stared at the words at the top of one of the last few pages of the report. "Horace Appleworth, cemetery fencing repair project, June, 2005, $2000."

She silently handed the report to Althea, pointing to the page. Althea read the words, then sat down at the conference table in the comer.

"What does this mean?" Althea asked.

Penny found the letter from Mike Pritchard that came with the report. She read parts of it out loud.

"The included flash drive is a copy of one found by Sally Boswick in Dick's desk. She put it in her computer, opened it and found the included list. She believes that this is a list of the money received by her husband in exchange for granting city contracts. She has yet to find the money, however, you will note that your client is one of those who bribed Boswick along with many others. Sally Boswick called our office and we immediately went to her home to collect the flash drive."

"We intend to present this evidence at trial and believe that it confirms that Horace Appleworth had bribed Dick Boswick in the past and when his bribe didn't work this time, he killed him. Would you like to discuss a plea?"

Penny looked up at Althea.

"It means that Mike has grounds to argue intent," said Penny, "that Horace had a reason to kill Dick, that he was frustrated and became so angry he killed him. But if he did kill him, and I'm not saying he did, I could argue that he didn't go there with the intent to kill, but then why did he have the gun?"

"I need Horace in here now. Althea, please find him."

An hour later the door burst open and Horace came rushing in. Althea jumped, then calmly said,

"She's waiting for you. Please go on in."

Horace walked into Penny's office. "What's happened," he asked.

Penny waved him over the conference table, handing him the report. Horace stood reading it. When he came to the list of names, he sat down abruptly in the chair at the table.

"I forgot about this," he began.

"You forgot," Penny said, staring at her client, her eyes wide.

"Yes, it was a long time ago. 1 was so upset about the murder charge, that's all I could think of. I remember now."

Penny said nothing, waiting for him to continue.

"It was a bad time for my business. If I didn't get that job, I was afraid I would have to lay off some of my guys. And when you do that, you can lose them for good. And they are good workers," Horace said softly, his elbows on his knees, holding the report in his hands, staring at it.

"Anyway," he continued, looking up, placing the report on the table with a thud, "when Dick suggested there was a way I could ensure I got the bid, I listened. The amount was not so great and he was right I could bury it as a cost of doing business, so I paid him and got the contract.

"But, and I want you to hear this--that was the only time I did it. I never did it again. I knew he was still taking bribes but I found work in other communities and was able to get along without Midvale Corner's business."

"And this time," Penny said.

"Well, this was a big job so I couldn't really pass it up. And, I hoped he had scammed enough money that he had stopped doing it. But, when I heard the rumor that Victor was going to get the job, I knew that my bid was fair and it made me angry that we might lose out. I also believe that we would do a far superior job."

"That's why I went to his office that night. I went to confront him but not to kill him."

Penny continued to look at Horace, unblinking.

"You know," she said, "that the Prosecutor will use this against you, but I am more interested in the other names on the list. We know Victor would probably have gotten the contract because we know he gave Dick money, but were any of these other names on the list trying for this job?"

Horace picked up the report, leafed through it, reading it carefully.

"I'm sure that Fiona Hollis, Canfield Construction, Best Builders, Victor and I were bidding. There may have been others. Fiona and Victor both paid for jobs in the past just like I did. We all resented it but didn't do anything about it."

"Did you consider going to the police. He was committing a serious crime and breach of the public trust." Penny said.

"We talked about it but we didn't because Dick had the commissioners in his back pocket and we didn't know how deep the corruption went. It could have gone all the way to the Prosecutor's office. We couldn't take a chance. He really had us."

Penny looked up at the soft knock on her open door. Looking up, she saw Kyle standing in the doorway.

"Come in," she said. "We need your help."

Kyle sat next to Horace.

Penny filed Kyle in on the events of the morning.

"Can you contact these people? Maybe they will talk to you. Some of them are out of business now and some have moved on, but others may still be around. I want to know what they have to say. And, of course we don't have much time, the trial is coming up soon and Mike is sure he will win. Here's a copy of this report. And we are assuming it's accurate, I don't know that it is. There may be more and where is all the money? In a secret bank account?"

"I'm on it," Kyle said, standing up and heading out the door.

When Horace rose to leave, Penny didn't like the dark look on his face.

"What are you thinking?" she asked.

When Horace didn't answer, she continued in her firm lawyer voice.

"I don't want you to do anything about this. It will only cause more trouble for you. Kyle is a good investigator. He will find the truth. Promise me you will stay out of it."

Horace sighed, his shoulders dropped and he looked at Penny.

"Okay, I'll stay out of it. I know some of these people and perhaps I could help?"

Penny shook her head. "No, I'll let you know what Kyle learns.

After walking Horace out the door, Penny went back to work on the questions for the jury. She, too, had to let Kyle do his job.

Chapter 22

Kyle took the report to his office, sat down at his computer and found the addresses of the most recent bribers on the list. He intended to visit all of them.

His first stop was the owner of Canfield Construction. At first, he denied any part of paying Dick bribes, but when he saw the report, he admitted paying the bribe once.

"I finally gave up on Midvale Corners' jobs," he said, "because Dick was getting greedy-he wanted at least 10% of the total cost of the job for him. That was too much to bury. I moved on. Am I in trouble? I sold the business and the wife and I want to go to Florida."

The big man sounded worried. He ran his fingers through his grey hair, looking at Kyle with a furrowed brow. After wishing him happy traveling, Kyle left the man to his thoughts. He went on to the rest of the names on the list. All denied bidding on the recent courthouse restoration job, many had decided the cost of doing business in Midvale Comers was too high and they sought work elsewhere.

Kyle determined that Victor, Horace and Fiona Hollis were the only ones in the running for the work. And he already knew that Victor had left $30,000 with Dick, which had since disappeared. That left him with the task of speaking to Fiona Hollis.

He pulled up in front of Hollis Lumber Yard, parked his car and went in the door.

"I thought 1 told you to stay away from here," said a female voice. Kyle turned to the sound. Fiona was standing at the back of the showroom, hands on hips, feet planted.

"I thought you might like to know that the prosecutor has a list of all the people who have bribed Dick Boswick for work in the past and your name appears on the list," Kyle said.

Fiona glared at him as if her stare could change the facts.

"Follow me," she said after a pause, heading back to her office.

Kyle entered the dingy office tucked in a comer of the building. There were no windows and the room smelled musty. The wooden desk, made of oak, was dull and the mismatched chairs in the room in front of the desk were covered in faded upholstery. The room had an air of neglect as if the people who lived there had given up hope.

Fiona waved Kyle to one of the chairs. He handed her a copy of the list of names.

"And just where did Mike Pritchard get this list? I'll deny bribing Dick for a job. Our work speaks for itself. Everyone knows we do good work."

Kyle told her that Sally Boswick had found the flash drive with the information, which she gave to the police.

"Where is the money?" Fiona asked.

"That hasn't been found yet," Kyle answered.

"So, exactly how do they know that these so-called bribes really took place?"

Kyle shrugged his shoulders, hands up. "I don't have an answer for that," he said, "but I'm sure they will find it. The police will search until they do.

"Are you submitting a new bid on the court house restoration job? I understand that due to Dick's death and the circumstances surrounding it, they are opening the bidding again."

"Of course, we are," said Fiona. "And I'm sure we will win. Victor may be out of the running. Horace will be convicted. That leaves Hollis Lumber Yard as the winner."

Kyle looked doubtful since he suspected that with Dick gone, some of those who had left the bidding wars would return if they thought the playing field was level.

Kyle stood to leave. He opened the door to find Luther Rahn standing right outside it. He seemed to be listening to their conversation. Kyle nodded at the man who hurried past him into Fiona's office, shutting the door with a thud.

Kyle made a note of the conversation and Luther's appearance when he got to his car. Driving off, he mused about Luther Rahn and his relationship to Fiona. His PI nose smelled something not right. He decided to talk to Detective Dunlap and compare notes.

As he drove toward the police station, his cell phone rang. Looking down at the number he saw it was Arney, accountant for almost every business in Midvale Comers, including his own. His phone was hand's free so he answered.

"Kyle," Arney said, "I have found something strange. I just left Randy Haywood's motorcycle shop with their deposits for the day. I was there balancing their checkbook so I offered to take the money to the bank. He had two large cash sales a couple of days ago and he still had the money in the safe and he wanted to get it in the bank."

"I counted it out-it was about $30,000 in cash. Most of it was hundreds and some of the money looked and felt quite strange."

Kyle could hear the undertow of excitement in Amy's precise voice.

"Strange how," he asked.

"The money has brown spots on it. Some of them are quite large. Now you know that our little group does investigation once in a while so I've had some experience with dried bloodstains and these spots look like blood to me. And some of the bills are greasy. What do you think 1 should do?"

"1 think you should meet me at my office and let me see what you're talking about. I'll be there in a few minutes."

Arney agreed.

Kyle came bounding up the stairs to his office to see Arney standing at the end of the hall by his office door. Briefcase in hand, a bright green scarf around his neck to ward off the cold, Arney smiled when he saw Kyle.

"I can hear Percy inside. He seems impatient," he said.

"He's been alone all day," Kyle explained, turning the key in the lock. The men entered the small office, a mirror image of Penny's at the other end of the hall. Kyle didn't have a receptionist so he used the reception as a conference room. A long walnut table stood off to one side, surrounded by several mismatched wooden chairs. Percy jumped up in one of the chairs ready for some attention.

Arney put his briefcase on the table and gave Percy's big head a few rubs. He snapped open the brief case. With his usual precision, Arney had stacked the hundred-dollar bills in piles of 50, held together with rubber bands. There were two plastic bags holding the money.

"I put the suspicious money, about $21,000, in this bag," he said, holding up the larger bag. He opened the bag. A strange odor assailed their noses. Kyle stuck his nose right in the bag, his eyebrows pinched together. He sniffed, stopped and sniffed again.

"It smells like turkey," he said. "And I think I can discern a whiff of copper. I bet those brown stains are blood."

"I think we should call Detective Dan. He will know how to proceed," Kyle said.

Kyle picked up his desk phone and called Dan's private number.

"Dunlap," said a voice.

Kyle explained what they had found.

"Is this the work of Althea and her group?" Dan growled. "Never mind, I'll be right there."

A short time later Dan walked in the door. He brought some equipment with him.

Looking at the plastic bag of money on the table, he poked at the contents with a pencil. Pulling a pair of latex gloves out of his crime scene duffel, he put them on then carefully reached in taking out one of the bills almost covered in a brown stain.

"This looks like blood," he said.

"That's what 1 thought," Arney said. "I wonder if it has anything to do with Dick's murder. Maybe the lab can test the blood for DNA?"

"I agree," Dan said. "I'll send it off to the lab."

"All of it?" Arney asked. "Randy is not going to be happy about that. After all, it belongs to him. And we know if the police get it as evidence, it could sit there for months. I need to call him."

"How about this," Kyle said. "We find the most damaged bills; make a note of them, take pictures of the rest of the money and then you can deposit it in the bank. Doesn't the bank have to destroy damaged bills and replace them?"

"Yes, they do," Arney answered. "We could ask the bank about that. If they have to replace all of them, maybe they could all be sent to the crime lab. First though I have to call Randy. Can I use your office for a little privacy?" he asked Kyle.

Detective Dan stood looking at the money, musing about its origin. Why a motorcycle shop? Then he remembered Kyle mentioning that Luther Rahn had recently ordered a brand-new Harley and paid in cash. Where did this money come from? And, if the stains were blood, how did they get there? And would they be able to get DNA from them and match it to a victim or a perp or ordinary citizen who cut himself.

Kyle thought he could see Dan's mind working. He knew Dan would get to the bottom of this.

Arney came back in the room. "Randy is on his way. I don't think he will object to a few of the bills being sent off to the lab, but I know his business hasn't been good and he has to pay the manufacturer for the bikes and meet his payroll."

The men stood musing about the money, now spread all over Kyle's table. In what seemed like a moment, Kyle's office door opened and Randy Haywood came charging in.

"What is this all about?" he asked, looking at Dan.

"Randy, we think that some of this money has blood on it and we need to send it off to the lab for DNA testing."

"How long will that take? I need the money to pay the Harley folks."

"How long do you think you can hold them off?" Dan asked.

"Probably till the end of this month, but after that I'll be in trouble with them. They don't care if this money is evidence."

"I know that bills that are whole but dirty or stained can be replaced at our local bank," Arney said. "We might have to give them notice since it is a lot of bills. It looks like a fourth of them are covered with some sort of stain and the bank has to send them to the Department of Treasury to be replaced, which could take some time. I don't know about that. I can call Hiram, the VP and ask him."

"Do that," Dan said.

Arney went back into Kyle's office to place the call. Dan proceeded to separate the damaged bills from the others, being careful to handle each one as little as possible.

Arney returned with the information that "the bank can replace up to $1000 of the bills right away, but they need a few days to replace the others and they want the damaged bills ASAP or they would have to consider it a loan to Randy and he would be charged interest."

"No way," Randy said, "I have enough debt. How long will it take to test it?"

"The State police lab can take weeks," Dan said. "And I don't have the budget for a private lab."

"I do," Penny said, entering the door. Kyle smiled and the other two men looked up in surprise.

"Kyle texted me and told me what was going on," she explained. "I am certain this is the money left at the crime scene. I placed a call to Horace and he agreed to cover the lab expense."

Kyle pulled out his cell phone, calling his favorite lab. After asking some questions and listening carefully, he clicked off.

"If we bring it in today, they can have the results in 24 hours, max. It will cost about $2500. Will Horace be okay with that?"

Penny nodded, "He gave me permission to go up to $3000 if necessary."

They decided that Dan should be the one to take the stained money to the lab. "I'll stop by the police evidence locker and get the vial of blood from Boswick," he said. "The lab will need it for comparison."

Dan noted the serial numbers of all the money and took pictures of the undamaged bills. They all knew that the chain of evidence had to be protected in case the money proved to be what they thought it was and Penny would need it in the trial. Dan got out the labeling stickers, carefully placing the money back in the bags and affixing the label to each one.

When he was done, the three left the office--Kyle and Dan on their way to the lab, Penny returning to her office, Randy and Arney off to deposit the $16,000 in undamaged bills at the bank.

Later that evening, Althea, who upon hearing the news of the stained notes, called a meeting of the Society, opened the door of the book store around 7 pm to see her friends already at their places, waiting for her.

"We have your favorite coffee," said Rose. "We're waiting for you to hear Arney's story."

Althea sat down, nodding to Arney, who proceeded to tell his tale. The others were pleased with the news.

"I am sure that the blood will prove to be Dick Boswick's," he said. "I think we can be sure that the killer took the money from him after killing him. The question is who?"

"Well, we know it isn't Horace," said Rose. "Did Randy tell you who spent all that money on a motorcycle? My goodness, I didn't spend that much on my car."

"Randy is pretty sure it was Luther Rahn," Arney said. "But for the life of me I can't see why he would have any motive to kill Boswick. He's been in prison for the past five years and didn't even know him. And he certainly didn't have any financial tie to him that we know of."

"Speaking of that, Mary, have you seen any new bids for the courthouse project?"

"Yes, so far we have ten, including the original three, Fiona Hollis, Victor Miller and Horace. I think we got more because word went out that maybe this time the procedure would be fair. Our temporary assistant city manager is known to be honest."

"I think we can eliminate the new applicants, although we should check them out. One of them could have killed Dick on the hope that the bidding would be reopened, 1 suppose," Althea said.

Rose nodded, "I know most of the new group, some belong to my church I can check their alibis if you want."

"That would be great," Althea said. "How soon can you do that?"

"I'll get on it right away," Rose answered. "We have our church book club meeting tomorrow. And I can call the rest on some pretext or the other."

"You're good at making up stories," Mary laughed. "It must be all that fiction you read."

Rose beamed.

"Okay," Althea said, "Let's meet tomorrow at our usual time. We should have the blood type results and more information. I know we are making progress."

The group cleaned up their table and moved to the door. They didn't notice Luther Rahn sitting at a corner table, leaning forward, listening. After they left he picked up his cell phone. When he was connected, he said, "I'm coming over. We need to talk."

Wednesday morning dawned with a surprise snowstorm. For reasons known only to the weather gods, the snow that was predicted to land far north came to Midvale Corners. Penny, up early with too much on her mind, was driving carefully down the unplowed streets to her office. JD, strapped in with his doggy seat belt, was making snuffling noises from the back seat.

"I know," Penny said, "you don't like being tied up back there, but this old Jag doesn't handle all that well in snow and ice. I want you to be safe."

As if to prove her point, the car started to slide around a curve in the road. Penny, hearing her father's directions in her head, down shifted and straightened the car out. She turned into the parking lot of her office, bringing the car to a stop next to Althea's old Ford Escort.

"You're here early," Penny said, opening the door to her office to the smell of coffee with a touch of cinnamon.

"Good morning," Althea said. "I have some things to finish up before the day gets busy."

Penny smiled her thanks. She wondered what she would ever do without Althea. She took her briefcase into her office and got ready for the day. She was deep in thought when she heard a light tap on her open door.

Looking up into Alex's hazel eyes, she smiled, "Hello, come in, have a seat," she said the words tumbling out of her mouth in a rush. She thought she might be blushing.

Alex grinned. "Hello, I wanted to give you what might be some good news," he said, sitting in one of Penny's client chairs.

Penny waited. "Ethan dropped by last night—just in time for dinner—strange, my mom didn't seem all that surprised. At any rate, he said he was going through his pictures from last summer in search of anything that could help Horace. He thinks he might have taken a picture of him without realizing it. He was taking lots of pictures for the Chamber project. He has them in several shoe boxes."

"He doesn't have them on his computer?" Penny asked.

"No, he doesn't like computers, he likes to hold the pictures in his hand. And he has the dates and times on the pictures—his camera does that. At any rate, he and my mom were going to go through the box for summer to see what they can find. She said she'd call you if they came up with something."

"That is so nice," Penny said. "I don't know how to thank them for their efforts."

"Well, we could take them out to dinner one night—not as a date, of course—just an evening out," Alex suggested. "My mom still claims that they are not dating."

Penny nodded, "Sure, it wouldn't be a date. Just the four of us having dinner."

Alex glanced at his watch, jumped up, causing JD to look up from his nap. "I have to get to court. You know how Judge Sanford will fine you if you're late. And with the recent murder of Dick, the security takes forever."

"Go," said Penny as Alex's long legs carried him quickly out of Penny's office. Waving good-bye to both women, he was out the door and on his way to a busy day in court.

Across town at the Hollis Lumber Yard, Luther paced back and forth in front of the door to Fiona's office. Hearing the click of the four-inch heels Fiona insisted on wearing, he turned to the sound. Fiona frowned, stopping at the door.

"What do you want?" she asked.

"I want my money. I want to move on," he answered.

"Keep your voice down," Fiona said unlocking and opening her door. "Get in here." She went into the office. Luther followed her. They stood facing each other.

"I need some money. Either give it to me or …"

"Or what? Don't you dare threaten me. It's not my fault you're broke—I've paid you each week for standing around. I don't how I'll justify that to my brothers. You must have had some money—you bought that fancy Harley."

"You know where I got the money for that. Now I need some money to leave town." He raised his hand.

"Don't even think about it," Fiona said, glaring at him. Realizing that it might be best to get him out of town, she told him to come back after work that afternoon.

Luther stomped out. Fiona sat down in her chair behind her desk. Her heart was racing, her breath shallow. She knew that Luther Rahn had a violent streak. She unlocked her bottom drawer, taking out the small pistol she kept there. She checked to make sure it was loaded, tucking it into her purse sitting on the floor where it would be handy if she needed it.

The morning moved slowly for Penny. She felt like all she was doing was waiting; waiting for the blood test results, waiting for the Court of Appeals to rule on the motion, waiting for Ethan to find the one picture in hundreds that might help Horace, waiting for—her mind raced to Alex—what was she waiting for there?

"Mike Pritchard's on the phone for you," Althea said, tapping lightly on the door. Penny jumped as if she had been struck by lightning causing Althea to jerk back from the door. "Sorry, I didn't mean to scare you."

Penny picked up the phone to hear Mike saying, "I don't care what you think, Dan, we have a trial coming up and I want a conviction. Oh, hi, Penny. I am faxing over the answer from the Court of Appeals. We won. We can question the jurors ourselves. And in the judge's chambers."

"That's great news. Will you draft the order or shall I?" Penny asked.

"Will you have time to do it? I am a bit swamped here."

"Sure, no problem. I'll send a proposed order over to you later today," Penny said.

"Good," Mike said hanging up the phone in her ear.

Penny got up, heading for the coffee. She stopped to tell Althea the good news. "I have to write the order so I'll get on it right away."

Penny returned to her desk with a fresh cup of coffee and a blank screen on her computer. She stopped for a moment to wonder what the argument between Dan and Mike was about and then began drafting the document. She looked up an hour later to discover a sandwich sitting on her desk and the wan November sun shining in the window. The order finished, she sent it as an attachment to Mike's e-mail and sat back to wait for his comments.

"Thanks for the sandwich, Althea, I didn't even hear you go out."

"You're welcome. I took JD for a walk while I was out. You were totally engrossed in what you were doing."

Penny's computer pinged announcing a new message. Penny opened it. Mike made a few changes to her motion, but nothing that she had to argue about. She sent the final copy to the printer. Judge Sanford still didn't have e-filing. He thought it was a little too "iffy;" he didn't have faith that things sent over the air could be accurate or safe. So, Penny put on her coat, put several copies of the order in her briefcase and left the office to walk across the street to the courthouse. Stepping out the alley door to her office building, she saw a soft snow was coming down, a remnant of the storm from last night. She was glad she had thought to put on her boots.

When she entered the court house, she saw it was brimming with people, going about their business with the county—one man, sitting on the bench in the hall, his old Golden Retriever at his feet, could be heard saying, "I don't know why dog licenses are so expensive. Look at him; does he look like he needs a license to exist?" No one seemed to have an answer.

As Penny opened the door to Judge Sanford's office, she shivered with a chill as if the storm outside had entered the room. She wondered how Julie, his long faithful secretary, managed but then remembered that she was the mother of five boys so she probably was well able to deal with one judge. Julie looked up, took the order and said, "Wait here, Penny, I'll take it to him for his signature. He's not that busy right now."

A few minutes, she bustled out of the office, motioning Penny to go into his office.

"I'm not happy about this," Judge Sanford began. He looked up, his dark eyes narrowed. "I'll go along with it but you tell Mike that I still want to see the questions two days before the trial begins. I'm adding that line to the order, then I'll sign it."

"Thank-you, your honor," Penny said. "I'll send a copy to Mike." She turned and left his office and went on out of the courthouse, relieved to get out into the relative warmth of the outdoors. She knew the Judge didn't like anyone to question his authority in his courtroom. But at least Mike was with her on this one.

"Penny," said a voice. Turning to the sound Penny saw the substantial frame of Detective Dan. "I have the results of the blood spots if you have a minute."

"Of course," Penny said, "Let's go back to the office and get out of this weather."

When the two of them walked into the office at the top of the stairway, Althea was coming out of the little closet that served as a kitchen and copy room. The room smelled like peanut butter cookies. "You're just in time," she said, "These cookies are from the Deli—Andrea brought them up—they were just baked and are still warm. I made fresh coffee. Kyle will be here shortly—I sent him a text when I saw the two of you coming from the courthouse. It is handy having an office that faces the courthouse, isn't it?"

Kyle and Percy came into the office waiting for the others to get their coffee and head for the conference table in Penny's office. Percy, after giving JD a rub to leave his scent so other cats would know this dog belonged to him, found his spot on the window sill. Kyle, coffee and cookie in hand, joined the three others at the table. Dan looked up from brushing cookie crumbs off his comfortable front to see six eyes staring at him.

"What?" he asked, grinning. "I take it you want to know what this report says."

"Yes," they said in unison.

"In a nutshell, the blood on the money matches Dick's. That fact tells me that the money was in the same room as Dick when he was murdered, but …"

"Who did Randy say gave him the money?" Penny interrupted.

"He thought it came from Luther Rahn, but he couldn't be absolutely sure since he sold two motorcycles the day he got that money. One to Luther and he took a $5000 deposit in cash from a Claude Black. I checked Black out. He's a biker who comes up with money but doesn't have a job of any sort. But he doesn't seem to have a record."

"So, the bloody money could have come from either one of them?" asked Althea.

"I think so," Dan said.

"What was the grease on the money?" Kyle asked.

"Turkey fat," Dan answered.

"Turkey fat?"

"Yes, and I found Luther this morning and asked him about it. He denied knowing anything about the blood on the money but admitted that he stored money in a frozen turkey in his mother's freezer. He said he had been saving it up over time, sending it to his mother and telling her to put it in the turkey. He was adamant that it was not from the bank robbery that sent him to prison."

In the midst of the laughter, Althea said, "It's a good thing Mrs. Rahn didn't decide to cook that bird."

"Did you find Claude?"

"Yes," Dan said, "he gave me an alibi for the night of Boswick's murder that I have to check out."

"What does Mike say about all this?" Penny asked, staring at Dan.

"He says it has nothing to do with anything. He wants to ignore the whole thing." Dan said, "That's why I'm bringing it to you. He would not be happy with me if he knew."

"No reason for him to know," Penny said. "It was a private lab. And we paid for it. If I want to use it in court, I'll have to give him a copy, but I'll worry about that later."

"Not to change the topic, but did you get a report on the fingerprints from my car blowing up?"

"Yes, here it is. It says there wasn't enough of a fingerprint to get a match, but there was a handprint that was clear. The good news it didn't match Horace but they had nothing else to compare it with so they couldn't get a match."

"Well," Penny mused, leaning back in her chair, "that's something."

"Do you want me to track down that Claude Black?" Kyle asked Penny.

"No, I don't think he had anything to do with Dick's death. Dan, will you check his alibi? And, Kyle, I would like to know if the serial numbers on the money Victor took out of the bank to pay Dick a bribe match the ones with the blood. Can you check that for me?"

"Will do," Kyle said, making a note in his trusty notebook. "I can contact Hiram, I am pretty sure that when that much is taken out of the bank, they keep a record of the bills. Should be pretty easy to check. I think Victor is in for a bit of trouble."

"Gordon will take care of him," Penny said.

Dan watched and listened to the conversation, pleased that they were going on with the investigation but concerned that they might get in trouble. He was especially concerned about Althea's group.

"Althea," he said, "What is that book club of yours doing? They could get themselves in trouble. Let the professionals handle this."

Althea nodded at Dan, "Don't worry, Dan, we're careful."

The group broke up. Kyle on his way to check on the serial numbers of the money, Dan to find Claude Black's alibi witness to be sure they could rule him out. Claude was a strange one and Dan was a curious fellow.

Althea, deep in her own thoughts, filled the little sink with warm soapy water and washed the dishes. After placing the last dish in the cupboard, she went back to her desk to close down for the night.

Penny came out of her office, "I think it is time to close up. It sure gets dark early now that the time has changed. I can't seem to get used to that."

Both women bundled up to go out in the cold. Even JD had a coat to wear that kept the snow off his back. He also had some boots that he didn't like to wear, however, Penny insisted when there was a lot of salt on the sidewalks. Licking the salt could make him sick. Penny was the last to leave turning out the lights, locking the door and setting the alarm.

Althea headed for the bookstore. Her group was straggling in as she walked in the door. Seeing that they were getting sandwiches from the Deli, she did the same, joining the group while she waited for her order.

Sensing the tension coming from the group, she smiled at each. Rose was the first to speak up.

"I spoke to all the people on our list of possible suspects and they all have an alibi. I don't think any of them had anything to do with Dick's murder. I'll say that none of them were sorry to see him gone—they didn't want him dead—they just wanted him out of office."

"I don't understand why none of them complained," Mary said. "I'm sure the Commissioners would have listened. And they could have told Mike. He would have a duty to investigate."

"I think they didn't want to cause any trouble," Rose said. "And Dick had them all convinced that he had the power to put them out of business if they complained."

The group shook their heads in unison. For a group of doers, it was hard to understand non-doers.

"Okay," said Rose, "it looks like we are left with the original three. We are sure Horace didn't do it and Victor admits he was there and gave a bribe, but I don't think he is a murderer. So, we are left with Fiona. And we have no evidence that she was even at the concert much less at Dick's office."

"What about that Luther Rahn? Did anyone see him there?" Arney asked.

They pondered that. "Well, Rose said, "we are pretty sure he was the one looking up explosives at the Library and Penny's car was blown up, probably by someone who didn't want her investigating

Dick's murder. He says that he was looking up the information for a customer at the Lumber yard, but I do wonder."

"But, what is his motive for killing Dick? He didn't even know him." Althea asked. "But do you think he could be a hired killer? Do you think that is possible? And, who hired him?"

"Of course, it is. But how do we connect him to the murder?" After pondering that question, the group disbanded with no answer.

In the meantime, the subject of their inquiry, Luther, was pushing his motorcycle through the gears. He loved the feel of the powerful bike between his thighs, the rush of adrenalin as he glided around the curves. The roads were clear, the day of sun had dried them off, the November sun was setting and he cruised along. He was planning to meet Fiona in an hour to get the rest of his money and then he would be out of this lousy little town and its lousy small-minded people. He was sick of all of it. He would cruise down to Florida—maybe the Keys—for sun, surf, chicks and booze, lots of chicks and booze.

Luther, intent on the road ahead of him, didn't notice the car behind him. With its lights off, it was like a ghostly presence, one not seen. He could see the curve ahead, a long-left hand bend with snow-covered fields on either side. He hunkered down, ready to flow with the bike as it started into the turn when he felt the push. The bike began to skid. He tensed, grabbed the handlebars, saw the tree coming and tried to straighten the bike out. It wasn't to be. The bike hit the tree at full speed. Luther flew in one direction, the bike in the other, bursting into flame as it landed.

"You don't threaten me," said a voice. "No one threatens me." Climbing out of the car, the figure went over to Luther lying motionless in the snow. Feeling for a pulse in Luther's neck and finding none, the person walked away. The car moved back and forth over the tracks in the snow and then drove down the road.

Chapter 23

The November morning was still struggling to get going when Althea opened the office door. She dashed to pick up the ringing phone.

Listening to the voice on the phone, she stood still, her eyes wide, then she grabbed the legal pad and pen always in the corner of her desk to take notes.

"Was it an accident?" she asked Dan Dunlap who had called with the news of Luther's death.

"It sure looks like it," he said. There were skid marks and then the bike went head first into the tree. It looks like Luther was thrown off the bike. We'll have to wait for the coroner; it looks like he broke his neck when he landed. He didn't wear a helmet, but I'm not sure that would have saved him."

Althea thanked Dan for calling, hung up the phone and sat down in her chair, still holding the pen in her hand.

"What's wrong?" Penny asked.

Althea jumped. "Oh, my goodness, I didn't hear you come in. I have news, but I'm not sure what it means. Luther Rahn was killed in an accident last night."

Penny stared at Althea. Kyle burst in the door.

"Did you hear the news about …" he started then stopped when he saw their faces. "I see you did."

Penny nodded. "Let's talk about this."

Coffees in hand, the three sat down at the small conference table.

"Assuming it was an accident, it means nothing to our case," Kyle started, "although the serial numbers on the money matched some of the numbers on the bills we sent to the lab."

"If that's so, that means that Luther was at the crime scene since we know at least some of those bills came from the money Victor paid to Dick. And we could argue that the only way that Luther could have the money is if he took it from Dick."

"I still don't see what motive Luther would have to kill Dick," Penny said. "But at least it will raise reasonable doubt at the trial. I can add Victor to the witness list but he can take the 5th and get out of testifying. Randy, Arney, Dan, the lab technician, someone from the bank to testify about the numbers to establish the change of evidence for the bills. That could add another day to the trial. Judge Sanford will not be happy. I better get to work. I have to let Mike know this development and he will object to the evidence so we will probably have to argue about it before the Judge." Penny rose to go to her desk.

Althea said to Kyle as they were taking their cups to the little kitchen, "Do you think Luther Rahn could have killed Dick? And, if so, why?"

"Luther has a violent record," Kyle said. "I think he would have done anything for money."

The two stared at each other. They parted without a word each deep in thought.

"There is no way Luther Rahn had anything to do with Dick's death," said Mike, roaring in Penny's ear. "And there is no way I'll let all the information get before a jury. And I know the Judge will agree with me. He doesn't want this trial, which will create a lot of publicity, to turn into a three-ring circus."

"We'll see about that," Penny answered. "I'll get an emergency motion in front of the Judge as soon as possible."

"Go ahead," Mike answered. "You'll lose." He hung up in Penny's ear.

Penny booted up her computer, found the form for a motion to admit evidence and started to assemble the facts she would need to win the argument. Mike was right about the Judge—he would not let in evidence that was extraneous and too far from the facts of the case and would cause the trial to drag out.

She started to think about the series of events and how they could relate and support each other.

Just before 5 o'clock Penny finished her motion. She dashed over the courthouse to file it and deliver a copy to Mike's office. The Judge denied her request for a hearing on the motion, saying he could decide the issue based on the briefs. Penny didn't hold out much hope that Judge Sanford would let the evidence in; he didn't like last minute changes.

On her way across the street back to her office she saw Althea heading for the bookstore to meet with the Society. I certainly hope they come up with something, she thought. I think I need a miracle about now.

After everyone had their coffees and snacks, Althea filled the group in on Luther's death. Mary jumped in; "I heard rumors that the police think Luther's "accident" was not an accident after all. According to the courthouse grape vine, Detective Dan thinks it might have been murder. There was a dent on the rear fender of the bike that did not fit with the accident theory. He thinks maybe Luther was pushed into the tree. Dan has asked his accident expert to reconstruct the event."

"That is really interesting," Althea said. "Who has a motive to murder Luther and is it connected to Dick's murder?"

"I think it is," Arney said. "If we assume that Luther killed Dick, we have to figure out his motive since he had no reason that I can think of to do that. But, Luther wanted money, and I think he was paid to do it and I think whoever paid him, decided he was a liability and shoved him off the road."

After some discussion, the group decided that was a viable theory and they also had an idea of who the killer might be. Althea said she would talk to Penny in the morning and see what she thought.

Chapter 24

As the trial date approached, Penny spent more and more time at her desk. She had her trial notebook organized into sections beginning with the questions for the jury and ending with a few notes for her closing statement. Horace came by often to check on progress, getting more and more nervous as the day approached. Penny didn't want to admit it, but she was nervous, too. This was her first murder trial, in fact, her first week-long trial and she was worried that she would let her client down.

JD and Althea sensed the tension in the office and left Penny pretty much alone to work out the kinks. However, on this morning, Althea needed to speak to Penny about the meeting the night before. Just as she was about to knock quietly on Penny's closed office door, Ethan came in with dog, Toby, in tow.

Ethan had a big envelope in his hand. He handed the envelope with a triumphant smile spreading across his ruddy face. While JD and Toby greeted each other as dogs do, he opened the envelope, pulling out three pictures and placing them on Althea's desk.

"I found what I am sure are pictures of Horace from the night of the concert. My camera prints the date and time on the pictures so I know they came from that night. I didn't stay at the concert as I told Penny. I didn't really like the band that night so I wandered around taking pictures trying to capture the evening light.

"When I do that I don't pay much attention to people, but I do get some in my nature shots. Anyway, isn't this Horace in the background?" he asked pointing at the first of the pictures.

Althea picked it up, got out her magnifying glass and looked at it closely. After some time, she said,

"I can't be absolutely sure. We need to get Horace in the same position to see if that is him. Let's see the others.

Althea looked at the other two. When she came to the last one, she smiled. "I do believe you are right—that view looks like him. I can see part of his face. Do you have the negative? We can ask Kyle to take it to his expert to have it blown up. The time on the photo says 8:30—do you remember where you were?"

"Yes, I walked away from the concert, past the city offices and on down to the trail that goes along the river. That is a great view in the evening. Anyway, I stopped and took pictures of the trees draping over the river and evidently Horace was sitting on the riverbank with his back to me. I was so busy looking for the right angle with the tree branches that I completely ignored the man. But I am sure that was him and I stayed there about 15 minutes and I know he didn't move. The negatives are in the envelope."

Althea walked over to Penny's door and tapped lightly.

"Come in."

"Ethan's here and he found some pictures that I'm sure you want to see."

In a few long steps Penny was in front of Althea's desk with the magnifying glass in hand.

"Ethan—that is Horace—I'm sure of it. Can we prove the date and time? This will really help. Oh, thank you, thank you."

Ethan blushed and grinned. "You will want to thank Mabel, too. She helped a lot. Will I have to testify at trial? That's a little scary, but I'll do it for Horace."

"Yes, said Penny, "but we will go over all the questions before then so you will be well prepared. It won't be too difficult."

"Althea," she said, turning to her, "can you have Kyle get these blown up and make copies. We will have to send a copy to Mike before the trial and we need copies for the 12 jurors. Oh, I know this will help a lot."

Althea nodded. Penny escorted Ethan and Toby, who had been sleeping next to JD, out the door. She was thrilled with the pictures. She knew they would help to establish at least a reasonable doubt for her client. She was sure of it. She went into her office to call Horace with the good news. Maybe the picture would jog his memory about where he walked that night.

The afternoon passed quickly. Althea took the pictures to Kyle to have them prepared for trial and looked in her books to find the questions Penny would have to ask Ethan to have the photos admitted into evidence. She knew that the questions had to be precise in order for the Judge to allow the jury to see them.

Around 3:30, Penny came out to the smell of a fresh pot of coffee. She went into the kitchen to pour some and get a cookie from the tin where Althea kept them.

When this trial is over, she thought, I'll need to go back to Weight Watchers and give up all these cookies. They can't be good for me, but right now I need the carbs. Gordon says that a trial is like running a marathon and I need to 'carb up.' At least that's a good theory.

Althea looked up. "What's so funny?"

"I am using the trial as an excuse to eat these delicious cookies. I didn't realize that my deductive reasoning drilled into me by my professors could so easily be used to justify bad eating habits. Okay, back to work," Penny started toward her office.

"Could you keep JD out here with you for a while? I've got piles of papers sitting all around the room for the trial and I'm afraid he'll mess them up—you know how he likes to circle around before he lays down."

"No problem," said Althea, laughing. "He can stay here with me."

Penny organized her stacks of papers into the parts of the trial; voir dire questions for the jury, her opening statement, which she would practice several times before the trial, a pile for both defense and prosecution witnesses with as much information as she could find about each of them, questions for them and thoughts on what points she needed from each for her closing argument.

Penny raised her head when she heard male voices in the reception area—it sounded like Kyle and Detective Dan. Curious, she opened the door. Both men turned smiling in her direction.

"What's up?" she asked.

"I have the blow ups of Ethan's pictures and I am sure that is Horace in the background," Kyle answered. He handed the photos to Penny. She looked at them closely.

"I think so, too. Althea, call Horace and ask him to stop by to look at them. They may jog his memory on where he was and maybe he saw someone else. What do you have Dan?"

Dan, who was sitting in the largest and most comfortable of Penny's client chairs, had a glint in his eye and a big smile on his ruddy face.

"I have two reports that are mighty interesting. First, remember the ear print we found on the outside of the back door to Dick's office? On a hunch, I took an ear print of Luther Rahn's ears and asked the technician to compare them. It turns out that the ear print belongs to Rahn. The technician tells me that our ears are almost as good as our fingerprints for identification."

"Do we know when the ear print was put on the door? Can we prove it was the same night that Dick was killed?" Penny asked.

"I'm not sure. I'll check with the cleaning staff to nail down exactly when they cleaned that door, but it is interesting. At least it helps confirm that Rahn was around Dick's office. I'll leave a copy of the report for you."

"Now, the second report is on the palm print we found on one piece of your car. I had a hunch about that one, too. That palm print belonged to Rahn, too."

"I'm not surprised," Althea said. "Remember Rose and Mildred saw him looking up explosives in the library. Now, I'm sure he blew up your car. What an evil man."

"What does Mike say about all this?" Penny asked.

"He still doesn't believe the car bombing had anything to do with Boswick's killing and he says we can't prove when the ear print was put there so even if the judge let the evidence in, it wouldn't help," Dan answered.

"I need to think about all this," said Penny taking the reports back to her office.

Dan and Kyle left, their tasks done for the day. Althea found Horace. He asked if Penny could come to him because it was late and he had to be in his house by 6:30. Althea said she would pass on the information to Penny.

A short while later, Penny came out of her office.

"Horace can't make it before his curfew," Althea said. "Can you go by his house?"

"Sure, I'll take the photos with me. I'm off to see Fiona—she agreed to meet with me and I may want to call her as a witness. I have some questions for her."

"You be careful," Althea said. "I don't like that woman and we of the Midvale Corners Literary Society think she may have something to do with Boswick's death. I think you should take Kyle with you."

"I'll be fine," Penny said. "I have J D and Pepper spray in my purse. That will stop folks a lot bigger than Fiona Hollis."

JD got up and stretched, coming over to leave with his mistress. Penny patted his head. "You can come, big fellow. You'll have to wait in the car, but it's not too cold today so you should be okay."

After Penny and JD left, Althea closed up the office for the night and headed home. As she was coming out the street level door of the building, she turned to her left and bumped into Alex Jeffries.

"Oh, I'm so sorry," she said looking up at him.

"Not to worry," he said. "Is Penny still in her office? I thought I would tempt her with a dinner invitation. She needs to take a break."

Althea explained the latest information from Dan and her concern that Penny had gone to interview Fiona.

"She shouldn't have gone alone," Alex said, his brow furrowed and eyes narrowed. He reached in his pocket for his phone. While Althea watched he called Kyle, explaining the situation.

"I agree; I'll meet you there. Good idea, call Dan. We might need the law," Alex said.

Alex turned on his heel and dashed off. Looking back, he said, "Sorry, Althea, but I need to go. Kyle and Dan will meet me at Fiona's"

Feeling a little relieved, Althea turned into the bookstore, her phone in her hand to call the members of the group. "We need to meet," she said to Arney, the first in the phone tree.

Chapter 25

Shortly after five, Penny arrived at the lumberyard as the employees came out the door heading across the parking lot to their cars. Entering the building, she noticed that only the security lights were on, making the shadows from the piles of lumber and huge saws extend far out on the floor. Breathing the smell of pine, birch and walnut, the woods that had been cut that day, she called out,

"Fiona. It's Penny Johnson. Are you in your office?"

"No," said Fiona standing next to Penny.

Penny jumped.

"Follow me," she said moving toward the back of the building. The two women walked without talking, each with their own thoughts. Fiona went into her office, walked around behind the desk motioning Penny to the lone empty chair in the cluttered room.

Folding her hands in front of her on her desk and sitting ramrod straight, Fiona shook her long blond hair out of her eyes.

"Well, how do you think I can help you with Horace's trial? I think he did it so I don't think I would make a good witness."

"That's not what I want you for," Penny answered. "I want to show that Dick was corrupt and demanded kickbacks."

"That's not news. And others may have given him money for contracts, but I certainly did not."

"Not so," Penny said leaning forward, watching Fiona carefully. "Mike Pritchard has a list all the moneys Boswick collected and when. Evidently he kept good records of his underhanded dealings. And your name is on the list as one of the more frequent contributors to his personal retirement plan."

"What does that mean? I am sure every contractor in town is on that list including your precious client. And I wasn't anywhere near Midvale Corners when Dick was killed. I had nothing to do with it."

"True, Horace is on the list, but Horace did not employ Luther Rahn who was in Midvale Corners that night. And you did employ him and, it seems, paid him quite well."

Fiona stiffened, her face blank.

"What do you mean?"

"Luther is dead. His motorcycle slid off the road and hit a tree. Dan Dunlap is not so sure it was an accident. The rear fender of the bike has an indentation that was not the result of the skid. The accident reconstruction expert is still piecing it together. It's his theory that Luther was helped to slide off the road."

"That has nothing to do with me. Maybe one of his enemies from the old days had reason to kill him," Fiona commented.

"I wondered that myself," Penny said. "Then we learned that the palm print found on my car—the Pepto Bismal pink car, that was Maureen's—was Luther's. At least that is how it appears from the preliminary report."

"That was one ugly car, it is probably a blessing it blew up, but why would Luther care unless he did it as a prank or a community service."

"No, my theory is that he wanted to get me out of the way. I was the only one who was continuing to look for Dick's killer. The prosecutor and most of the police had signed off on the murder. They figured my client had motive, means and opportunity and that was that."

"And," Fiona said, "they are right."

"Not exactly," Penny said. "Since I was the only one still saying he didn't do it, Luther must have felt threatened. And, what did he have to do with Dick's death? I think he killed Dick and took the money that Victor admits he left with Dick. The police found an ear print on the door leading into Dick's office from the outside; remember his office was the only one that had an outside door. Detective Dan check the ear print against Luther's and it matches. We also know that the money Luther used to buy his motorcycle had Dick's bloodspots on it and matched the serial numbers of the bills that Victor took from the bank the afternoon before he met with Dick."

"Why would Luther kill Dick—Victor or Horace are the more likely murderers—maybe Dick demanded more money from Victor or Horace thought the bidding would be reopened if Dick was killed," Fiona said, leaning back, confident that she had solved the whole matter.

"Now, if you don't need anything more from me, I plan to go have a nice meal and look forward to the announcement of the awarding of the restoration contract, which I am sure will be to me."

"Not so fast," said Penny, leaning forward. "I think I know why Luther is the killer. He wanted money. Not all the money found at Luther's or paid to Randy from Luther came from Victor." Pointing at Fiona, she said, "And, I'm pretty sure some of it came from you."

"The gun that killed Dick belonged to Jake Rahn, Luther's uncle. Luther had ample opportunity to steal the gun. It was so old that he figured it was untraceable. Even though it was registered to Horace, Jake Rahn admitted that he bought the gun at a gun show several years ago. I think there is plenty of evidence connecting Luther with the death of Dick and with you."

Fiona stared at Penny.

"I think that is quite enough," said a voice.

Penny turned to see Sally Boswick coming through the doorway to Fiona's office with a large pistol in her hand.

"She knows too much, Fiona," said Sally. "We need to get rid of her."

"Sally?" said Penny. "What are you doing?"

"Oh, please," said Sally. "Fiona couldn't do this on her own. She's not that smart. All she wanted to do was threaten him. I wanted more than that. He was a cheater and a crook. Now I have all his money. Stupid man, he hid it in the chest in the basement. Did he think I wouldn't find it? Now, let's go. Come on, Fiona, time to take Penny for a drive."

Sally waved the gun at Penny. "Get up."

Penny stood slowly. Sally got behind her and pushed.

Penny started walking, wondering how she was going to get to the pepper spray. Fiona grabbed Penny's briefcase and the three women started walking out into the shadowed building.

The women left the building and started across the parking lot. The stars and the moon were blanketed with clouds and the streetlights were dimmed in the lightly falling snow. It was so dark Penny could barely see where she was walking. She knew if she got in the car with Sally and Fiona, she was as good as dead.

Fiona handed Penny her briefcase. "Find the keys to that old heap. I'm sure no one will be surprised that you skidded off the road in that death trap. And if that dog tries anything, Sally will shoot it."

Penny opened the briefcase, grabbed the keys and the pepper spray. She turned suddenly and pushed the button on the canister. Nothing happened. Sally grabbed it laughing.

"You lawyers are so cheap—you should have bought a new bottle of that stuff. We're going for a ride and you can die in your precious car. You and that stupid dog."

"Halt," said a male voice. "Put your gun down, Sally. It's all over."

Sally grabbed Penny around the neck and whirled in the direction of the voice. Headlights from four cars flooded the scene with light.

"I'll kill her." Sally said pushing the muzzle of the gun hard against Penny's head.

"No, you won't," Dan Dunlap said, pointing his pistol at Sally.

"No, we won't let you," Kyle said, standing to the other side of Sally, pointing his pistol at her.

Sally stood still for several seconds; seconds that seemed like hours to Penny. Feeling Sally's hold on her neck loosen, she jerked free, landed on her knees then was up and dashing toward the headlights. Sally swung towards Kyle and raised the gun. Shots rang out. Sally fell to the ground.

Fiona, who had been standing still, staring at what was happening around her, started to run. One of the policemen took after her, bringing her to the ground with a thud.

Penny felt strong arms around her. Looking up she saw Alex's concerned face. He put his long coat around her and led her away.

The Emergency Medical Team dashed over to Penny who waved them away. "I'm okay—go check on Sally."

Dan and Kyle were kneeling by the fallen Sally. Penny could see that she was moving. Dan picked up her pistol.

"Sally Boswick, you are under arrest for the murder of Dick Boswick," he said.

Sally started to answer when the EMTs arrived to check her over. "It doesn't look like a life-threatening wound, but she is losing blood, Dan. We should have her patched up pretty quick, but she needs to go to the hospital. I think she will need a surgeon to get the bullet out. You can question her there."

They loaded her into the ambulance. Fiona was sitting in the back of the police car, hands handcuffed, looking shocked.

The ambulance was soon on its way, siren blaring.

"You need to go to the hospital, too. I want you to be checked out to make sure you're all right," said Judge Gallagher, leaning into the passenger side of Alex's car where Penny was sitting.

"Dad, how did you get here?" Penny asked.

"I called him," Althea said. "I knew he would want to know what was going on."

Penny looked over to see the entire Midvale Corners Literary and Investigatory Society staring at her. She laughed and turned to Alex.

"Okay, take me to the hospital before the whole town is here to check on me. Oh, goodness, here comes Mother. She looks upset. Mom, I'm fine. Is JD okay? He's barking his head off."

JD, released from the car, ran to Penny and was soon transferred to Alex's car where he licked Penny's face until she made him stop. Judge Gallagher drove the Jag and Maureen took the family car. The cars loaded up and they drove off to Midvale Corners Hospital.

"I need to call Horace and Mike," Penny said. "I think we have solved Dick's murder and there will be no trial."

"I agree but let's get you checked out first. Your knees look a little sore," Alex said, giving her a worried look.

A short time later all including JD, who was given special permission since he was a retired service dog, were in the waiting room of the hospital. Penny was being checked over by an intern, Sally was in surgery; Fiona was screaming for her lawyer and Dan was trying to get statements from all the witnesses to the events.

"Everybody, be quiet. This is a hospital and people are sick and I need to talk to you individually. Who wants to start?"

"I'll start," Althea answered, proceeding to explain how her group came to the conclusion that Sally and Fiona were the co-conspirators to Dick's murder.

"All the clues pointed to them. Sally and Fiona have been friends since grade school. When Sally learned about Dick's affair, she turned to Fiona for advice. Fiona wanted to threaten Dick with exposure, but Sally had a meaner streak. She hired Luther to kill Dick and Fiona agreed because she thought that with Dick dead, the bidding would reopen and her bid would win. Fiona decided she had to kill Luther because, we think, he was pressuring her for more money. I don't know if Fiona knew he was going to blow up Penny's car. Maybe he did that on his own. One thing I am sure of is that Horace Appleworth had nothing to do with Dick's death."

"I agree," said Penny coming into the waiting room with bandages on her knees.

Everyone came up to her, their faces concerned.

"I'm fine," she answered before anyone could ask. "Just a few scratches. Kyle and Dan, thank you for saving me. That stupid pepper spray; I guess it was a little old. If it had worked, I could have handled that situation. Can we do this later, Dan? I want to go home."

"Okay, but first thing in the morning. Your office, okay? Kyle, I need you there, too."

Penny nodded. "We'll be there at 9:30."

Everyone left and order was restored to the little hospital.

Chapter 26

Althea arrived at the office first, loaded with fresh fruit, bagels, cream cheese and donuts for those with a sweet tooth. She pulled down the large coffee pot. She knew this was going to be a busy day indeed.

The door opened.

"I know it was my bullet that got her," said Dan holding the door for Kyle. "You guys at the CIA were never good shots."

"Oh, and you boys at the FBI are better?" Kyle retorted. "I don't think so."

"Well," said Penny coming in with JD, "since both of you use the same model Glock and the bullet found was really mashed up, it will be hard to know which of you shot her. It doesn't matter to me, I'm just thankful you were there. Otherwise, JD might be homeless."

"Not to worry," laughed Althea, "he can always come live with me."

Horace and Ryan came in the door. Penny smiled at them and for the first time since Horace called her several weeks ago, received big, honest smiles from both of them.

"I can't believe that this is over and this ugly tether will come off my leg. Can I take it off now? It really is uncomfortable," said Horace, hanging his coat on the hall tree stuck in the corner of Penny's office.

"No," said Penny. "If you do, the police will come and drag you off to jail. I'll schedule a hearing as soon as possible, but in the meantime, you must still abide by the terms of your bond or Ryan will lose his money. Remember I told you courts work on written orders and the only order we have is the one that specifies the conditions of your bond."

While all were getting their coffee, Penny went into her office and placed a call to Mike Pritchard. She was sure he heard the news.

Mike answered with a gruff "Hello, Mrs. Johnson, I think I know why you're calling. Dan put a copy of his report on my desk sometime early this morning. It looks like you were right all along and your client had nothing to do with Boswick's death. But what were you thinking to go off by yourself to confront Fiona Hollis?"

"I wasn't really by myself," Penny said, defending herself. "I had pepper spray and JD."

"Right, pepper spray that didn't work and an ex-bomb sniffing dog that can bark. At any rate, I suppose you want to get in front of the judge as soon as possible. I talked to his clerk and we can have a few minutes right after lunch. She put us in at 1:30. Is that alright with you?"

"Wonderful, shall I draft the order of dismissal and cancelling the bond?"

"That would be helpful. I'll review it before the hearing," said Mike.

Penny hung up the phone, smiling to herself, thinking that Mike was a lot pleasanter now. She went out to the office to tell Horace the good news.

Later that afternoon, Penny stood at counsel table with her client before Judge Sanford. Mike came striding in a few minutes later. He smiled and chatted with the members of the press who were filing the courtroom.

"All rise," said the bailiff at precisely 1:30. Calling the case of the People v Horace Appleworth, file no: CH 12-12009, he handed the file to the Judge.

"I see we have a development in this matter," said Judge Sanford. "Mr. Prosecutor, you have a motion?"

"Yes, your honor, in light of the recent developments, I move that the matter of the People v Appleworth be closed, all charges dismissed, the terms of Mr. Appleworth's pre-trial release be removed and the bond returned."

"Mrs. Johnson, I trust you and your client have no objection to my granting this motion," said the Judge.

"No, your honor, we agree with the motion. My client is relieved that this matter is over."

Judge Sanford nodded. "The motion is granted." He signed the order, handing a copy to Penny.

Turning to Horace, he said, "Mr. Appleworth, I apologize on behalf of the court for all this unpleasantness. I am sorry for this inconvenience."

Horace, who saw this as slightly more than an inconvenience, bit his tongue and nodded. Following Penny's instructions, he said, "Thank you your honor, I am relieved that the real killer has been found."

"If that is all, we will move on to the next matter," said Judge Sanford. "Before you go, would the lawyers approach the bench?"

Mike and Penny looked at each other and then went to the bench.

"First, I want to congratulate you, Penny, for your zealous defense of your client. You are following in your father's footsteps. He was an outstanding defense attorney before taking the bench. And I trust you will be, also."

Turning his attention to Mike, he continued, "Mr. Prosecutor, I am upset with your rush to judgment in this matter. I suggest that in the future you let your police officers do their job before you file charges against innocent citizens."

Penny and a chastised Mike thanked the judge and returned to their respective counsel tables, put their files in the briefcases and proceeded out the door. The reporters followed.

"How does it feel to be a free man, Horace?"

"What happens next, Mike?

"This a win for you, Penny, how does it feel to win your first big case?"

Mike stepped up to take the lead. "We are pleased with the result and thank Mrs. Johnson for her assistance. We will prosecute Mrs. Boswick and Ms. Hollis to the letter of the law. We cannot have the citizens of Midvale Corners in danger. It is regrettable that no one called to my attention that our City Manager was taking kickbacks. All of this could have been avoided, I think."

Horace and Penny smiled at the reporters and posed for pictures. Horace agreed that he was pleased to be a free man and said, "If it weren't for Ms. Johnson's persistence and the assistance of the Midvale Corners Literary and Investigatory Society and Detective Dan Dunlap who believed in me and helped make all this come about,

I would be a sorry man. I'll be so glad to get this ugly thing off my leg," he said, pulling up his pant leg to show the tether.

Penny said she was pleased that the matter was successfully resolved.

The reporters had what they needed.

Penny and Horace immediately headed to the police department where Dan removed the tether. Ryan appeared to collect the bond he posted and they were off for a celebratory lunch at the Country Club restaurant.

Ryan drove to the Club. He and Horace were talking about the turn of events, busy making plans for the future, relieved that the case was resolved. Penny sat in the back of the car, pleased with her win, which would help her practice. She knew it would bring in more business, but she also knew that Mike was not pleased with the loss, no matter what spin he put on it. She knew her future dealings with the prosecutor's office would be more difficult.

Bringing herself back to the present, she saw Horace staring at her.

"I can't thank you enough for believing in me," he said. "I thought it would never end. And to think you were almost killed. It was all so horrible."

"You're welcome, Horace. I had lots of help from Althea's Society and the people of Midvale Corners. Sometimes justice takes time but will win out in the end."

The End